Murder Most Holy

FIVE STAR

Murder Most Holy

Mike Manno

To Amy;
Best wishes;
Mike Manno

Five Star • Waterville, Maine

This novel is a work of fiction. Names, characters, places and incidents are either the product of the author's imagination, or, if real, used fictitiously.

First Edition
First Printing: June 2006

Published in 2006 in conjunction with Tekno Books and Ed Gorman.

Set in 11 pt. Plantin by Elena Picard.

Printed in the United States on permanent paper.

Library of Congress Cataloging-in-Publication Data

Manno, Mike, 1949–
Murder most holy / by Mike Manno.—1st ed.
p. cm.
ISBN 1-59414-387-0 (hc : alk. paper)
I. Title.
PS3613.A568M87 2006
813′.6—dc22 2005037390

This book is gratefully dedicated to
Theresa Martin
whose words can move a soul.

Acknowledgements

There are too many people I have to thank for their assistance with this work: First, my wife, Luanne, who never failed to support me; Kim and the gang at the Tuesday Writers Group for their often biting, but always good-natured criticism; the folks from Love Is Murder who made the proper introductions; John Helfers, the acquisition editor; my editor, Hugh Abramson, who let Stan be Stan; and finally, my wife's good friend, Marie Callas, who patiently line-edited the final manuscript before submission. To them and to all those who, over the years, offered tips and suggestions, I owe you a big "thank you."

Chapter One

There is something commanding about a ringing phone. It rang at eight-forty Saturday morning on what was to have been the first day of my honeymoon. Notice the tense: was to have been. Naturally, my first thought was not to answer it. Of course, it might be Diane. But I really didn't want another explanation from her; she had said it all Wednesday night. It rang again, so I decided to answer it, not because it might be Diane, but because I am a cop.

"I wasn't sure whether or not to call you today." It was my boss, Captain Hodges.

I told him I didn't mind.

"I think I have something to take your mind off Diane. I won't force it on you. A car bomb killed a young nun this morning in Forbes Island."

"Yeah, well, I appreciate the diversion, but why us?"

"Her father's the newspaper publisher. Seems he's been feuding with the local police chief and politicos. She bought it in his car. This is a political hot potato and the locals want this out of their hands, like right now. The Commissioner got the call a few minutes ago from the Attorney General."

"So you want to give me a murder investigation? Kinda like a non-wedding present."

"If you're up to it. I'll understand if you want to pass."

"Can I get my two weeks back?"

"Anytime you find another bride."

For the first time in two days, I smiled. "You're on."

Captain Hodges commanded the Special Investigations Unit. It was small and, theoretically, an elite unit, designed to be the investigative arm of the state police. I had only worked in the unit about four months, much to Diane's displeasure, since we were tasked to play cops and robbers all over the state.

"You have a passenger. The lawyer who teaches at the academy. There may be some bad politics here and the AG wants him along."

"Yes?" I hesitated.

"Well, you've worked with him before, haven't you?"

"Not alone."

"Well," he said. "Make the best of it."

The drive to Forbes Island from the state capitol takes about three and a half hours. What makes it so long and difficult is that there's no direct route. The only way to make the drive is to follow several of the state's worst two-lane highways through about a dozen small burgs that no one has ever heard of, and in which even fewer live.

Forbes Island is not what you would call a thriving metropolis, not even by Midwest standards. It is just about what its name implies, an island unto itself. Situated northwest of the state capitol, its nearly forty thousand inhabitants are almost divorced from the rest of the state, a situation that I daresay was considered beneficial by most of the citizens of the state, Forbes Islanders or otherwise.

My rumpled, bow-tied companion on the drive was Parker Noble. For nearly twenty years he worked on the Attorney General's staff, prosecuting the state's leading criminals. Lately, he spends most of his time teaching at the law enforcement academy and serving as a liaison to the state police. Parker was quiet during most of the ride. With his small, five-foot-five-and-one-half-inch frame, thin mustache, even thinner hair, and his ever-present bow tie, it was hard to see how he was once a premier prosecutor.

"Sorry to hear about your girl."

"It happens. Said she didn't like the travel."

He said something, but it sounded like little more than a groan. Then he started talking about Forbes Island. Every once in a while he would stop, grunt, wheeze a little, rearrange the tobacco in a pipe he never seemed to be able to keep lit, then start in on another story. Finally he turned to newspaper people.

"When I started with the AG's office, one of my first cases involved the murder of a newspaper editor in Booneville. You know where Booneville is, don't you, Stanley?"

I hate it when he calls me that. You put up with a lot when your name is Jerome Leonard Stankowski. "Stan" is the best of a bad situation, but "Stanley" just drives me up the wall.

"Yes, Parker, I know where Booneville is."

"Interesting case," he said. Then, like the absent-minded professor, he picked the newspaper up from his lap, turned to the sports page, and just left me wondering what had happened that was so interesting in Booneville. "Hey," he said, "looks like your old team made an interesting trade."

"That was a while ago and it wasn't quite my team, Parker. What was so interesting in Booneville?"

"I hear you could have made it, Stanley. They say you had the right stuff."

"That's part of the game, Parker. Who'd they trade for?"

"Bolinski. Did you know him?"

"Why would I know him?"

"You know, Bolinski, Stankowski. You're both Polish."

I had to bite my lip to keep from saying something insulting. "No, and I didn't know the Pope, either."

"Good man."

"I wouldn't know, Parker. I don't go to church much these days."

"I meant Bolinski." He turned back to the sports page. "He hit over .350 in Denver."

"The ball carries out there, Parker. Air is lighter."

He just grunted something and turned back to the paper.

"Booneville," I finally said. "What happened in Booneville?"

"Damnedest thing, Stanley. Damnedest thing. Remind me to tell you about it sometime." Then he grunted something, waved at the window, and went back to the sports page.

When we arrived in Forbes Island, the police dispatcher was able to give us directions to the crime scene. We were directed to an older section of the city in what seemed to be an exclusive residential area, built up on small, wooded lots. By the time we arrived, the local police had already completed the preliminaries and were keeping the news media and the just plain curious at bay.

The car was still sitting in the driveway, near the rear of the house. It was a late-model Buick, or what was left of a late-model Buick. Actually, the outside of the car didn't seem too bad. It looked, more or less, like a car that had been vandalized by culprits who didn't stay around long enough to complete the job. It was only when you were near enough to look inside that you could see what had happened.

The police chief, Joseph Edwards, met us. Edwards, dressed in khakis and a navy blue polo shirt, was an unimposing man of thin build with sharp features, gray eyes, and close-cropped blond hair, probably in his late forties. He escorted us inside the house. "The dead woman is Anna Marie Winborn, twenty-five," he said. "She was killed about five-thirty when she tried to start her dad's car. Her dad suffered some kind of attack shortly after. He's at the hospital. May be touch and go for him. Neighbor is a doctor. He's there with him now."

Parker asked, "This girl was a nun?"

"Yeah. From what Doctor Burnelli, that's the neighbor, told us, she was here visiting. Had just arrived yesterday."

"Where was she going so early in the morning?" Parker asked.

"Probably church," the chief replied. "St. Cecilia's has an early morning Mass at six-thirty, I think. But that's just an educated guess. All we really know is she was going somewhere in her father's car. That was the old man's Buick. Anyone who knew him knew it was his car."

Parker started to poke around the living room. Although it was fairly large, the furniture arrangement made it appear small and cozy. Chairs and couches faced each other over a glass coffee table so as to encourage conversation. "Did anyone else know she was here?" he asked.

"That we don't know, yet," Edwards said. He looked a little perturbed as he watched Parker root through a candy dish. "Her brother might be able to tell you that."

"Anybody else live in the house?" I asked, as Parker helped himself to the candy.

Edwards turned towards me but kept an eye on Parker.

"No. Old Man Winborn was a widower. His son, Michael, lives in an apartment across town. He was here earlier, and then went to the hospital to be with his dad."

"Just the two of them?" I asked.

The chief nodded. "You mean the kids? Yeah, just Michael and Anna Marie. Michael is about three years older."

"Married?"

"No. Do you want to see the car? There's a deputy sheriff here with some military experience in explosives."

I started to say yes, but Parker shook his head and indicated that he'd rather look around the house first. The inside of the house was much larger than it looked from the street. Behind the formal living room was a family or recreation room. It contained a TV and a game table. Next to it was a large kitchen. On the stove, ready for use, were clean but empty pans. Parker rummaged around the kitchen for a while, looking into the cabinets and the refrigerator.

"What are you looking for, Parker?" I looked at him and arched my eyebrows.

"Something to eat, Stanley."

I stepped closer to him and whispered, so Edwards wouldn't hear, "Parker, you can't eat the food here. Besides, you just ate on the way here."

He closed the refrigerator door, looked it up and down as if he were checking the seal, and said, "No matter, there's nothing there anyway."

I nodded and watched silently as he continued his examination of the kitchen, hoping that he wouldn't find something to eat or drink.

Apparently satisfied with the kitchen, he left it to make an inspection of the rest of the house. The girl's room was neat. Her bed was made and her clothes were folded, except for a short, black habit hanging in the closet. The attached bathroom was as neat as the bedroom.

Her dad's room was different. It was disheveled, as if someone had made a quick exit. The bed was unmade, and the shade on the bedside lamp was crooked. The room's condition was consistent with someone being suddenly awakened and staggering out of it.

Parker went to the dresser, where he started to poke through a fistful of change he found there. Then he started turning the pennies over.

"What are you doing, Parker?"

He turned to me. "I'm looking for wheaties," he said, and then turned back to what he was doing.

"Parker, what are 'wheaties'?"

"Wheat pennies, Stanley," he said, not bothering to look up. "You know the kind. The old ones with wheat on the back. Not the newer ones with the memorial." He looked at me and smiled. "I collect them, you know."

For a minute, I half expected him to start putting the pennies in his pocket. I breathed a sigh of relief when he didn't and wondered whether my main job here might be to baby-sit Parker. He made a cursory examination of the rest of the house, looking into closets and drawers. It all seemed as neat as the girl's bedroom, but he didn't seem too interested in any of it. On the way out, he took more candy from the dish. The chief was on the front stoop, waiting.

"The guy from the sheriff's department is still here," the chief said, leading us back to the car. "Not an expert, mind you, but until the ATF arrives and we get things back from the lab, he's the best we have." He introduced us to Deputy Paul Chase as we walked to the car.

"Like I told the chief, this looks simple enough. Homemade. Apparently, it was rigged to go off as soon as someone started the car. We'll know more later, especially after the experts come, but I don't think it would take an expert to rig." He looked at Parker. "You know, it's possible that the guy could have missed."

"How so?" I asked.

"It wasn't a very powerful bomb. It didn't do any more damage than necessary."

Parker walked around the car and looked into it from the passenger's side. "Deputy, that could mean an expert, couldn't it?"

Chase shook his head. "Either that or a sloppy amateur. We'll know soon enough."

"My instinct," I said, "is that the nun was not the target."

"No," the chief said. "From what we gather, she was just home for a visit. The doc next door says the visit was planned as some kind of surprise, so that would seem to indicate her old man was the target, and he had plenty of enemies. You'll find that out soon enough." He stopped long enough to watch Parker unwrap another piece of ill-gotten candy and pop it into his mouth.

"His daughter, on the other hand, was popular in spite of her dad," he continued. "I think she broke half a dozen hearts by going into the convent. I remember when Anna Marie was in high school. She was very popular—cheerleader, homecoming queen, top of her class—and pretty. You wouldn't believe how pretty she was. Not sexy or gorgeous, just plain pretty. Not ever in any serious trouble, and not an enemy in the world.

"But her old man, now that's another story. Cranky and getting worse the more years he spent alone. He was a widower. Anna Marie's mother died while she was in junior high, I believe. Don't off the top of my head remember the year, just that the girl was in school."

He paused for a moment, as if to relax his mind, and just stared into the air.

"Could the girl have had any enemies? An old boyfriend or something?" I asked.

"I don't see how," he replied. "Besides, as far as we know, no one knew she was here." He paused. Then he continued: "The old man used that paper of his like a battering ram. No one or no thing was safe. Rumor has it that he has the goods on everyone in town and plans to use them. I don't really know, but it wouldn't surprise me. We all have skeletons, you know."

Parker stood there looking at me and nodding his head. There was a long silence while he surveyed the neighborhood. A few neighbors stood across the street, chatting with a uniformed officer standing with them. Finally, Parker broke the silence. "Are you talking to anyone?" he asked the chief.

"No. We checked the neighborhood. No one saw or heard anything. Until it blew, that is. I figured Doctor Burnelli and Michael would be the first ones you'd want to talk to, so, under the circumstances, we haven't spent a lot of time with them. I thought it best to wait for you." Edwards looked at me as if he wasn't sure if he had made the right call on that. He looked down at Parker. Parker looked up at him, smiled, and unwrapped another piece of candy.

"Doesn't look like the old man will be much help, though," Edwards said.

I asked for directions to the hospital. Edwards offered to take us there, but Parker mumbled something incoherent and headed back to the car. Unfortunately, he took the driver's seat while I got the directions from Edwards. Forbes Island wasn't that big of a place and the directions were easy to follow. The only problem with the ride to the hospital was that Parker was driving. To say that he is an erratic driver is an understatement. I made a mental note to keep the keys out of his sight.

"Looks like we may have a town full of suspects. This fellow Winborn sounds like a real ogre," I said.

He just grunted as he swung the car around. He turned through a break in oncoming traffic into the hospital's parking lot. I just sat quietly while he parked right in front of a rather conspicuous sign that read, "Doctors' Parking Only."

"Parker . . ."

"State plates, Stanley."

We quickly found Dr. Burnelli. Slightly stooped, with receding gray hair and a full mustache, Dr. Burnelli was a short, slight man. Even so, he was still a little bigger than Parker. He took us to a small conference room. Parker asked if we could see Winborn.

"No, Mr. Noble," he apologized. "Mr. Winborn, Chuck, is in intensive care. I'm very concerned about his heart. He was not well to begin with. He's had heart problems for several years. I can't state it for a fact, but I think he's had several small attacks. I kept telling him to slow down. I think he was just starting to listen, and then this . . ." he drifted off. Parker gently brought him back to the issue at hand.

"He was so excited about this week. Having Anna Marie home again was all he talked about." His voice started to break

"Did anyone else know she was coming home this weekend?" I asked.

"Besides Chuck, only Michael and I knew. Michael and Chuck went to Grand Bay to meet her plane. We all met at the house for a little reunion. The five of us sat around talking and laughing, just reminiscing about old times."

"Did you say five?" I asked. "I thought only you, the brother, dad, and the girl were there."

"I'm sorry, Mr. Stankowski, there were five of us. You're right about the four. That's how it started. But right after we got back from dinner, Anna Marie called a friend to come over."

I asked, "Who was the friend?"

"Margo Roberts. Dad's a dentist. Best friends from school," Dr. Burnelli said.

"Where did you go to dinner?" Parker asked.

"Christie's, it's our version of upscale. Why?"

I answered for Parker, "We're wondering if anyone might have seen Anna Marie in town before this morning."

Dr. Burnelli looked puzzled. Parker said, "We will need to know who the bomb was intended for, Doctor. We don't want to jump to any conclusions yet, but if someone saw her at the restaurant, it would mean that she could have been the target."

"I see," the doctor said. "It would be very hard to see why anyone would want to harm that sweet little thing."

"I know, Doctor," Parker said. "What about Michael?"

Burnelli's eyes widened. "But she was his sister."

"No, no, Doctor," I said. "Not as a suspect." He looked relieved. "We mean: tell us about him."

Burnelli relaxed. "Michael's worried about his father. Michael's not the extrovert or the success that his sister is, er . . . was." He paused, starting to tear up again. "I'm sorry. It's just that we were all so close. Michael is like a little, lost puppy. If it weren't for his dad, he wouldn't have a thing. Simply depended on him for everything."

"How so?" I asked.

"Michael is very loyal to his father. It won't take you long to see that his loyalty tended to isolate Michael from his peers. He tied himself to his dad, so to speak; now he works for his dad at the newspaper. With Michael, it's probably more emotional than anything, especially with his dad being a widower and his sister gone." He paused. "Anyway, we can talk later, but I think for Michael's benefit you should talk to him now, then let him be by himself."

Dr. Burnelli showed Parker to the room in which Michael was waiting. We watched through a glass partition as Dr. Burnelli announced our presence. He motioned for Parker to enter. Michael stood up. Good God, I thought, he's even smaller than Parker!

Michael was thin, with sandy hair. His eyes were bulging from a face of sharp features. He wore wire glasses with thick, pop-bottle-bottom glass that accentuated his eyes, almost making them look like a frog's when he looked directly at you. His appearance made me wonder how this guy could have a sister as pretty as the chief had said Anna Marie was.

Dr. Burnelli made the introductions. "These are the gentlemen, Michael. This is Mr. Noble and Sergeant Stankowski." He left us alone with Michael.

Michael slumped back into the chair and for a brief moment looked relieved to be off his feet. Parker and I pulled up chairs closer to Michael.

"I'm sorry, fellows, I don't think I can say much more. I've already been over this with the police once." His voice was deep, almost too deep for his body.

"How's your father, son?" Parker asked.

"Doctor Burnelli says things are touch-and-go. He's got a bad heart, you know." Michael hung his head and looked at the floor. "This has been such a shock. I guess he wasn't as well off as I had thought. Oh God! My poor dad. I know he's not the most popular person in town, but he's the only family I have. I knew I'd have to face this someday, but I didn't think it would be this soon."

Parker looked over at me, then eased forward in his chair and put a comforting hand on Michael's shoulder. "Is there something I can get for you?"

"No thanks, Mr. Noble. I'll be all right. It's just such a great shock."

"I understand. If you don't mind, we do have to ask you some questions." He nodded at me and I took out my note pad. "Now your sister arrived last night, correct?"

"Yes. Well, no. Actually, she arrived late afternoon. About four-thirty."

"You and your father met her at the airport?"

"Yes."

"Where did you have dinner?"

"At Christie's. It was Mom and Dad's favorite place to take us when we were little." Michael looked up and smiled. "Anna Marie was so happy to be back home with us. She was especially happy to see Dad again. I think she felt a little guilty about leaving him alone to go into the convent."

Parker readjusted his seat. "And who was present for dinner?"

"Myself, Dad, and Doctor Burnelli."

"Not Margo?"

"No. Sis called her after dinner."

"Did you see anyone you knew at the restaurant?" I asked.

Michael bit his lip, as if straining for a thought. "No. My dad knows some of the staff but, other than that, I don't remember anyone."

"No one came up to you and said hi or anything?"

He shook his head.

Parker leaned forward in his chair, towards Michael. "Did anyone other than you and your dad know that your sister would be coming home?"

"Just Doctor Burnelli."

"You said something about your sister feeling guilty about the convent. What did you mean?"

"Well, about leaving Dad alone, you know."

"How long was she gone?"

"About four years. My mother died when I was in high school. Ever since, Sis kind of took care of Dad. I was already out on my own when she left for the convent, so I think she felt sort of guilty for leaving Dad alone. Do you know what I mean?"

Parker said he thought so. Then he asked if either his sister or his father had seemed preoccupied about anything, or if there was anything that seemed unusual to him.

"No, nothing out of the ordinary."

Parker sat quietly for a minute, so I asked the next question: "When did your sister call her friend?"

"Shortly after we got back from dinner. Anna Marie insisted on calling her. Margo came over about seven or so. Sis wanted to surprise her friends. She and Margo were best friends."

Parker started to fidget with his pipe again. "Well then," he said, "besides Doctor Burnelli and this Margo, no one outside the family knew your sister was in town."

"That's right."

Parker continued, "Michael, I know this is difficult, but please think hard. Did your father ever receive anything that could be considered a threat against his life?"

Michael nodded. "Kooks and crackpots. Every once in a while. I know he's not a loved man, but we never took them seriously."

"Perhaps you should have," Parker said.

"Perhaps."

"Do you know of anyone who would like to see your father dead?"

"Plenty. It'd take quite a while to compile that list."

"Any come to mind?" Parker asked.

"Go through the old editions of the *Independent*. You'll see for yourself. Like I said, he wasn't the most popular guy in town." He looked at me, and then turned to Parker. "Do you mind, Mr. Noble? I'd really like to be with my father now."

Parker said no. Michael stood up, but I said I had another question. Both Parker and young Winborn looked perturbed. Michael, who had started to stand, sat back down.

"Do you know where your sister was going this morning?"

He shook his head. "No, maybe to morning Mass. Nuns do that. But that's just a guess."

Parker, with a nod, gave Michael permission to leave. I followed Parker out into the hall. He frowned, reloaded his pipe under a "No Smoking" sign, and said, "Let's find that doctor again."

Dr. Burnelli was brief. He went over the same ground as Michael.

"His standing in the community? Well, Mr. Noble, Chuck is one of those men who you either love or hate. Really, there isn't much left, as far as he's concerned. I suppose some think him a hero. But if you're putting together a list of suspects, you'll have to list half the town."

Parker looked at me, gave a dejected sigh, thanked the doctor, and, with me in trail, took his leave. Silently he walked back through the hospital corridors. The disinfectant odor had just cleared my nostrils as we stepped out onto the front steps. Parker poked me.

"Hey," he said, pointing to a strange car. "Isn't that where we parked?"

It was getting late and I was hungry. A uniform took us to the city impound, where we picked up our car. From there we drove to the SuperSaver Motel on the main highway and checked in. Unfortunately, it had only one room free, but when the innkeeper said he'd have plenty of rooms tomorrow, we agreed to double up for one night.

Next to the SuperSaver was a small café. It was just the kind of diner that Parker preferred, small and plain with a basic meat and potato menu. We settled into a booth and ordered.

"Okay," I asked, "where are we going?"

"You tell me, Stanley."

"All right, here's what I see. No one knows that the girl is in town, so it is logical to think that the killer was after her father. He had enemies. She didn't. . . ."

"Unless it was someone in the family," Parker interjected.

"Unless it was someone in the family," I agreed, "or the secret was not kept as carefully as Doctor Burnelli thought. I suppose someone could have seen her at the restaurant, but that still leaves the why. Why would anyone want to do in the girl?"

"Granted," he said, "but remember what I've always said about Parker's first law: Never rule out the obvious."

"I wasn't in any of your classes," I said. "I don't know your first law from your last."

He paused long enough to relight his pipe and take a sip of his coffee.

"Next time it goes out, leave it out, Parker."

"You would never have made it in the old days, Stanley." He put the pipe in the ashtray. "Look, here's my point. Someday, if you make an arrest, you'll charge someone with the murder of a nun, not her father. That person will go to trial and you will be called to testify. The guy's lawyer will ask you what you knew about the girl, if she had a secret lover, ever had an abortion. Never mind that none of it is true. He'll ask anyway. And as soon as you say, 'I dunno,' he's going to suggest your investigation was incomplete. 'My client is being tried for the murder of someone he didn't even know and who the cops don't even know anything about.' That's what he'll tell the jury. Then he'll ask why his client is being tried for the murder of someone that he didn't even know."

I shook my head. "I don't know, Parker. I'm a cop, not a lawyer, but don't you think you could explain to a jury that the killer just got the wrong person? After all, it's a simple matter to understand."

"You're right," he said. "But in the hands of a skillful lawyer, it won't seem that simple. I know how they operate. It will become much more complex. So, we still need to check out the girl," he added. "Now, what about the bomb?"

"I think whoever did this apparently knows something about explosives. He was professional enough to know just how much stuff to use to get the job done."

"Or," Parker added, "amateur enough to almost not get it done. When we finish eating, I want you to check out this Margo girl. Your job is to find out all you can about this nun. You can drop me off at the police station. The uniforms will give me a ride from there."

"Whoa, Parker. Who's in charge here? You're just a tag-along, remember?"

He finished his coffee. "That I am, Stanley. That I am. Now, drop me off at the police station, and you go find this Margo."

Taking orders from Parker was not like taking them from another cop, but this was a logical place to start, so I dropped him off and went to check out Margo Roberts. It wasn't long before I was across town at the home of her parents, Dr. and Mrs. James O. Roberts.

Mrs. Roberts, who was very free with her opinions of the Winborn family, introduced me to her husband and daughter. I gathered a few particulars about the family. Dr. Roberts, a dentist, was not acquainted at all with the Winborn family, except for Anna Marie. Mrs. Roberts, a housewife and part-time dental assistant, knew both the Winborn children.

Margo was about twenty-three or -four and almost cute. I really don't know any better way to describe her, but maybe it was just the day. She appeared to have a nice figure; her brown hair was straight and parted in the center and hung behind her ears. Her eyes were red and watery, and she dabbed them with a tissue. After declining her mother's offer of coffee cake, I asked her about Anna Marie.

"Thinking back on it, I really think Anna Marie always wanted to go into the convent. I remember during school she just wasn't as interested in the boys as the rest of us girls. Good heavens! She was popular enough, but it just didn't seem to matter. You know," she blushed, "I sometimes wished I was as pretty and as popular as she was."

"Now don't you go saying any such thing," Mrs. Roberts said. "She's just saying that, Sergeant Stankowski. Why she's just as pretty and could have been just as popular as that poor, dear Winborn child. Don't you agree, Sergeant?"

"Edith," Dr. Roberts said, "just let Mr. Stankowski do his job and stop fondling over Margo."

Margo smiled, blushed, and dabbed her eyes again.

"Men," Mrs. Roberts replied. "Why, they just never know what it's like to grow up a woman."

I agreed with Mrs. Roberts and turned back to Margo, "Miss Roberts, was there anything unusual last evening, anything that may have given some clue as to what happened?"

"No. I'm sorry. Really, I haven't had much contact with the family since Anna Marie left for the convent. Once in a while I'd see Michael; we'd say 'hello' and that would be it."

I asked her to tell me what took place at the Winborn home last evening.

"Well, not much. I arrived about seven-thirty or so. Like I said earlier, Anna Marie called me about seven or so and asked me to come over. I got there a while later. Her dad and Doctor Burnelli were already there. Well, we started talking about old times—you know the kind of stuff—and Doctor Burnelli was telling some funny stories about Michael and Anna Marie as they were growing up. We had drinks and snacks and talked and talked. And that was about it."

I asked if she knew that Anna Marie would be coming home for a visit.

"I had an idea. She wrote to me from the convent, but I didn't know the date. She said her plans were not firm, but that I'd be the first to know. I don't think she told anyone else. It would be just like Anna Marie to come home quietly, so no one could plan a big fuss over her."

"Anything else about last night?" I asked.

"No," she said. Then she smiled. "Yes, Michael." She

looked at me and her eyes sparkled through her tears as she remembered. "You know, he tried to keep his father from serving drinks. Said it wasn't fitting for a nun. Can you imagine that? His own sister! Well, I'll tell you, we were ready to bust a seam laughing at him."

"That's it?" I asked.

"That's it. I left around one-thirty; we had a little mini-breakfast. By the time I got to my car, I noticed Doctor Burnelli and Michael were leaving too. I'm sorry but, you know, everyone loved Anna Marie. No one would have done this to her." Margo paused. "Now her father, that's another matter."

"How so, Miss Roberts?"

"Oh, all that stuff with his newspaper. I think everyone hated him for one reason or another. He wasn't too bad in person, but that paper of his was enough to drive people nuts. I'm sorry, I'm no real help. I wish I could be." Tears started welling up in her eyes again.

"You can help. If you think of anything I might be interested in, would you give me a call?" I handed her my card. "We're staying at the SuperSaver Motel, or you could call the police station and leave a message for me."

So far, that was it, nothing. Sister Anna Marie Winborn was just what she appeared to be: a sister, a daughter, and a nun, nothing more sinister than that. Of course it was early in the investigation and I didn't really expect to find out anything more than I did.

When I arrived back at the motel, I found Parker sitting on his bed in his boxer shorts. It always amazed me why some men want to wear little basketball uniforms under their clothes. Now me, I prefer jockeys with regular T-shirts. But that's not Parker. He looked ridiculous, like a skinny athlete with black, calf-length socks.

"What did you find out?" he asked.

I told him the whole story and asked what he had learned.

"I found out what we already knew. This Winborn fellow had a lot of enemies. I've combed through library copies of the *Independent* for the last several months, and I've gone through police file after police file 'til I'm sick of looking. How fast can your people locate files?"

"Depends on whose we want."

"We'll need that little computer thingy of yours in the morning."

Then he slipped into a pair of pajamas and started fiddling with the TV.

"What are you looking for, Parker?"

"The Nashville station. Do they have the Nashville station here?"

"Do you know how far we are from Nashville, Parker?"

"The cable station," he said. "You know, car racing and country music. It's Sunday night. Mrs. Skosh and I never miss the Statler Brothers."

"It's Saturday, Parker," I said. He just gave a big, dejected sigh. With that, I decided to take a walk. Diane was still on my mind.

It sounded like a fire alarm at first. Then I heard some mumbling and Parker's voice. Finally, I found the light and noted that my watch said four-sixteen—that's a.m.—as in Sunday morning. Parker was on the phone, but by the time I got my bearings, he was hanging up.

"That was Doctor Burnelli," he said matter-of-factly. "Charles Winborn just died."

Chapter Two

Sunday was one of those bright, sun-drenched days that seemed to have been made for fun, not work—especially when that work included murder. Even the heavy motel curtains couldn't keep out the light.

Parker wasn't there when I woke. I suspected he got up early and went to church. I showered and dressed quickly and went out for coffee and what I call a jog, which is more of a brisk walk. I wasn't surprised when I found Parker, rumpled suit, bow tie, and all, in the room when I returned.

"You're to call that Margo girl," he reported indifferently.

It's not that unusual to be called back by an interviewee. Sometimes those calls turn out to contain the best leads. When I reached her, her first words were: "Is it really true about Mr. Winborn?"

I assured her it was, but I couldn't help feeling a little dejected if this was all she wanted. My spirits picked up as she continued, "There was one thing I thought about that I don't think I mentioned last night. It probably won't help, but I thought I should tell you anyway."

"Okay, what is it?"

"Remember you asked yesterday if there was anything unusual about Friday night? Well, I think there was. Anna Marie and I were alone for a short time, and she asked me about a friend of ours, Buffy Coyle. Her real name is Frances Jean, but we always called her Buffy, because when she was little, she used to look like that little girl on the TV show. Oh, what was the name of it?"

"I know which one you mean. Go on."

"Well, she, Anna Marie, said something about having wanted to invite Buffy over, too, but her father wouldn't let her. Then we were interrupted, and she never did finish what she was saying. Now I got to thinking about that, Mr. Stankowski, and the more I thought about it, the more I thought it might be important. You know, her dad would have done anything for her. I don't think he felt the same way about Michael, but he sure doted on her. It just seemed funny, that's all."

"Miss Roberts, what do you mean when you say Mr. Winborn doted on his daughter, but not Michael?"

"Well, I remember things from a few years ago. It always seemed that whatever Anna Marie wanted, her father would get it for her. Maybe it was because he was a widower and she didn't have a mother, or maybe it was because she was the youngest. I don't know, but she never was left to want for anything very long.

"Why, she was always the best dressed and never lacked for any spending money, even though she didn't have any type of after-school job. And she always seemed so blasé about it, as if she didn't really care one way or the other. I guess that's because she really had more spiritual things on her mind.

"Now, take Michael, on the other hand. He was always working, and he seemed to adore his father and would always speak right up and defend him at the drop of a hat. And with his dad, that wasn't always so easy. Somehow, I just got the impression that all the favoritism went to Anna

Marie, who couldn't care less, and nothing went to Michael, who was really devoted to his dad." She paused, then added, "Oh yeah, there's one other thing."

Parker had already left for breakfast and I was getting hungry, so this better be good, and quick.

"What is it?" I asked.

"Buffy works for the newspaper."

When I arrived at the diner, Parker was already there. So was Chief Edwards, in uniform. Parker was reviewing a file that the chief had given him, and the chief was looking uncomfortable. I sat down and ordered coffee, oatmeal, and half a grapefruit. Edwards smiled at me and looked as if he was relieved to be joined by another cop. I decided not to say anything about Margo Roberts' call until Parker and I were alone.

Parker handed me the file. "Tell Stanley," he said to the chief.

Edwards turned to me. "Like I was telling you yesterday, this guy Winborn had plenty of enemies."

"But what's that got to do with this stuff?" I asked as I started perusing the file. "This has got to be at least fifteen or twenty years old."

"A lot," he said. "This file is part of a larger one involving a local drug ring that was operating here about sixteen years ago. Normally this wouldn't be relevant at all, except that at that time there were reports of the involvement of some prominent people in the county. There was never any direct connection with anyone, but my cop's hunch is that it was true. Then things just shut down. Kinda like they took their profits and ran, so to speak."

"How does this relate to Winborn?" I asked, as my breakfast came.

"One of the guys supposedly involved in this was a man named Berrigan. Herbert Berrigan. Became a very successful businessman, among other things."

"And you think Winborn knew?" I asked.

"I'm almost positive," the chief said.

"And so a businessman has a shady past?" I took a bite from my oatmeal. "Is that enough for murder?"

Parker sipped his coffee and nodded to the chief to continue.

Edwards drew a breath and looked me square in the eye: "Bert Berrigan?"

Whatever it was, it went over my head.

"Bert Berrigan," the chief repeated, "Herbert Casey Berrigan."

"The congressman?" I wondered if this was why the Attorney General was so quick to send Parker. We sat in silence as I paged through the file. Finally, Edwards finished his juice and left.

"The AG wants this wrapped up quickly," Parker said. "He thinks things like this have a tendency to get out of hand."

"He knows?"

"Yes, I talked to him this morning, right after the chief called me. Seems that this is one of those open files that continue to haunt you cop types. Anyway, after things quieted down yesterday, Edwards remembered the file and wondered if there was any connection. Don't you wear a suit when you work?"

"I don't like ties, Parker."

He took a sip of his coffee and went back to eating. "You know, this is a heck of a breakfast for three ninety-nine. Look at all this: eggs, bacon, potatoes, hotcakes. You ought to try it."

"Parker, what else did the AG say?"

He shot me that look of his, shrugged his shoulders, and then went back to his breakfast. "You eat like a bird."

That's just like Parker. He gives me something to think about, then drops the subject. Of course, I'm beginning to think he likes food better than crime. Anyway, after breakfast, as we walked back to the SuperSaver, I told Parker about Margo's call. When we entered the small lobby, the manager waved me over. He had a message from the capitol. Parker had apparently called and requested some department files.

"That stuff you wanted, Parker. They have the material for download." I turned to the manager. "Is there an extra phone jack I can plug into? The ones in the rooms can't be unhooked."

"I have a small conference room. Right this way, Mr. Stankowski."

I let him show Parker the way, while I retrieved my laptop. When I returned, Parker was fiddling with the room's TV, trying to find the country station again.

"Here, Parker, just plug this in," I said, handing him the phone cord.

He looked at me with a blank expression, but took the cord. "I was looking for the pre-race show, Stanley."

I turned on the computer. It didn't take long for the modem to make the connection. Just a few keystrokes, and the information was loaded into my laptop. Parker was still trying to find the Nashville station, as I began to scroll through the information.

"Bingo."

Parker looked up from the TV. "What'd ya get, Stanley?"

"A file for one Joseph Ryan Edwards."

"See if the guy here has a printer, and you can print out a hard copy. I hate to read on those tiny screens." He turned back to the TV and his racing program.

The SuperSaver didn't have the kind of printer I needed, so the first thing I did when Parker and I finally arrived at the Forbes Island Police Department was to locate one that worked with my laptop. I printed out the file, careful not to let anyone see it was the chief's. I gave the hard copy to Parker. He folded it and put it in his breast pocket.

Officer Richardson, whom we had met yesterday at the crime scene, was there, along with Deputy Sheriff Paul Chase. We were ushered into the chief's small office. It was windowless. Wood paneling covered the walls, forcing the ceiling light to struggle to illuminate the room. The chief made the re-introductions. Parker took a seat between Richardson and Chase. I pulled up a folding chair and put it next to the chief's desk.

"I don't have any of the lab work back from your office," Edwards said to Parker, "but Chase here has had some experience with explosives. He was on the scene yesterday and can give you some preliminary thoughts. Chase."

Chase cleared his throat. "Okay. You know, it's been a long time since I've seen anything like this. But it was a black powder pipe bomb. Just enough to do the job. Look here, I got pictures."

Chase spread blowups across the chief's desk. The photos graphically illustrated Anna Marie's death. Anna Marie, or what was left of Anna Marie, was nearly unrecognizable. The interior of the car looked as it did when Parker and I arrived, except the remains were still present.

"The powder was detonated by an electrical charge from the car's battery," he said. "The lead went to a wire under the dash, the ground to the seat belt anchor. The guy who set this didn't even need to know which wire to tap into; almost any would do. Once power went through the wire, a spark detonated the powder under the girl's seat," Chase explained. "It's a rather crude, but effective, detonation."

"Deputy," Parker said, "what type of knowledge of explosives would be needed to rig this thing?"

"Aw, heck, not much. Just a simple electrical connection, a little black powder, and boom."

"How much black powder would be needed?" I asked.

Chase turned to me. "About a pound," he said. "Very easy to get around here. It's used by a lot of sportsmen with muzzle loaders."

Parker asked, "What?"

He turned back around to Parker. "A muzzle loader. Used a lot by deer hunters. One pound would do the damage we saw. That's how it's sold, by the pound."

"Would somebody with a military background be able to do this?" Parker asked.

"Sure would. But this is almost too simple for a someone trained in military ordnance. This is the kind of stuff you can read about on the Internet."

"How about a trained ordnance technician with limited means?"

"Sure." He nodded. "But there's just one thing I don't understand yet. I don't know if the perp knew just how much explosive to use or was just lucky. The device wasn't big. Could be a lucky amateur or a good pro."

Parker nodded as if he was taking this all in. "What about the ATF?"

"Tomorrow. Best they could do, with that church bombing in Omaha," the chief replied. "And then, only one man."

I asked, "Are we checking the sources for the powder?"

"Yup, but we'll probably come up dry. Too many sportsmen and too many sellers."

"Where's the car?" Parker asked.

"In the city garage," the chief said.

"Thanks, Deputy," said Parker. "Anything else, Chief?"

"Richardson might have something."

"Well, not really," Richardson said. "We dusted the car for prints but, right now, zip. No one in the neighborhood reports seeing or hearing anything unusual. The last we know the car was driven was Friday evening. Winborn and his son went to pick the girl up at the airport in Grand Bay. According to the doctor next door, the car was never moved after that.

"The party for the girl broke up about one-thirty Saturday morning. No one in the house remembers hearing anything outside. That leads us to believe the device was probably planted sometime between one-thirty and five-thirty, when the blast occurred."

"Could it have been planted earlier?" Parker asked.

"Of course, it's possible," Richardson said. "But that would have been pretty risky. My best guess is that whoever did this came after the party had ended."

"I suppose that if someone came by during the party, he might be alerted to the fact that the girl was home and the bomb might kill the wrong person," I said.

"Unless someone wanted to kill the girl," Parker added.

"Or didn't care who was killed," the chief said. "Someone motivated by revenge might only care that he was inflicting pain on the old man. Killing the daughter would do just that."

Richardson said, "In any event, I think we can assume it was placed after the party."

"I agree with the officer," Edwards added. "Remember, besides the next-door neighbor, there were two others present, Michael and the girl's friend. Both had their own cars. Anyone who came during the party would have seen the extra cars and probably waited until all was quiet."

Parker stood, bent over the desk, and started to sift through the photos. "You're probably right," he said. I noticed he reached inside his jacket, as if to see that the papers I had given him were still there. "You're probably right, Chief," he said again.

Frances Jean Coyle wasn't the easiest person in the world to find. She had an unlisted phone number and a new address, but I found her anyway. I also found out that her friend was wrong: Buffy Coyle didn't work for the newspaper. She had been fired.

"Quit, not fired, Mr. Stankowski, and let me make that very clear. And it's pronounced 'cole,' like Old King Cole. Not like 'coil,' a wire."

She took me by surprise. "I'm sorry," I stammered. "It's just that it had a 'y' and an 'le' in it."

"I know. Everyone tells me that. It's like the stuff you get from the ground, 'coal.' Just live with it. Now, what else do you want?"

Buffy Coyle didn't sound much like a Buffy. Neither did she live in the kind of place you'd expect a Buffy to live. It was a small, ground-floor apartment in an old house located in what appeared to be a low-rent neighborhood.

"Look, it's all I can afford, okay? I've been out of work three months. That bastard promised to blackball me, so I had fair warning I'd be without a job for some time. First thing I did was to find a nice, cheap place. I have a little money saved, but not that much. Winborn said it'd be a cold day in hell before I got a job without his recommendation. Well, he was right."

"Okay," I said, "let's back up a little here. Start from the very beginning."

Frances Jean Coyle, Buffy to her friends, classmate of Anna Marie Winborn and Margo Roberts, graduated from the state university with a degree in journalism and a lust for adventure and idealism. The adventure ended in the big city with an overly attentive and married editor. The idealism ended with Charles Winborn's brand of journalism.

She sat cross-legged in an overstuffed chair. Her arms were on the chair's arms. She gave me a steely look.

"I think it started with that 'ladies' club.' The paper didn't like having a house like that in town. So, Mr. Winborn rented an apartment right across the street from it and had a photographer take the pictures of everyone who went in and out. One of the pictures ended up in the paper. I must say, it was an effective way to force the girls out of business. But putting that man's picture in the paper just never seemed right to me. But I let it pass and never said too much about it."

She took a deep breath, and then continued.

"Then, during the tractor plant strike, the *Independent* rode the strikers so hard that they became the laughingstock of the whole area. And when the union wanted to put an ad in the paper to give its side, Old Man Winborn refused to print it. Like that's wrong," she said, making a small fist. "First Amendment and all that stuff. I don't know who was right or wrong in the strike, but we only printed one side. A lot of people got hurt over that, and I think what we did was wrong.

"We were always taught in journalism school to honor the truth. You can't really do that if you won't print the whole story and let everybody have their say, can you? The truth, the whole truth, not a half-truth mixed with a pack of lies. Isn't . . . oh, it really . . . it really gets me mad all over again to even talk about it."

Why, I asked her, did she quit?

"Why? Oh, a lot of reasons. The straw that broke my back was what that asshole did to Tom Foley. Foley was a decent man. I know, I helped cover city hall."

"Foley, the mayor?" I asked.

"Yes. Soon to be the ex-mayor, if Winborn has anything to say about it. He just hounds Foley. Poor guy can't do a thing right."

"Lies, Miss Coyle?"

"No, not lies. Worse! Half-truths. Winborn and that damn newspaper of his would tell just enough of the truth to make it impossible for someone to defend himself. Winborn was good at that. You talk to Tom Foley and ask him about the campaign against him. I'll tell you this right now: you can believe what Foley says."

There was a long pause. I could almost see the hate bottled up in her. I let her sit still for a minute. I cleared my throat, then asked her, "Did you know that Mr. Winborn died this morning?"

I watched for her reaction very closely. Buffy Coyle was obviously a pretty little girl, and by little I mean just that, tiny. But today, whatever attractiveness she might have had was overshadowed by her venom.

"Good," she cried. "I'm glad." There was another pause; then she looked relieved. Her prettiness started to return. Her face, once drawn and tense, relaxed. She allowed herself to slump back into her chair. Now there was a twinkle in her eye when she returned my glance. Her small chest heaved as she inhaled. Extending her lower lip beyond her upper, she blew a wisp of hair from her eyes as she exhaled. Then she smiled.

"Wanna celebrate?"

The duty nurse at the hospital directed me to the Pancake Inn, Dr. Burnelli's usual mid-Sunday afternoon habit.

"I'm not so sure that I would say Chuck ignored Michael or loved him any less than Anna Marie. I found the relationship quite natural. Perhaps I've been doctoring these people around here too long, but I didn't see anything unusual.

"You see, Stan . . . Can I call you Stan?"

I nodded; everybody except Parker did.

"You see, it's not that unusual for a close relationship like Chuck and Anna Marie's to develop under the circumstances. A man loses his wife, a young girl her mother. She tries to ease her own grief by taking care of her father, doing what her mother would have done, becoming the woman of the house, so to speak."

"Like a young boy taking his father's place?" I interjected.

"Exactly. He'll try to keep his mother as he thinks his father would have wanted. You see that happen all the time. What is not as prevalent is the father-daughter situation after a mother dies. But it happens the same way.

"Chuck needed that, as most fathers would, but especially Chuck. All he had was his family. I don't need to tell you how folks around here felt about Charles Winborn. It was only natural that he would become very attached to his daughter."

He poured himself another cup of coffee, blew on it, and took a sip. Replacing the cup on the saucer, he continued.

"Now, with the boy it was a little different. When his

mother died, Michael was at an age where he was too big to cry and too little to know it's all right to cry. We each cope with tragedy differently, Stan. Michael's method was to become aloof. Yet, he couldn't break from the family. He still needed their support, but couldn't outwardly depend on it too much. The classic case of a young boy struggling to be what a boy thinks a man should be.

"Michael was treated about as he expected and wanted: no sympathy, no tears. But he grew more dependent on his father and his father's approval than he realized. And his father responded, giving him exactly what he needed, no more and certainly no less. So what you have is what from outward appearances is a father doting on his little girl while apparently indifferent to his son. Not exactly the case. Chuck was very good to Michael; after all, it was Michael who would someday have control of the *Independent* and who was trusted to carry out the Winborn family mandate."

"Which was?" I asked.

He frowned, "I suppose it was to keep Forbes Island clean. Chuck attacked evil wherever he found it. I suppose he wanted Michael to do the same thing."

"Evil?"

He nodded, "Vice, corruption in high places. Wherever Chuck saw it, or thought he saw it. Evil, Stan, is in the eye of the beholder."

Remembering Parker's admonition to never rule out the obvious, I asked Dr. Burnelli if he knew of any reason why anyone would want the girl dead. The answer was as I expected: "Who would want to kill Anna Marie? Now, her father, that's a different matter."

I found Parker at the *Independent*, sitting at Winborn's desk in a large, well-adorned office. He always seemed to enjoy it that I didn't have as much news as he did. As a matter of fact, he seemed to enjoy it a little too much. I told Parker what Buffy Coyle and Dr. Burnelli had told me, but he didn't even look up from the pile of newspaper clippings he had spread all over the desk. Just a few "ahas" and "is that so?"

Finally, Parker looked up: "Okay, Stanley, if you are so sure of yourself, follow up on this Buffy Coyle thing; but first, I need your help.

"I've been going over these clippings. Seems Winborn's latest duel was with a developer named Costello over a zoning matter. I'm ahead of you about Mayor Foley," he said. "It seems this Foley was the typical, ambitious politician. Only this one was born with a silver spoon in his mouth, on the way up, before the *Independent* got hold of him."

Just then we were interrupted by a partially balding man, about fifty, who entered with two cups of coffee in paper cups. Parker quickly introduced the intruder. "This is Mr. Rhodes, the Managing Editor of the *Independent*. Detective Sergeant Stankowski, Special Investigations."

Rhodes was tall and, like me, casually dressed. He handed one of the cups to Parker and offered the second to me. I declined. He apologized about only having two cups. "I can run back for more."

I told him no. He took a seat next to me, in front of Winborn's desk.

"Ace and I have been talking, Stanley . . ." Parker started.

"Ace?" I asked.

"Oh, that's me," Rhodes said. "Everyone calls me Ace."

Parker gave me a stern look that said "don't interrupt," and continued, "Ace was telling me about the mayor. Why don't you tell Stanley what you just told me?"

Rhodes took a quick sip from his cup. "Foley comes from a fairly well-to-do clan and had for some time made it an open secret in party circles that he wanted to run for Congress. Somehow he was persuaded that he would have a better chance if he held some local office first, so he ran for mayor with our endorsement. In fact, the old man encouraged him to run."

"You mean Winborn?" I asked.

"Yes." Rhodes leaned forward, putting one elbow on his knee. "You know, normally these local offices are the kiss of death to a politician with higher ambitions. You get caught up in all the petty, Mickey Mouse local squabbles that make a lot of enemies and few friends.

"But Foley was different. He seemed to stay above most of the fray. In fact, he was doing quite well by all accounts until Winborn turned on him. The first problem came over the appointment of Chief Edwards. Foley wanted to promote Edwards when Chief Sanders retired. But Winborn considered him soft on crime."

"Why?" I asked.

"Edwards was one of those 'good ol' boy' types. I think he thought Edwards would let too many things slide. Well, the boss exploited this when Edwards changed policy on the so-called victimless crimes—prostitution, simple possession, and pornography. Edwards tended to leave the little stuff alone. Well, Winborn went ballistic over what he called the 'moral decay' in the police department."

Rhodes stopped just long enough to take another sip of his coffee and, with his free hand, rubbed what was left of his hair, as if to assure himself it was all still there and in place.

"The latest with Foley has to do with his insurance

agency. It seems that Foley's agency took over the city's group policy shortly after he became mayor. The boss thought that was suspicious and went after him for it."

"What about this zoning matter Parker was mentioning?"

Ace looked a little puzzled. "To tell you the truth, I haven't been able to figure that one out. The developer is Roscoe Costello, and he doesn't have a bad reputation as real estate people go. Never was able to figure it out."

"Did he take on people just for the hell of it?" I asked.

Rhodes just shook his head, "Who knows? It may have just been a power thing with him, but I suspect there might be more behind it."

He spent the next hour taking us through old files of the *Independent.* I was able to examine the ladies' club photos Buffy had told me about. The guy whose photo had so angered Buffy was someone by the name of Milo Becker. I asked Rhodes about him.

"Becker sold cars. Was pretty good at it, from what I heard. Had a wife and two small children. He heard about the photo and came here begging the boss not to print it. Winborn just smiled and printed the picture anyway. The guy's life came to an end after that. Wife left him. She took the kids. He lost his job and home. Just became a laughingstock."

"Whatever happened to this guy?" I asked.

"Funny thing about him," Rhodes said. "You would have expected him to leave town. He didn't. He stayed right here. He works one of those quick shops on the south side."

Chapter Three

Sunday evenings in Forbes Island apparently provide little in the way of recreation or entertainment. A drive through the city found nothing, including the diner next to the SuperSaver, open. Had we known the city better, perhaps we would have had more of a choice for dinner. As it was, we finally found dinner at a little truck stop on the highway that bypassed the city.

I followed Parker into the smoking section of the restaurant, where he promptly lit up his pipe. He ordered the "Hungry Man Special" and a root beer. I had the roast beef sandwich and coffee. Parker doesn't usually talk much while he eats, and this meal was no different than any other I had attended. I did the talking; he did the eating. Once in a while he would pause, point at me, nod, and grunt approval; then, without missing a bite, he would go back to his food.

When he finished, he ordered another root beer, stoked up his pipe, leaned back, and said, "Well, Stanley, what do you think?"

"Parker, I just told you what I thought. Weren't you listening?"

He shrugged.

"Okay, Parker. Once again, you've got so many people either scared of, or hating this Winborn, and they all could have a motive. You've got the congressman, the mayor, Becker, the real estate guy, and God only knows what you have in that report on the chief . . ."

"You didn't look?" he interrupted.

"Parker, when have I had a chance? Geez, even Buffy Coyle had a motive. I suppose, if you keep looking, you'll find that Michael and Doctor Burnelli did, too."

He just smiled. "Motive isn't part of the crime."

"Huh? What do you mean, 'motive isn't part of the crime'?"

"Just what I said. Motive is not an element of the crime."

"Parker, is this some of your legal mumbo-jumbo?"

"No. It's the truth. You don't need a motive to prosecute a crime." He finished his root beer. "Granted, a jury would like to hear a motive, but you don't need one for a conviction."

I stared across the table at him for a long minute, trying to decide how to respond.

"Then what are we talking about, Parker?"

"Nothing, just passing the time." He waved for another root beer. "We're going to have to be careful with this, Stanley. These kinds of investigations can get touchy. Too many important feathers can be ruffled."

"You don't need to tell me that, Parker."

"Good. Glad to hear it. Now, let's go see Becker," he said. With that, he got up, handed me the check, and walked out to the car.

We drove to the QuicKing store on South Beaver Road, where we were told Becker worked. We were too early to catch him; he was scheduled for the overnight shift. With a flash of my shield, the day manager was happy to give us his home address.

Becker lived in half a duplex in a run-down neighborhood not far from Buffy Coyle's. His was an older building with fading gray paint. It had a dry wooden porch that creaked when we crossed it. We knocked. He was home.

He was a tall man, about my size: six-foot, medium build, with jet-black hair. He was wearing only a T-shirt and jeans, and he needed a shave. He looked tired. We could hear a TV in the background when he opened the door. I showed him my identification.

"And this is Parker Noble from the Attorney General's office," I said.

"Yeah," he said, "you're here about Winborn. It's all over town." He didn't invite us in. We asked about the publisher. There was a long pause. "Are you here to take me in?"

Parker explained the process. "Right now we're just asking questions, Mr. Becker. We're gathering information, and trying to figure out what's going on." Parker stopped. Becker peered down at him. Parker began again. "We understand that you had a run-in with Mr. Winborn some time back," Parker said.

Becker studied Parker. "If you're from the Attorney General's office, you a lawyer?"

"Yes."

"Then you know I don't have to talk."

"We just want to clear a few things up," Parker said.

Becker looked at us. He ran his hand over his head, smoothing down his unruly hair. "I don't have anything to say. Good night, gentlemen." As quickly as that, he closed the door. Parker and I looked at each other. Parker had that look in his eye. I usually know what that means. This time I didn't.

* * * * *

When we got back to the SuperSaver, the clerk gave us the key to a second room. Finally, I would be able to get comfortable outside of Parker's view. Naturally, Parker made me pack my stuff to move to the new room. He said he would call Tom Foley while I unpacked.

My room was across the hall and just down from Parker's. It was identical to Parker's, except it overlooked the parking lot, whereas Parker's overlooked the main highway and a park across the street. It also only had one double bed; Parker's had two. I didn't have much to move from Parker's, and only one bag from the car, so it didn't take me long to get settled. I got back to Parker's room as he was hanging up the phone. "That was Foley," he said. "He'll talk to us after he sees his lawyer."

"So, when are we going to see him?"

"Whenever. He'll call us." He turned on the TV with the remote, then fiddled with it a little. "It's Sunday. Want to watch the Statler Brothers with me?"

Parker never ceased to amaze me. Here we have a good suspect who wants to see his lawyer, and he'll just sit there watching TV waiting for his call. Now, me, when a guy says, "I want to see my lawyer first," he moves to the top of my list. But not Parker. He never seems to be in any hurry. I think they teach them that in law school.

"I don't think I'd be as good a company as your . . . your . . . what's the name of your landlady friend again?"

"Mrs. Skosh."

"Yes."

"Yeah, she's very nice. The three of us watch TV every Sunday night."

"The three of you?"

"Yes, can't forget Buckwheat Bob."

"I don't want to hear about your dog, Parker." I excused myself and went back to my room. Parker asked me to have my office run the names we had generated thus far, so I called them in as soon as I got back to my room.

I looked outside. It was still light and it seemed too early to retire. I started to wonder what Diane was doing; then I remembered that the chief's file would still be on my laptop, so I thought it might be a good time to look it over, since the computer screen didn't bother me like it did Parker. I was just reaching for it when the phone rang. The voice on the other end was cheerful.

"Hi. This is Buffy. Remember me?"

"Yes. This morning."

"You didn't take me up on the celebration. Should I be mad?"

"Miss Coyle . . ."

"Buffy."

"Okay, Buffy. . . ." That was all I could get out before she cut me off. She gave me directions to a bowling alley not far from the SuperSaver and told me to meet her there in the bar.

I went, mostly out of curiosity. When I arrived, she was sitting alone in a corner booth. She almost looked too young to drink. She wore a pink short-sleeved blouse and a pair of black jeans. Her mousy brown hair was pulled back into a ponytail. She already had a beer. I ordered from the bar, then joined her.

"Hi," she said and smiled. I could see a little blush in her cheeks, and her pale blue eyes sparkled. She was not the Buffy I had first met. This Buffy was sweet. She ran her finger around the top of her glass, almost as if trying to tease it. "It's Sunday. I was alone. You don't mind, do you?"

I said I didn't.

She sat quietly for a few minutes, and then took a dainty sip of her beer.

"I really loved Anna Marie," she said. She looked past me and appeared to bat away a tear. Turning back to me she smiled. "I want to help you get whoever got her."

"Then just tell me what you know, Miss Coyle."

"Buffy."

"That's right, Buffy."

She blushed. "I haven't been feeling much like a Buffy lately." She circled the top of her glass with her finger again. She looked up. "You have a nice face. How old are you?"

I could feel myself blushing. "Miss Coyle, I'm supposed to ask the questions."

"Buffy," she giggled, then took another sip of her beer. She smiled. "You know, I'm starting to feel like a Buffy again. You married?"

I smiled. "Twenty-nine, and no."

"Why?"

"Why twenty-nine, or why not married?"

There was a little impish grin on her face.

"Why not married?"

I smiled. "It's a long story."

"Is it because you're a cop?"

I shook my head no. There was no reason to go into the story with her. "I didn't start out being a cop."

"What were you then?"

I took a sip of the beer. "You really don't want to know."

"Sure do." There was a slight twinkle in her eye. "Tell me."

"Promise not to laugh."

"Is it that bad?"

I had to chuckle. "No. I was a baseball player."

"What! Really? What team did you play for?"

"I signed with Detroit after college."

"Wow! You were a Tiger?"

I shook my head. "No, nothing like that, but I did pitch against them once. I was signed by the Tiger organization and sent to their double-A farm team in Erie."

"Pennsylvania?"

I nodded. "The Sea Wolves. 'See friends, see wolves.' " I had to smile. "That was kind of a marketing thing. Anyway, I was a pretty good right-hander. Second-year injury ended my career."

"I'm sorry," she said. "But how did you pitch against the Tigers?"

"They tried to play their triple-A teams once in a while. When they played Toledo, I was called up to pitch. Held 'em to two runs in six innings."

"That's too bad. So you think you could have made it, you know, to the Tigers?"

"I would have made it."

"That's a bad break. Does it bother you?"

"It did. Once. Finally you learn to deal with what life gives you. This is a good job and it gives me time to work on a master's. Enough about me. How about you?"

"Twenty-five. Never married." She paused and smiled. "Almost."

"Almost twenty-five or almost married?"

"Married."

"What happened?"

She took a long look into her beer glass. "It didn't go." She looked up and smiled. "You deal with what life gives you." She gave a weak smile. "Do you have anyone special?"

"Right now, just Parker."

"Who's Parker?"

I had forgotten. She hadn't met Parker yet. "The guy I'm working on this case with."

"Oh, your partner. Is he as cute as you?"

"No. He's not really my partner. In fact, he isn't even a cop."

She giggled again. "If he's not a cop, what's he doing with you investigating a murder?"

"Well, that's another long story."

"I've got the time."

I smiled. "Parker is a lawyer. He works for the Attorney General."

"Then why is he here? Shouldn't he be in court?"

I smiled again. "Well, Parker is kind of hard to explain. He used to prosecute. He was part of what they call area prosecutions. That meant he went all over the state, prosecuting cases that were either too difficult for local prosecutors or presented some kind of conflict for them. Kinda knows everybody and thinks he knows everything."

Buffy leaned over the table. "Stan?"

"Yes, Buffy."

"Would you buy me another beer?"

I smiled and motioned for the waitress. "You know, Parker always says, 'Anybody who drinks beer will steal.' "

She giggled. I was beginning to feel a little more comfortable. Two more beers came.

"So how'd ya get this guy as a partner?"

"He thought he was washed-up as a lawyer. It seems that he was promised a judgeship, but it never came. He got dejected and quit. The AG is his friend and found a new home for him. He teaches at the academy and puts on legal seminars for local cops. Otherwise, he just kinda hangs around and goes wherever he is sent. I've never worked with him alone before. Anyway, he always thinks he's in charge."

She smiled. "I suppose if the Attorney General sends him, he kind of is in charge."

I had to smile, too. "Well, if you look at it that way."

"Is he married?"

"Widower. No family. And you? You were going to tell me about almost getting married."

She smiled. Her little body relaxed. "His name was Kevin. He was a dreamer. Too much of one. I just couldn't play Sancho Panza while he chased windmills."

"This morning I got the impression you were somewhat of a dreamer. What happened?"

She shrugged. "Life. The only real windmills are potholes." She fingered her glass again, looked up, then down into her glass. "Maybe there are just too many dreamers. Maybe we don't all belong together."

"How long ago, Buffy?"

"Just about the time I left old Winborn. Life is funny, isn't it? One day you're on the top of the world looking down, and the next you're on the bottom looking up." She wiped her eye with a napkin. "You know, I was really looking forward to seeing Anna Marie again. She would have understood. I wrote to her and told her all about Kevin. I didn't tell her I quit the paper. Just told her Kevin and I split. She said she would be home for a visit, and we could talk."

She looked into her glass again. "You know, Stan, when we were in high school, I always used to tell her about my boyfriends. And every time one of them left me, she'd sit up all night with me while I cried. I cried all day yesterday when I heard she died. I really loved her. She would have been the best nun ever. I'll miss her. I don't think guys understand the kind of friendships we girls have."

"You said something this morning about not being able

to get a job without Winborn's recommendation. How could he hold you back?"

She shrugged again. "Simple. I told you about my first boss, Handy Andy. Naturally he won't give me a recommendation, and Winborn didn't. Well, it looks like I've spent the three years since graduation goofing off. Not a very good impression for a potential boss." She ran her finger around the top of her glass again. "Well," she said, after a brief pause, "this isn't about me. It's about my friend."

She sat silent for a minute. She blotted her eyes again with the napkin. Finally, she reached both arms across the table and took my hand in both of hers and pulled it to her still-moist cheek. She rested her head in my hand. Then she smiled and looked at me. "Would you take me home?"

Chapter Four

Six-thirty came early Monday morning. I was flattered at Buffy Coyle's come-on Sunday night, but I hadn't taken her up on her offer. Instead, we stayed in the bar until after midnight. I resisted the urge to tell her about Diane, but I did learn a little more about Anna Marie, her dad, and the newspaper. So, I guess you might say my night was short, but profitable.

I showered and dressed in a sport shirt and slacks. On the road, I was a little more casual in my dress than was Parker.

I knew he would not be up for a while. No matter where we are, Parker never seems to be in a big hurry to start the day, and no matter what time he gets up, you don't want to talk to him until he has had his breakfast. This Monday was no different.

I grabbed a quick coffee to go from the diner and started out on my usual morning walk. I am not what you would call an exercise buff, but I always try to take a brisk walk in the morning before starting my day. Over the years I've found it's a good way to get my blood circulating and heart beating, and it doesn't remind me of those training camp wind sprints like a jog would. I find it's also a good time to think.

I went over in my mind what we had thus far, which was

a city full of suspects who'd like to see Charles Winborn dead. Before leaving my room, I had taken a quick peek at the Edwards file I had received yesterday. For some reason, it seemed incomplete. Parker seemed to think something was questionable about it, too, or at least that's how he acted when he asked about it at dinner.

My walk around the SuperSaver took me through a nice little park area. There were several people already out walking, a few with dogs. Funny, every woman I saw reminded me of Buffy, not Diane. I began to feel a little bad that I hadn't taken her home. Then I wondered when I'd see her again. I started mulling over more questions I'd like to ask her. For most, to be honest, I already knew the answers. But the questions could still be used as excuses.

Then it dawned on me. Buffy knew Anna Marie was going to come home. She said so last night. If Buffy knew, did anybody else? Margo Roberts knew she was coming, but not the exact date. What about Buffy? Did she know the date?

There's my question, I thought. It was a perfect excuse to call her later.

I wound my way back to the SuperSaver. The morning traffic around the motel was starting to pick up. Morning rush hour in Forbes Island wouldn't be like it is in the capitol, but the cars were starting to stack up anyway.

When I got back to the motel, I picked up a copy of the morning *Independent*. It was only a five-day daily, so this was its first issue since the explosion that killed Anna Marie. The headline on the front page was what I expected:

PUBLISHER, DAUGHTER
DIE IN WEEKEND MAYHEM

On the front page there was a large picture of Charles Winborn with Anna Marie in her novice habit. The picture painted her as pretty as everyone had said she was. The chief must have been right; she probably did break a lot of hearts when she entered that convent.

Her father, on the other hand, looked stern. There was little family resemblance between father and daughter. Michael looked more like his father. Anna Marie must have taken after her mother and, from the looks of things, her mother must have been very beautiful.

As I walked back to my room, I could hear Parker stirring in his, so I grabbed my laptop and took it to the conference room so I could download anything new from headquarters. I had hoped that I would have reports on Becker, Berrigan, and Foley, but, realistically, I expected only one, maybe two, by now. After my download, I left a message for Parker that I would meet him at the diner. He finally arrived about twenty-five minutes later.

I was casual, but Parker came into the diner in his usual rumpled suit and a little bow tie. I noticed both were different than the ones he wore Sunday.

"Morning, Stanley," he grumbled as he sat down. I showed him the paper. He just stared at it, saying nothing. Finally, the waitress came and he ordered and got his coffee.

"It says we were sent in by the AG," I said.

Parker grunted.

"It mentions you, Parker. But I didn't see where it mentioned me."

Parker looked back at the paper. His finger traced the story on the front page, and then he turned inside, where he picked up the trail again. "Here you are," he said. "It says here, 'Noble is leading a team of state agents investigating the bombing.' That's you. You're the 'team of state agents.' "

He took the sports page and gave me the rest. He didn't say another word until his food came and he ate. Then he started to get a little more talkative. Finally, he announced our morning itinerary.

"Ace Rhodes called me this morning. He got hold of Winborn's lawyer. We have an appointment with him shortly."

I asked about Edwards and Foley, but he waved off my question. "The lawyer is expecting us around nine. Now Stanley, let me finish my food."

Quentin Collier, Charles Winborn's lawyer, looked and acted every bit like an attorney named Quentin should. He stood nearly six feet, and was immaculately dressed in a three-piece, pinstriped business suit with a starched white shirt in which he actually looked comfortable. A burgundy tie, with a matching pocket-handkerchief and gold cuff-links, set off his clothing. He was topped with a reassuring shock of gray hair above just enough facial lines to give him the look of character, not age.

Parker opened the interview carefully, telling Collier about the bits and pieces of information we had already collected. I was always amazed at the great deference Parker showed his fellow lawyers. Parker expected the same from me. "They are all fellow members of the justice system, and just because you are sometimes on different sides is no reason to show disrespect," he had once told me. Myself, I always thought that showing respect to a lawyer was like saluting an enemy officer in wartime.

"It looks something like this," Parker said. "We have ample numbers of people who, for various reasons, would like to have seen Charles Winborn out of the way. We know of no reason why anyone would like to see Anna Marie dead. I needed to know if anybody had a grudge against Anna Marie, so I think we can rule her out as the intended victim.

"Our basic assumption is that the old man was the target. So, what we have is a lot of people with a lot of public reasons for wanting him dead. I need you to tell me if there were people with private reasons to see Winborn—or his daughter, for that matter—dead."

Collier looked a little puzzled and slowly lit a cigarette, which then had Parker scrambling through the pockets of his suit jacket for his pipe. Collier looked across his great mahogany desk, first at Parker, then at me. "Do you mean something like blackmail?"

"I mean just that sort of thing, Counselor," Parker said. "You were familiar with his affairs. Is there anything you can tell us that could help us piece things together?"

"I'm sorry, gentlemen. I wish I could help. All I can tell you about is his will. Most of Chuck's financial affairs were handled through a Jeffrey Fielding. He's the business manager for the newspaper. If there were anything amiss in Chuck's finances, he'd be the person who might know. But, if you are suspecting anything like that, I doubt if even Fielding would know. Chuck had a way of keeping some things very close to the vest."

He laid his cigarette ash in the large tray on his desk. He carefully tipped his cigarette against the bottom of the tray. The ash came off in one piece. "As far as I know, there was nothing irregular; but remember, I wasn't in the best position to know."

Parker asked Collier how Winborn held ownership of the newspaper. "Were there any partners or stockholders we should know about?" he asked, trying to relight his pipe.

Collier nodded. "Contrary to public opinion, Chuck didn't own the paper outright," he said. "He may as well have, though. The effect was the same. He controlled a family voting trust that held the paper's stock. The trust was set up by Mrs. Winborn's family. Her father, John Benson, turned the trust over to Chuck and Libby—that was Mrs. Winborn's name, Libby—just before he died. Chuck and Libby were to receive the income from the trust for as long as either of them lived and was able to vote its stock, thus giving Chuck control over the paper's operations. The trust naturally favored the grandchildren, Michael and Anna Marie; however, Chuck was given some discretion over the final allotment each child would receive. Of course, under the circumstances, Michael will now inherit it all."

I asked how the trust would have been split had Anna Marie lived.

"It would have been split evenly." He stopped to brush an errant ash off his suit jacket. "No one outside the family would have received anything, except for a few small bequests. From what I know, there would appear to be no financial motive to see Chuck dead."

"Except for the children," Parker noted.

"Rule Anna Marie out," Collier said. "She had no need or use for money. As for Michael, he only needed to wait."

Parker looked puzzled.

"You didn't know?" Collier asked.

Parker shook his head.

"Charles Winborn had cancer. It was a slow form of it, low-grade lymphoma, but it was still fatal. He had another year, maybe two, two and a half tops."

* * * * *

Chief Edwards was waiting for us when we arrived at the police station. Because of the position the chief had been put in by Winborn's paper, the state was effectively in charge of the local gendarmes, at least as far as this investigation was concerned. Edwards, for his part, was cooperative, although obviously uncomfortable in his position. As soon as we arrived he gave us the news that the funerals for the Winborns would be held Wednesday morning, with a rosary said at the funeral home tomorrow night. He said the original plan was to have funerals tomorrow, but the nuns from Anna Marie's convent needed the extra time to make travel plans to Forbes Island. After the funeral, the nuns were going to take Anna Marie's body to the convent for internment there.

"Sad thing about the girl," Edwards said. "The old man almost deserved what he got, but the girl . . ." his voice trailed off. Although he looked pained, I wondered if it might be a look of guilt.

In response to Parker's question, Edwards said that as far as anyone could tell—and he had several men tracking these things down—no one outside the group at the Winborn home Friday night knew Anna Marie was home.

"Oh," I said. "That reminds me. Buffy Coyle knew she was coming home, but I don't know if she knew the exact date. And Margo knew, too, but not the date."

"And when were you going to tell me, Stanley?" Parker asked.

"I told you about Margo yesterday."

"And this Buffy?"

"I just found that out last night."

Parker looked perturbed but said nothing. I knew the subject would come up later.

Edwards said, "There's an ATF agent at the garage with an ordnance officer from the local guard unit. Would you like to see what they are doing?"

Parker got the directions from Edwards and we left. As soon as we got into the car, he started in on me. "What do you mean 'last night'?"

I explained Buffy's call and my trip to the bowling alley. I also told him what had transpired.

"Are you crazy? Slipping out to a bar to see a girl who could be a suspect? What do you have up there, sawdust?"

"Parker, I think I know what I'm doing. I handled it right."

He shook his head as if in disbelief. "Did you at least learn anything?"

"Yes, Parker."

"I mean something that will help us with this investigation."

I thought as I drove. "Buffy knew Anna Marie was coming home."

"You said that."

"It wasn't what you are thinking, Parker."

Parker was quiet, but he seemed satisfied. He lit his pipe as I pulled into the city garage area.

"Okay, Stanley," he said. "No more nocturnal activities with suspects."

Deputy Chase was in the garage with an Agent Fellows from ATF and a Major Osborne from the guard unit. Chase made the introductions.

"Here's what we have," Fellows started. "This is a simple device. It was wired into an ignition wire under the dash. A car lamp with the bulb broken appears to have been used to ignite the bomb. It was a pipe bomb filled with about a pound of black powder."

Fellows led us to the car.

"The pipe was set under the driver's seat on a quarter-inch iron tray. We can't tell if it was fixed on the tray or not, but that was enough to direct the force of the explosion upward. Without the tray, it is possible that the occupant might have survived. Might have."

Parker asked, "Is this anything that you would need any real expertise to rig?"

"Well, not really," Fellows said.

Osborne added, "A layman, Mr. Noble, might think that the pipe bomb would automatically kill the driver. Like Fellows says, maybe not. Putting the iron plate under the pipe, directing the force of the explosion, indicates more than a lay knowledge of explosives."

I asked if anyone had checked on the source of the powder.

"Like I said yesterday, too many suppliers," Chase said. "There are deputies asking around the county, but no one remembers a single purchase."

Parker looked at the federal man and pointed to the car. "Mr. Fellows, is that the way you found it?"

"Pretty much. We had to take some things out to examine them. We're reassembling them now. Just to see if we missed anything. Would you care to see?"

"When will you be finished?"

"In about an hour."

"Good," said Parker. "We'll be back after lunch."

We had left the police station without printing out my daily download from headquarters, so we headed back there. We got our printouts, but they only included Becker and Foley. Outside the station, Parker stopped and looked at the reports. Then he handed them to me, folded to show each man's military record. Both were Army ordnance.

* * * * *

Before we had left the police station, Parker had gotten a recommendation for a lunch counter across the street from the station house. It was called Billy's Dugout, probably because you had to descend half a flight of stairs from the sidewalk to get to it.

Parker, over my objections, led the way to the smoking section. "Next time, Stanley." We both ordered. Parker took the new printouts and gave me Edwards' from yesterday. He pointed out the problem with the chief's report. There was a four-year gap in his career.

"What do you make of this, Parker?"

"I don't know. He was born and went to school in Virginia. If I were you, I'd check with Virginia state police. I'd have your people do that today.

"As for these other guys, looks like we only have two right now, Becker and Foley . . ." His voice trailed off as he became distracted by something behind me. I turned to see what he was looking at. It was Buffy. Her shoulder-length hair was free from last night's ponytail. She was dressed in a pair of faded jeans and a bluish-gray tank top that didn't quite cover her midriff. She looked great. She also looked about fourteen.

She made a beeline straight to me. "Oh, hi, Stan. I missed you at the motel. So I checked at the station. They said you'd be here." She turned to Parker and put out her hand. "You must be Mr. Parker. Stan told me all about you last night. I'm Buffy."

Parker was the picture of disbelief. His jaw dropped, and his eyes nearly jumped out of their sockets. He took her hand, shook it, and looked at me. Parker was ashen but he didn't say a word.

Buffy used her butt to push me over in the booth and

scooted in beside me. She took a sheaf of papers from her purse and laid them down on the table.

"Here's all my notes," she said. "I sat up most of the night writing these out. I told you I was going to help you catch that guy." She looked at me and smiled. "I enjoyed last night."

Parker was having a conniption fit. He just looked at me. Finally, he started to say something. His lips were forming words but no sound was coming out.

"I need a Coke," Buffy said, as she bounced out of the booth and down to the end of the counter.

Parker turned back to me. Sound was starting to come out of him again, but he was only able to utter one word. "Lolita?"

"I can explain, Parker."

"And she's going to help? This better be good," he said. He turned and looked at Buffy. I didn't know if it was in amazement or in horror.

Buffy came back with two drinks. "Here, Mr. Parker, they said you had a root beer."

Buffy smiled. Parker was speechless, again. I had to bite my lip to keep from laughing at his reaction. He said nothing. He just drank the root beer.

"When do you want to go over this stuff, Stan?" she asked.

Now it was my turn to feel uncomfortable. "Buffy, we have to go back to the garage."

"Okay," she said, "I'll come."

Parker reached across the table and patted Buffy's hand. "Young lady, we're going to examine the car in which your friend was killed. I don't think you'd enjoy that."

Buffy looked at me for support.

"He's right, Buffy. You shouldn't see that."

Buffy smiled and looked at Parker. "Its okay, Mr. Parker. I'm cool with it now. I know Anna Marie would want me to help."

Parker gave me that look again.

"Miss Coyle . . ." he started.

"Buffy. It's Buffy Coyle. It's pronounced like Old King Cole. Not like coil, like a wire."

Befuddled, he just looked at her.

"It's in the spelling, Parker," I said. "You see. . . ."

He held up his hand. "Never mind, Stanley. Miss Coyle, if you'll excuse us, Stanley and I need to finish and get back to the city garage."

"Okay," she said. "But I'm coming, too."

There seemed to be nothing we could do or say to dissuade her. When we left, she followed us in a little pickup truck.

Deputy Chase and Agent Fellows were still there when we arrived. The car looked much the same as it had when we first saw it Saturday. "Really, we only needed to put the passenger's seat back in," Fellows said. "We took it out to pick up particles."

"Poor Anna Marie," Buffy whispered. "Show me how it was done. I want to know."

Fellows looked at Parker. Parker nodded and Fellows took us to the car. "Under here," he said, pointing under the dash, "is how the bomb was triggered. See this wire? This is the lead to the bomb. Most of it was blown away, but this part is left. It was wired here." He pointed again.

Buffy leaned in to see better. The car door was open, but she leaned in such a way as to not touch anything. "Show me again," she said.

Fellows looked at Parker, who nodded, and then repeated the lesson.

Buffy got down on her hands and knees and looked under the dash. "This wire?" she asked.

"That's right, Ma'am."

"Then what?"

Fellows pointed to where the driver's seat would have been. "The bomb was here. Another wire was attached to the seat-belt mount, here."

Buffy looked closer at the seat-belt mount. She looked at Fellows and pointed under the dash. "You mean it was connected by this black wire?" Fellows nodded. "And the other end was connected here?" He nodded again.

Buffy looked at the seat-belt mount again. She reached in and took a little piece of red wire that was flaking off. "And it was attached here?"

Fellows nodded.

"Why?"

"Why what, Ma'am?"

"Why two wires?"

Fellows looked at Parker, then at me. Finally he turned back to Buffy. "It needs a lead wire and a ground wire to make the right electrical circuit. Otherwise it won't work."

"Oh," she said. When she got up, I could see she was trying to blink back the tears. The color had left her face. She tried a half smile, then, head bowed, walked out of the garage towards her little truck.

Chapter Five

We didn't have much time to examine the car. Ace Rhodes paged Parker at the garage, and soon we were on our way back to the newspaper office. Rhodes met us in Winborn's private office. He closed the door.

"I didn't tell the police about this when I called you," he said. "But I found this envelope here this morning."

He opened a panel behind Winborn's desk. "I never knew this was here. I was trying to get some papers that fell behind the credenza. Here's what I found," he said, handing Parker a large manila envelope.

Parker took the envelope, sat at Winborn's desk, and opened it. It contained a single file folder marked "Edwards." In the file were yellowed newspaper clippings, and there was little doubt regarding whom they were about:

ROOKIE COP SUSPENDED AFTER ARREST

Police Chief Martin Gillmore today suspended Durham Police Officer Joseph Edwards for using excessive force in arresting a Negro shoplifting suspect at a downtown department store.

Pending the completion of the investigation, Gillmore said Edwards would remain on administrative leave. Edwards could be dismissed from the de-

partment if the results of that investigation warrant it, Gillmore said.

According to witnesses to yesterday's arrest, Edwards struck the suspect with his nightstick several times after the man had been subdued. Some witnesses had reported hearing Edwards using a racial epithet during the incident.

For Edwards, this is his second brush with the law since his appointment to the Durham police force last spring. Earlier, his former wife Peggy had charged him with assault. . . .

Parker looked at Rhodes. "Does anyone else know about this?"

"No. Like I said, I just found it this morning. That's why I left the message I did. I didn't want anyone at the cop shop to know."

"Did he have files like this on everyone?" I asked.

He shook his head. "I know that's the rumor, but this is the first time I've seen anything like this."

"If he had any more, do you know where he'd keep them?"

"No. I'm surprised I found this one. You might check his house."

"I know you are a newsman, Ace, but for now I'd like you to keep this quiet," Parker said.

"This isn't just another crime story to us, Mr. Noble. This hit home. This was our family. I'll do whatever you want."

"Good. Keep looking for more files," he said.

We had no sooner left the newspaper office when we received word that Tom Foley was ready to meet with us. He wanted to have his lawyer present, so PD told us to call him first.

Tom Foley's insurance business was, as residents put it, "on the square." In the local vernacular, it meant across the street from the county courthouse. Like many Midwestern cities, Forbes Island was built around a city square on which stood a local monument or courthouse. Inside, Foley's suite contained three rooms: Foley's office, a small conference room, and a larger reception area where his secretary was. His private office was small and crowded, filled with those little mementos that mark the progress of one's life and career. Tom Collier, Quentin's younger and much less distinguished-looking brother, was there to represent the mayor.

After some small talk, I discovered that Quentin and Tom did not practice together, and, in fact, were not exactly on the most friendly of terms.

Tom leaned forward in his chair. "Quentin's philosophy is simple: Poverty sucks. Mine is a little different. Having a license to practice law is more than having a license to print money. When you hang out your shingle, you're saying to the world: Champion for hire. Law is an experience, a life force of its own. Law is a demanding mistress, and her lover must forsake much to keep her satisfied. Quentin sees the law as a means to another end, money. The end I see is justice. Just different philosophies. But that's not what you're here about. Perhaps another time."

For a minute I was taken back. For a minute—no, for only the briefest of a split second—I began to think that some lawyers might be due the respect Parker gave to them. But then I swallowed hard and the feeling passed.

Parker, who had been nodding in agreement, came quickly to the point. Addressing Tom Foley, Parker reminded him of the situation in which he found himself: he wasn't a suspect or anything like that, not yet anyway, but we'd be remiss if we didn't consider his past relationship, which was mostly bad, with the late Charles Winborn.

"After all," said Parker, "there is a reason the state is investigating this matter. It is because of the bad relationship Winborn had with so many people who might influence the investigation. The state wants to see this done on the up-and-up; that's why we have to consider your involvement."

Tom Foley looked the part of a "man's man." There was just enough gray on his temples to give him a trustworthy look, without appearing old. He wore a light blue button-down shirt, tie, and no jacket. He leaned back in his chair, fidgeted with a paper clip from his desk, then looked at Collier. Finally, he looked back at us.

"I understand. If anyone had a grudge against Charles Winborn, it would be me. I've been over this with Tom, and I think the best thing is to just answer your questions as honestly as I can. Go ahead."

"You know your rights?" Parker asked.

"Tom explained them to me. I know I don't have to say anything."

I looked at the lawyer. He nodded towards me. I asked Foley what had started the feud between the mayor and the newspaper.

"I'm not exactly sure. Chuck, early on, had encouraged me to seek public office. I wonder now if he was really sincere or if he was just talking. But shortly after I took office, his attitude towards me changed. He never liked Joe Edwards, considered him soft on the crimes that Chuck wanted ended, mostly vice things, like pornography and prostitution. I think the break really came when I appointed Joe chief. Joe had been assistant chief and was really next in line for the job. But Chuck saw it as some sort of compromise with morality, a compromise that he disapproved of. Shortly afterwards he became a one-man crusade to put morality back into Forbes Island. He rode us hard."

Foley spoke in a soft, measured, confident manner.

I asked about the insurance scandal the newspaper reported.

"Nothing to it," Foley said, showing the same confidence. "This is an independent insurance office. One of the companies we sell group policies for is Metro Mid-American Insurance from Lincoln. So did the Wess Allen Agency. Some years ago, long before I became mayor, Wess sold a group policy to the city. About a year after I became mayor, which," he turned and gestured to me, "remember, is only a part-time job, Wess retired. Since we were the only other agent Metro had in the area, the company assigned the policy to us for servicing."

He shrugged. "All the public was told by the newspaper was that I got the city's business after I became mayor. Period. No explanation as to when and by whom the policy was originally sold. No explanation about the company's assignment to us or anything like that."

He tossed the paper clip back onto his desk. "It was a smear, and Chuck Winborn knew it was a smear and used it to ruin me. The election is in a couple of months, and at this rate I'll be lucky to get my own vote."

"Was Winborn supporting another candidate?" Parker asked.

"No. I really think he did some of these things just for spite."

The discussion continued in this vein for some time. Tom Foley answered in the same confident manner, but I could tell he was frustrated by the entire situation. He took us through a list of Winborn's prejudices. It seems that in addition to immorality, Charles Winborn despised unions.

At this point, Tom Collier broke in. "My law partner represented the union involved in the big tractor plant strike. There's a tractor assembly plant here, and the employees walked out at the end of their contract. The company was trying to force them into a wage reduction that the union was resisting. Well, to make a long story short, Winborn used the *Independent* to crucify the strikers. Not one favorable word was printed about them, and public opinion eventually turned against them.

"The union tried to fight back, but couldn't. It tried to put an ad in the paper to give its side, but it was refused. It even tried to do some hand-billing, but the larger print shops in the area, who do piece work for the *Independent*, were pressured into refusing the work. Some small shops did print the bills, but it was too little, too late. By then half the strikers were back at work, and the union was broken. This left a lot of bitterness in the community."

I continued to listen as Foley's lawyer laid out the facts of the union dispute and other controversies in which Foley and the newspaper had been involved. And as I listened, I could hear Buffy's words describing the same incidents, and I remembered her advice: "You can trust what Tom Foley says."

It was late afternoon when we had finished with Foley and, naturally, Parker wanted to find a place to eat. Rather than travel back to the diner by the SuperSaver, Parker decided to try a place called the Family Hour Café across from the Forbes County Courthouse and within sight of Tom Foley's office. As we walked to the entrance, I noticed Parker taking a long look at the courthouse building.

"I don't think I've ever tried a case here," he said. "In fact, I'm sure of it. I've been in most of the courthouses in this state, but not that one."

"Don't worry, Parker," I said. "I'm sure that before this case is over, you'll have a chance to go in and look around."

I followed Parker to the non-smoking section. "I think I'd like that," he said as we sat down.

"You think you'd like what?" I asked.

"To see the inside of the courthouse," he replied.

Sometimes, talking with Parker required a bit of concentration. It wasn't unusual for him to start a conversation, drop the subject, and then, without warning, pick it up again.

"Is there any particular reason why you'd like to see the inside of this courthouse?" I asked.

"They're all so interesting," he said as the waitress approached. He stopped talking long enough to look at the menu. He ordered the "Chef's Family Special," complete with salad, soup, a slice of pie, and a root beer on the side, to go along with his coffee.

"Courthouses have character," he continued after the waitress left. "Many seem so similar, but if you look closely, you'll see the interesting little differences in each one. Most around here have three stories, and the main courtroom is on the top floor with other public offices on the floors below. But once in a while you'll find one that has the courtroom on the main floor. You wonder at what the townsfolk of a hundred and fifty years ago were thinking. Why so many would put the court on the top, as if it were the pinnacle of the local government, and others put it on the ground floor?"

He looked serious as he spoke of courthouse architecture.

"Character, like some old ballparks have," I said.

"That's right, Stanley. Character."

"Parker, I'm beginning to think you have too much time on your hands." I smiled.

"No, seriously, just think about it. Next time you go into one of them, take a good look around. Look at the intricate woodwork and design, the polished brass, the paintings on the walls. When these buildings were built, the government and courts meant something to these people. That's why they are usually so beautiful."

I was a little puzzled at the direction this conversation was taking. "What are you saying, Parker? Don't you think the people today would build that nice a building?"

"No, I don't. Remember, at the time these old courthouses were being built, they were an economic boon for the city. Cities competed with one another for the site of the county seat, so they could have the courthouse. It meant becoming not only the governmental center for the area, but the economic one as well. Having the courthouse in your city meant economic growth and prosperity. County seat towns never failed. It was only natural that the towns that won the competition to host the county government wanted something special to house it."

"Well," I said, "you know history better than I do, so I'll take your word for it. I suppose that's why the state made so many counties. Spread out the prosperity."

"No," he said. "That's not it at all. Remember, when counties were being laid out there were no phones or cars. The only transportation was a horse. The state laid out its counties so that a farmer, anywhere in the county, could ride into the county seat, take care of business, and be back home in one day. That's why the large number of counties and why the competition for the county seat."

"And what does all this have to do with the Winborn case?" I asked.

"Nothing. I just thought you'd like to know."

"Tell me, Parker, do they teach you all this trivia in law school, or do you just come by it naturally?"

He started to give me that look, but then our food came, and, as usual, it provided the perfect distraction for him.

We returned to the SuperSaver and settled down around the small table in Parker's room. He took out the latest printouts we had for Milo Becker and Tom Foley.

"After our little visit with Foley today," I ventured, "I'd have a hard time seeing him involved in this mess."

"Oh, you do, do you?" Parker said. "And just why is that?"

"Two reasons. First, Buffy. Everything she said about Foley, he verified. And second, Tom Collier, I think, is an honest man."

Parker looked at me with a slight smirk on his face. Then looked down at the printouts. "You sure about that, Stanley?"

I wasn't amused. "Why not?" I asked.

"Because. First, never judge a person by his lawyer. I've seen too many evil men who have good lawyers and good men who have bad lawyers. Second, as far as that girl is concerned, start thinking with your head. Remember, she also had a reason to want to get even with Winborn. Here," he said handing me both printouts, "look at this."

I looked at the printouts and couldn't help but to feel a little sheepish, again. According to our records, both Foley and Becker had military records. Both were in Army ordnance. Foley had been an officer, Becker an enlisted man. Becker also had been busted a grade for fighting. Becker's demotion came as the result of an Article Thirteen administrative action. The initiating officer was Captain Thomas Foley.

"Looks like both our boys were at Fort Sill together," Parker said.

"And knew each other," I noted. "Ordnance. Isn't Fort Sill the home of the artillery? That would fit."

"Also looks like Becker was in and out of trouble for some time after he got out of the Army," he said, pointing to another part of Becker's report.

Parker was right. Becker's record for the first five years after his military discharge contained numerous entries, everything from assault to marijuana. But for the last fifteen years or so he'd been clean.

"Check when he married," Parker told me. "Most of that record is petty stuff, the kind of thing a man can put aside when he starts a family."

"But what might he resort to when he loses it?" I asked.

"That's a good thought, Stanley. We'll need to get more on Becker. For now, he's the only person we know who had a strong motive to see Winborn dead and the apparent means to pull it off," Parker said.

For once I was right. Parker would never think so, but I knew as soon as Becker had refused to talk, he was hiding something.

"Yes," Parker said, reading my mind, "but don't jump to too many conclusions. Remember, Tom Foley wanted to see his lawyer first, and you found that suspicious. Now you're ready to clear him because you like his lawyer, and this little girl that has your fancy likes him, too. Don't overlook that there is a connection between Foley and Becker. You'll want to find out exactly what that is."

Parker re-folded the reports, and continued. "And don't

forget, we are still investigating the death of a nun. Right now, as far as we are concerned, Winborn's death might have been just collateral damage."

I hate getting told my business by a lawyer, especially this one. But I had to admit—at least to myself, never to Parker—that he might just be right about some of this.

"There may be a connection between Foley and Becker, Parker, but what would that have to do with Buffy?"

Parker just smiled and gave me that look again. "Look, go get your gizmo and make a further inquiry on Becker and Foley and see if your people have the congressman's file yet. I think that's the only one we've requested and are missing. You go do that now; I've got to call Mrs. Skosh. Buckwheat Bob wasn't eating yesterday, and I want to see if he's okay now."

I let Parker call about his dog and went to the conference room near the front desk, where I was able to plug in my laptop. I framed the request for more information on Becker and the mayor. As soon as it was sent, the little beep from the computer notified me that another file was ready for download. The file name indicated it was Congressman Berrigan's. I loaded it and took the computer back to Parker.

He was just getting off the phone when I entered. He was pleased to report that Buckwheat Bob was back to eating again. He told me to open Berrigan's file. I did.

"Well, I'll be," he said, looking over my shoulder. "I've never seen anything like that. What do you make of it, Stanley?"

I didn't know either, but there it was, clear as day on the mini-screen: FILE EMBARGOED BY ORDER OF DIRECTOR, FBI.

Chapter Six

Tuesday morning was overcast, which matched my mood. Parker had dismissed me Monday evening so he could call the Attorney General at his home about Congressman Berrigan. I could understand the sensitive political nature of the matter, but naturally, as a cop, I resented being cut out of the loop. As irritating as that was, however, I took personal offense at Parker's suggestion that I ought to watch my contact with Buffy. He was right, of course. But I still took offense.

So naturally, after a night of more tossing and turning than sleep, Buffy was on my mind when I finally arose. As usual, I picked up a quick cup of coffee and started out on my morning walk. There was a slight chill in the air, so I wore a windbreaker. As I watched the people in the park, my thoughts drifted back to Buffy. She was nothing like Diane, and I wanted her to be on the level, although I knew Parker had his doubts. I was also confident that Tom Foley was on the up-and-up, too. If I was right, both could be invaluable as investigative resources.

Because of the cool weather, I had hurried my morning ritual and was back at the diner next to the SuperSaver at a rather early hour. It was too early for Parker, or so I thought. To my surprise, he was already there waiting for his order when I arrived.

"This is a little early for you, isn't it, Parker?"

"Mrs. Skosh called this morning," he replied. "Buckwheat Bob took a turn and had another bad night. Then the AG called about this Berrigan stuff. I'm really worried about Buckwheat Bob."

"Parker," I said, "what did the AG say?"

"About Berrigan or Buckwheat Bob?"

"You asked the Attorney General about a basset hound?"

"Yes, he's a very canine-conscious individual. As a matter of fact, he knows Buckwheat Bob."

"Parker, about the congressman."

"Oh, that. Well, it's none of our concern."

Parker's order was delivered. It consisted of three eggs, three pancakes, three sausage patties, and hash browns.

"Where do you put all of that," I asked, "and why is it none of our concern?"

"You don't want to know about my dog?"

He could be very irritating.

"No, Parker. I don't want to know about the dog. I want to know about the congressman."

"None of our business," he replied. "Pass the ketchup."

This was irritating with a capital *I*. I ordered a bowl of bran flakes and coffee and tried to collect my thoughts.

"Okay, Parker, you win. What next?"

"We look for a murderer."

"Where? What are we doing next?"

"What do you think, Stanley?"

"I think there's something strange about this congressman thing, that's what I think. And I'd like to know why we're being called off."

"We're not being called off. What gave you that idea, Stanley?"

"Let me tell you, Parker. First, we can't get the congressman's file. Second, you talk to the AG, then tell me it's none of our business. That sounds like being called off to me."

"Stanley, there are just some things you're going to have to take on faith. Let's just leave it at this: The AG has determined that the congressman is not a suspect. Now, tell me, what have you got planned for today?"

Sometimes my irritation with Parker can boil over to anger. I could feel my temperature rising, so I thought it best to cool down before responding.

"Aren't you going to tell me about your dog?"

He looked up, smiled, then started on a long exposition on canine ailments and Buckwheat Bob's medical history since puppyhood. Listening to Parker, I almost began to feel sorry for him. That stupid dog was the laziest mutt I had ever met, but he meant something to Parker. I don't know exactly how long Parker had been a widower, but it was obvious that the dog was the only family—and maybe the only friend—that he had. In all the time that I had known Parker, he had only mentioned the dog and his landlady, Mrs. Skosh, no one else. By the time my cereal came, he was on heartworm and discoloration of fecal matter, and I began to understand just why he might be alone.

"Parker," I interrupted, "I want to follow up on this Becker fellow. I have a hunch about him."

"Hunch?" He looked a little taken-back. He sat straight up, looked directly at me, and just blinked three or four times. "What kind of hunch?"

"I don't know. He seems like an odd duck. He stayed here after the newspaper ran the picture that ruined his life. He has ordnance training and a criminal history. Besides, he refused to talk earlier."

Parker continued to look at me with a vacant stare. It was almost like he was trying to understand what I was saying. He didn't say a word for the longest time. Then he took a sip of his coffee and said, "Okay, Stanley. You go after Becker."

That was it. My assignment for the morning was to check out Becker. And I knew just whom I wanted to do it with, too.

I dropped Parker at the police station. It was about nine-thirty when I reached Buffy's. I had called first and she was expecting me. Unlike yesterday, she had on grown-up clothes when I arrived: a blue skirt with a pink blouse and a light gray jacket. She had her hair pinned up and looked more like a librarian than anything else.

"Do you like it?" she asked.

I did and told her so.

There was a sparkle in her pale blue eyes when she looked at me. "I wanted to look professional. I don't think Mr. Parker liked my other look. So I wanted to look like a good detective while I was helping you two."

"Buffy, this is all unofficial. You're a source, not a detective."

"A valuable source, Mr. Policeman." She reached up and touched the tip of my nose. "And no better source you will ever have." She smiled, obviously pleased with herself.

"As long as you understand. Now, it's just the two of us this morning . . ."

She leaned into me and put her arms around my neck. "Good, that's the way I'd like it."

I reached around and unhooked myself from her hug. I felt uncomfortable. Was I letting this girl compensate for the loss of Diane? I could feel myself trying to suppress a smile. "Not now, Buffy. We have work to do first."

"You mean we have to crack the case before we play?" she teased. "Isn't that what you cops say, 'crack the case'?"

I smiled. There was something attractive about the little girl in Buffy Coyle. "Something like that. Anyway . . ."

"You want to look over my notes?" she asked.

"Becker, I want to know all about Becker."

"Who?"

"Becker. The guy in the picture. The ladies' club."

"Oh, okay." She scrunched her face. "Well, he sold cars, I think."

"Yeah, Ace told us that much."

"Who?"

"Ace. Ace Rhodes. One of your bosses at the paper."

"Ace?" she cried. Then she started to laugh. "Ace, my ass. That bald-headed geek. He's the only one who calls him Ace." She stopped long enough to try to control her giggling. "You know what his name really is? I'll tell you. It's Acel. Acel. Can you imagine that? He thinks Ace makes him sound like a real newsman. What a phony. Acel Rhodes, two-bit phony."

"Is there anybody at that newspaper you like?" I asked.

"Yeah, maybe Michael. Maybe. But Acel? Not my cup of tea. Now, captain," she saluted, "what orders do you have for me?"

It didn't take us long to get to Becker's. He was out. I figured he might be at work, so we drove over to the QuicKing. We parked along a side street and I sent Buffy in for two sodas.

"That's him," she said when she returned. "I remember when it happened. He came into the office and was begging us not to run his picture."

"What was his demeanor then?" I asked her.

"He was really upset. His eyes were red and watery. Old Man Winborn just laughed. The guy begged, but the old man just laughed."

"Did you know Becker before that?"

"No. No one did." She ripped the end off her straw wrapper and tried to blow it at me. It wouldn't go. "He was just another guy on the street."

"Think, Buffy. Did he look like he was mad enough to hurt someone?"

She relaxed a little in her seat, frowned, and then took a sip of her soda. "Might have been. I don't know, Stan. I was just so embarrassed by it all that I wanted to crawl into a hole. Maybe."

"What did you cover besides city hall?"

"The courthouse. Police. You name it."

"Do you know how to locate someone who's moved?"

"Come on, Stan. I wasn't a cop, but I was a pretty fair reporter. If they haven't changed their name or are in a witness-protection program, I probably can find them."

"Good," I said. "Find Mrs. Becker for me."

I dropped Buffy off at the courthouse and met Parker at Billy's Dugout. He was already there when I arrived.

"This is twice in one day, Parker."

He barely looked up from his plate. "Huh? What do you mean twice?"

"Twice. You beat me to the table. Twice. You did it at breakfast, too."

He just looked at me and kept eating. I ordered the soup of the day and told him I was looking for Mrs. Becker. He just nodded and kept on eating.

"What did you do today, Parker?"

He stopped eating and looked at me like he was really

perturbed. “I’m eating. Can’t you see? I’m eating.”

“Sorry, Parker.” I wanted to say more but didn’t dare. Why I have to put up with this torture I’ll never know. Some days when I’m with Parker, I can just picture my career dead-ending.

“Tell me,” he said, apparently noticing my irritation, “what else you did.”

I could feel myself turning beet red. Naturally, I didn’t dare say I was with Buffy. He looked up as my soup arrived.

“Did it take you all morning to decide to look for Mrs. Becker?” he asked.

“No, Parker. If you must know, I had Becker staked out.”

“Where was he?”

“At work.”

“What was he doing there?”

“He was selling sodas.” I hated working with this guy.

He finished his meal and pushed away the plate. “Hmm,” he said, raising one eyebrow. “I think this is the break we need.”

I was just ready to tell him what I thought when I noticed his stupid smile and the look. I had to smile back. “Okay, Parker, what did you do?”

“I’ve been checking into this Edwards thing. The old newspaper clipping is for real. He was on the Durham police force and was kicked off for using excessive force on that black shoplifting suspect.”

“African-American,” I corrected.

“Whatever. Anyway, he was kicked out.”

“Then how’d he get a job here?”

“Not so hard to do,” he said, “if you have a few friends in the right places and can forge a document or two. His real problem is that stuff with his ex-wife. They now call that domestic abuse, and, if you have a conviction for that on your record, you can't carry a weapon."

"And so?"

"And so, if that newspaper article ever came to light, Edwards loses his job and his pension."

"Where does that put him?" I asked.

"Right in the middle of this thing, Stanley. From what I can gather, after the Durham incident, Edwards moved, changed careers for a time, earned an associate degree from a community college in Ohio, and then re-entered police work out here. Naturally, he assumed that his earlier stint in Durham would never be known. And, normally, it wouldn't."

He waved for more coffee. "Remember, when he entered the field here, there was no police academy or special background checks. You could hire on with a small-time force some places by just being sober. Then you just move up to a little larger force until you find what you like."

"But how did Winborn know?" I asked.

"Wrong question, Stanley. It isn't as important how Winborn found out as it is to know if Edwards knew Winborn knew about it."

"Does he?"

"Didn't ask. I think we'll just have to let this one play out a little first."

"Why not confront him now?"

"Patience, Stanley. There'll be time for that. Right now we need his cooperation."

It was about two o'clock when we pulled up in front of the offices of R. T. Costello and Sons Construction Company. The company offices were located several miles west of the city's main business district. Parker had driven, so the trip was more eventful than most. But we did manage to make it in one piece, and for that I was thankful.

A quick flash of my state identification was all we needed to be ushered into the office of Roscoe Costello, who, in spite of the name of the company, was the sole owner and proprietor of the business. He had a large, spacious office. His desk was at one end, and a long, conference-sized table was opposite it. It was covered with papers and blueprints. Costello was a heavyset man with thick hair, probably in his late forties. After the opening pleasantries, Parker got right down to business: What about the feud between Costello and the paper over the zoning change?

"Look, Mr. Noble, I don't know what got into old Winborn over this matter, but there was no feud between us. Actually, I hardly knew the man. All I know of this matter is that he opposed the zoning for my new development." Costello reached into his desk drawer and took out a cigar. Parker, naturally, reached for his pipe.

"Forbes Island is a no-growth area," Costello explained. "You guys from the state capitol should know that." He lit the cigar and blew the first blast of smoke into the air. "We need new, clean, affordable housing if we are going to attract new business to this area. There's a new industrial park being developed just south of the city limits, but that will do the community little good if we can't house the workers it'll attract."

"So what was Winborn's beef?" I asked.

"That's got us all baffled. The area in question is currently farmland, about fifty-five acres. I have an option on the land, but it'll do me no good if I can't build on it. And, of course, without the zoning change, I can't."

Parker asked about the plat.

"That work's already been done," Costello said. "That

was almost the first thing we did. We filed the plat, pending city approval of the zoning. The city staff has already reported favorably, as expected, but the zoning board killed it. A couple of those guys are . . . er, were . . . in Winborn's pocket. One is an advertising salesman for the *Independent*. They're simply not going to do what Winborn doesn't want done."

I asked if Winborn had ever opposed any previous development.

"No," he said, blowing more cigar smoke, "and that's the strange thing. He'd always been pro-growth and pro-business. This is the first time that he'd ever tried to block anything like this. Sorry, I wish I could be of more assistance."

We talked another half an hour about the city, but he wasn't much more help. Before we left, he gave us a small area map on which he noted the location of the land he wanted rezoned. "If you find out what's up, I'd sure like to know," he said.

"What do you make of it?" Parker asked on the ride back.

"I don't know. This one baffles me, too. Unless he's not telling us something. Otherwise, there seems to be no reason for Winborn's stand." Parker was driving again, so I asked, "Where are we going?"

"Back to Foley's. I think we want to ask a few questions about Specialist Becker and a certain Article Thirteen. As far as Costello is concerned, I'd forget about it for now. My guess is that Winborn had some financial interest in the property not being developed that even Costello doesn't know about. Costello's got too much other stuff going for him to mess around with murder."

It didn't take us long to get back to Foley's insurance office, where we were recognized by his secretary and shown right in.

Parker asked Foley, "You don't mind if we ask you a few questions without your attorney, do you?"

Foley looked a little surprised but smiled, "Do I have a choice?"

"Yes. If you say no, we'll leave."

Foley motioned for us to sit down. "Ask away."

"I'd like to know about your military experience."

Foley fidgeted a little. "I suppose you already know. I was in ordnance."

"And so was Milo Becker," Parker stated.

The smile, or what was left of it, faded from Foley's face. "And your point, Mr. Noble?"

"No point, Mayor. Just an observation. Want to tell me about Becker?"

Foley readjusted himself in his seat, then looked directly at Parker. "Becker was from the area when he was assigned to my unit at Fort Sill. I think he thought the hometown connection meant a little more than it did. He tried to get away with a little too much, and I had to put my foot down. We both ended up back here, and that's about that."

"What was your relationship with him after you returned from the service?"

"Nothing, really. He moved to Forbes Island sometime after I returned. He worked for Stevens Ford, was assistant manager. I never bought a car from him, but I did look, once.

"He had a family and was a fairly quiet person. Kept to himself. But I knew who he was, and he was always friendly when we met. Liked to discuss old times, you know. Probably more because he knew the mayor than anything else. Why?"

"What happened after his picture appeared in the newspaper?"

Foley shook his head. "I think most people around here felt kind of sorry for him. His wife left him and Mrs. Stevens fired him. Had he been alive, Old Man Stevens would have been amused, but not the missus! Becker was gone before the day was out."

"Was he a violent man?"

"Small-time stuff in the Army. Nothing more."

"What if I told you he had a criminal record between the Army and here?"

"Depends on what type of record. Young Becker could have been a hothead. Bar fights and the like. I'd be surprised if he was involved in anything more serious."

"Like murder?"

Foley didn't respond. He looked at me, then back at Parker. He shrugged. Parker nodded, thanked Foley for his time, and we took our leave.

It didn't take us long to get back to the SuperSaver from Foley's office. I must say that Parker's driving had improved somewhat. We went directly to Parker's room.

"Are you still sure of this Foley guy, Stanley?"

"Yes." I tried to sound definite but wasn't as convinced as I tried to sound. "His story is plausible. Don't forget, enlisted men and officers live in different worlds in the Army."

"Don't forget, Stanley, he didn't volunteer any of this when we first met."

"But we didn't ask, either," I interjected.

"Who's sounding like a lawyer now?" he said.

I sometimes feel like he deliberately sets these traps for me to walk into. "Now what?"

"You keep on Becker. And see if you can find anything out about that piece of land Costello wants. Probably nothing, but it'll tie up a loose end and might end a line of inquiry."

"Or open one," I ventured.

"Or open one," he agreed.

When I returned to my room, I found a small, pink envelope waiting for me on my nightstand. I made sure I was alone before I opened it. It was from Buffy.

Bingo, mi capitán. 122 Prospect, Grand Bay.

I smiled and put it in my pocket.

Chapter Seven

Parker and I had a quick dinner. Well, quick for Parker, that is. Then we went to the funeral home for the Winborn wakes. The local news media had made quite a production of the crime and it was estimated that the crowd would swamp the small mortuary.

When we arrived, we found that the crowd estimates were correct. The funeral director had to move the caskets of Anna Marie and her father from the normal viewing rooms to the chapel to accommodate the large crowd. The chief; the mayor; both Colliers; Quentin, the distinguished, and Tom, the lesser; and Dr. Burnelli were all there. Also present were Ace Rhodes, a score of police officers we had briefly met, most in civilian clothing, and a small group of nuns I assumed to be from Anna Marie's convent.

Although it was a double wake and both caskets were closed, it was fairly easy to determine who came for whom. The dozens of younger mourners, along with the nuns, gathered on one side of the room before Anna Marie's casket. The older mourners gathered on the other side of the room, nearer to the old man's casket.

Straddling the two groups was Michael. Having just lost his sister and his father, he looked strangely awkward trying to make small talk with all of those who wanted to express their condolences. On the far end of the room near the head of Anna Marie's casket, Buffy, dressed all in black, was visiting with Margo Roberts. Both were crying; I thought it best not to bother either of them.

Parker and I stayed in the back, unobserved and out of the way.

"You take me to the neatest places," I whispered to Parker.

A small smile started to escape from his lips. "Shhhh," he said, "you don't want me to make jokes at your wake, do you?"

"What makes you think you'll live that long?"

"I eat right," he replied.

Before I could respond, Margo and her mother approached. "Hello, Mr. Stankowski. Is this the Mr. Parker Buffy told us about?" asked Margo.

I made the introductions, noting that it was Mr. Noble, not Mr. Parker.

Mrs. Roberts started first. "I can understand her making that mistake, Mr. Noble. Why Buffy and that poor Winborn girl were almost as close as Margo and Anna Marie were. I'll bet this is really hard on her. She is such a delicate child, you know." She turned to look across the room at Buffy. "Looks like she's been crying all day. Poor, poor girl, isn't that right, Margo?"

Margo nodded agreement and turned to me. "How's the investigation, Mr. Stankowski? Was I able to help?" she asked.

I told her yes, she was a big help. Then Parker started on a long-winded explanation of how crimes are investigated, the things he looked for, and how most criminal cases that are lost, are lost because of shoddy police work. Of course, he didn't bother to mention the lawyers and judges who won't let us use our best evidence. That would make too much sense for a lawyer to realize. I was ready to interrupt and defend my brethren, when Mrs. Roberts saved me from the trouble.

"That is so interesting, Mr. Noble. I could just spend the whole evening listening to your stories. Why, my club has speakers the first Tuesday of every month. I don't suppose you'd be interested, would you? Why, you'd draw the biggest crowd of the year. Oh, please give me your card, so I can get hold of you."

Parker looked resigned to his torture, and I wasn't going to do anything to save him. As he shuffled through his pockets for a card, I followed Margo's gaze as it turned to Michael.

"I really feel sorry for him," Margo said softly, still looking at Michael. "He's like a fish out of water." She turned to me. "He doesn't have any other family. And to lose both your sister and father together, this has to be hard on him."

I looked back at Michael. Outside of his attire, he looked the same as when we met Saturday at the hospital. Those thick glasses still accentuated his bulging eyes. He still resembled a frog, albeit a sad one.

"He looks a little odd, but I can't put my finger on it," I said to Margo.

"Oh, that's just Michael. He can't match anything," she said. "Look. He has two different shades of green. He'd never make it in the fashion world."

"Oh, Margo. He's always been that way," Mrs. Roberts said. She took a long look at me. "So many men can't put the right colors together. They have no taste for fashion. You do a nice job, Mr. Stankowski. That is a very nice sports coat and tie. I told Margo that the other night after you left, didn't I, Margo? Margo is very good with colors, too. I've always said that. You two are both very good with colors. Why I bet you'd both be able to pick out wonderful wardrobes."

Margo blushed. Mrs. Roberts smiled and looked at the card Parker had given her, the one with the gold Department of Justice seal on it. She turned to him. "Deputy Attorney General? Why, Mr. Noble, I am really impressed. You know, I didn't vote for your boss in the last election. I did the time before that, though. It was because of that garden club thing, remember? Or am I thinking about someone else?"

"Madam," replied Parker, "we don't investigate garden clubs."

"No, no, I'm right. It had something to do with that medicine they were growing. Oh, I'm sure I can remember. I have such a good memory about these things, you know. It was a garden club. Some old ladies and, oh, what else?"

"Oh, yes," he said. "I think I know which one. The garden club members were marijuana growers. Is that the case you are talking about?"

"Oh, yes, that's it, Mr. Noble. Why, you have such a good memory, too."

"I remember that case now. We had to prosecute because the local attorney wouldn't." He turned to Margo and me. "These little old ladies were growing marijuana for what they claimed were medicinal purposes. They called themselves the True Health Garden Club," said Parker.

Mrs. Roberts looked pleased. "Yes, I do believe you are right. Oh, can you tell my club that story? The girls will love it. Oh, Mr. Noble, if you would favor us, please." Then she turned to me, "Oh, Mr. Stankowski, please help us get your boss to come."

The words "your boss" hit me like a brick in the head.

There was a smirk on Parker's face. Mrs. Roberts continued, "It would be the highlight of our year. And you could come, too, Mr. Stankowski. Why, Margo would be there, and afterwards we could all go out for dinner."

"Mother," a sheepish Margo said, "I think we'd better leave these gentlemen alone. They're going to start the rosary soon and they don't have kneelers in these pews. If you don't want to kneel on the floor, we'd better get one of those other kneelers before they're all taken."

And with that, they excused themselves.

I turned to Parker. "You made a hit."

"And you and Margo are fashion plates."

"I didn't know we were going to have to kneel, Parker. I thought they did away with all this stuff. You're Catholic; you should have said something."

Parker just gave me that look. "You're Polish, Stanley. If you did your Sunday duty, none of this would come as a big surprise to you." He turned away to survey the crowd again.

Buffy was now standing with the group of nuns. She was holding the hand of one in both of hers, while the tears were streaming down her soft cheeks. Soon the older nun put her arms around Buffy, like a mother comforting a daughter. As she held her, I could see Buffy's little body shake as she wept into the nun's habit. I had an urge to go to her and hold her too, but the situation, not to mention Parker's presence, caused me to resist. Instead, I watched as Buffy mourned the friend she had loved.

The formal part of the wake lasted another forty-five minutes. The Winborn family priest read some prayers, a few people spoke, then one of the nuns led those present in the rosary. The nun would lead the group with part of the prayer, and the audience would respond with the ending. The small group of nuns, which by now included Buffy, gave by far the loudest response. Those who didn't get out in time were forced to kneel throughout the service, but a small few, Margo and her mother included, at least had something nice on which to kneel.

After the rosary, no one seemed to be in any hurry to leave. Most just began milling around, chatting with old friends and offering kind words to Michael. Presently, the priest made his way to Parker and me.

He was big, at least six-six, and looked like he had played football in college. "Would you be the gentlemen investigating this sad occurrence?"

"That would be us, Father," Parker replied, introducing us to the priest.

"Glory be to God. Well, I'm Father Dan, Daniel Hennessy. Well, Glory be to God. We know how important your work is. I'll keep you both in my prayers . . . in my prayers."

"Father," Parker said, "perhaps you can help us."

"Oh, yes, yes. Anything. Anything I can do."

"Father, if Mr. Winborn said anything, or you know anything that might be helpful . . ."

"Oh, Glory be, I wouldn't have the slightest idea. I'd have to think about that. I guess in my business, we don't think that way."

"I understand, Father," Parker smiled. "But if you think of anything that would help us find a motive for what happened . . ."

"Oh, oh. A motive. Yes, I suppose that would be helpful. Glory be. Probably someone who disliked Charles. So many did, you know. So many did. But Anna Marie, well, well, poor girl. Sweetheart she was. Poor, poor thing. Well, well, a motive, huh? Well, I'm not very good at these things, but I'll do what I can. Let me think on this. Maybe he said something. Maybe. Call me at the rectory."

With that he smiled, mumbled something, and started to leave.

"Oh, Father," I said. He turned back. "Can you tell me what your Mass times are?"

He smiled, "Sunday at eight-thirty and ten-thirty. Hope to see you there."

I know I blushed. "I've not been in quite a while. And daily?"

"Six-thirty every day, seven on Saturday. You can start back anytime, you know," he said with a smile, then turned and walked away.

We watched the priest leave, and Parker turned to me. "I'm glad to see you on your way back to the Church. Very good, Stanley."

"Parker, I'm not interested in church; I just wanted to know if there was a daily Mass. That would explain where Anna Marie was going. Give me a break, I'm just doing my job."

"Ahh," he said, "and I was starting to have such high hopes for your soul." I just looked at him and smiled. As we turned back to survey the crowd, I felt a tinge of excitement. I could see that Buffy, eyes still red and puffy, was making her way towards us with one of the nuns in tow.

"Stan, Mr. Parker, I want you to meet Mother Mary Frances. She was Anna Marie's superior. These are the gentlemen I was telling you about, Mother. I told her my real name is Frances, too."

Mother Mary Frances looked about seventy. She was short, about Buffy's height, and had a face full of character—not age. Parker, ever the gentleman, took the nun's hand and made a mock bow. "It is our pleasure, Mother.

May we express our condolences on your loss? Since we arrived here in Forbes Island, all we have heard is what a wonderful young lady your Anna Marie was."

"Yes, Mr. Parker . . ."

"Noble."

"Thank you, Noble," she said, smiling. "Yes, she was a most wonderful child. And to see all her friends. What a blessed life she had. We all believe that we have a sister in heaven now, talking right up to the Lord on our behalf."

"Noble, Mother, is my . . ." He stopped, shook his head, and smiled. "Well, thank you. Your faith is most inspiring."

"And what a wonderful family she must have had. She talked so much of her late mother and brother. And to have friends like this," she said as she hugged Buffy. "How blessed could she have been?"

"Yes," Parker said. "She was blessed."

"And her father, what a lovely man he was. Took care of her even in the convent. What a blessed person he was."

Parker and I exchanged glances. I tried not to betray any emotion.

"Yes, Mother. He must have been a wonderful man. Took care of them very well," Parker said.

"Oh, yes, and that was so hard to do with Anna Marie's condition."

We exchanged glances again.

"What condition?" he asked.

"Oh, you didn't know? That would be just like Anna Marie. She had multiple sclerosis. It was in its early stages, but her father took care of everything. Oh, and for a small order such as ours . . ." she started to say, as she began to choke back her words. "A small . . ." She blotted her eyes with a tissue, "But to do that for us and his daughter, well, Noble, it was just so wonderful."

She began to cry, and Buffy handed the elderly nun a handkerchief.

Parker looked at me. I could tell he was still irritated by the name thing. I made a mental note to straighten Buffy out about it.

"I'm sorry, gentlemen," she said. Reaching out, she touched our hands. "May God grant you strength in your work." Then she turned and, with Buffy now as the comforter rather than the comforted, she returned to the small group of nuns on the other side of the room.

I did not need to remember the name thing. Parker brought it up as soon as we left the funeral home.

"That poor old nun is there thinking my last name is my first name. This Buffy-person was a reporter. Now I know how they mix all those things up. First name. Last name. Can't they ever keep anything straight?"

"Well, look on the bright side, Parker. You made a big hit with Mrs. Roberts."

"Yeah, well, I'm just happy there's a Mr. Roberts."

"It's Doctor Roberts, Parker. And I suppose with the right kind of woman, you can be irresistible."

He gave me another one of those looks. "And I thought I was the fashion guy. All right, the funeral's tomorrow and we'd better go. I must say, your little friend dressed better for the rosary than she did yesterday."

"And she was even better this morning," I said before I realized what I was doing.

"I thought you had Becker under a stakeout?" he said sharply. "Or were you staking out some other type of territory?"

I couldn't tell if he was mad or not. As we got into the car, he fumbled around for his pipe. As I drove away,

Parker filled the air with a cloud of pipe smoke.

"Parker, she's really . . ."

"She's really what, Stanley? A friend of one victim who despised the other victim? Stanley, you're playing with fire."

Parker sat in silence for the rest of the drive. The only sounds were his matches trying to keep his pipe lit and me asking him to crack open his window. When we arrived at the SuperSaver, he didn't budge from his seat. He was thinking, and as long as he was thinking, I wasn't about to move either.

Finally he spoke. "Look, I noticed a little tavern down the road. Let's go back for a nightcap." Since I wasn't carrying my weapon, I agreed.

The Pine Run Inn was small, and rather well lit for a tavern. Parker led the way to a booth and started to fiddle with his pipe again, but finally put it away. He ordered a Scotch and water and I ordered a beer.

"I know what you're going to say, Parker . . ."

"Anyone who drinks beer will steal," he said with emphasis.

I wonder about him sometimes.

"Where are we now?" I asked.

"Tell me about this Buffy character."

"There isn't much to say, Parker. She was Anna Marie's friend and wants to help."

"Help us? Or help herself to you?"

"Its nothing like that," I said. "I'm aware of her position in this, and I've been keeping things on a professional basis."

"What is that professional basis, Stanley? Investigator to suspect? Interviewer to interviewee? Colleague to colleague?"

Our drinks came and I took a sip from my beer. The first sip was mostly foam.

"Look, Stanley," he continued, "I know you're upset over your wedding, and that's to be understood, but don't go trying to patch a broken heart with someone on your witness list."

I took another drink, this time sans the foam. "Look, Parker, she was on the inside with the paper. She knows the Winborn family and a whole lot of other people around here. She can be of some help. She was the one who found Mrs. Becker for me."

"Where?"

"Where did she find Mrs. Becker?"

"No, Stanley," he said in exasperation. "Where is Mrs. Becker?'

"Grand Bay. I'm planning on taking a trip over there tomorrow."

"Okay, Stanley. I won't second-guess you. Just be careful on this one. Don't find yourself in any embarrassing spots. Remember," he said, lifting his drink to his lips, "you may have to explain this relationship to a judge and jury someday."

"Noted. Now, Parker, where are we?"

Parker finished taking the sip from his drink. "Tonight, not much further than we were earlier. We didn't learn much except that Anna Marie had MS. So, it appears there may be even less of a reason that she would be the target of a killer."

"And, we know there was a morning Mass where she could have been headed," I said.

Parker nodded, "I don't know what we'll find there, but I think we should go to the funeral."

"Why? Wasn't the wake enough?"

He smiled through a little twinkle in his eyes. “Let’s just say I like to watch people.” He took another drink from his glass. “Okay. After the funeral, check out this Mrs. Becker. And one other thing, Stanley.”

“What’s that?”

“I want you to call in for another file.”

“Whose?”

“Buffy’s.”

Chapter Eight

Wednesday was another bright and sunny day, so nice that I did not want to go to a double funeral. In fact, I spent most of my morning walk trying to think of a way to avoid it. Afterwards, I met Parker for breakfast at the diner next to the SuperSaver. As usual, I arrived first, and, as usual, Parker wasn't up to any real conversation until after he had eaten his food.

"That's pretty heavy eating for a funeral, Parker."

He just grunted, then looked up. "It's a double header, Stanley. Don't they require more energy?"

"Pitchers don't pitch two games in a row, much less two games in one day. Parker, about this funeral thing . . ."

"But you know about the other players, don't you?"

"Yes, Parker. About the funeral . . ."

"They play two. We're going, Stanley. What'd you find on Buffy?"

"Nothing yet. I'll plug it in after breakfast."

"Mrs. Skosh called this morning."

"And how is Buckwheat Bob?"

"Much better today, thank you, Stanley. Looks like he had some kind of twenty-four-hour bug."

"Is that a week in dog time?"

Parker didn't look amused, but it didn't seem to hurt his appetite any. "The AG called, too."

"Did you tell him the good news about Buckwheat Bob?"

"As a matter of fact, I did; and he was greatly relieved," he said, then went back to his food.

"Well, Parker?"

He looked up. "Well what?"

Parker was, without a doubt, the most irritating man I've ever had to converse with on a regular basis. "Well, what did the AG want? I'm sure he didn't call you just to see how the dog was doing?"

"It would be just like him to do just that," he said.

There was a long pause while Parker put jelly on his toast.

"Parker?"

He looked back up at me. "He wanted to tell us that Berrigan was in the clear."

"How do we know that, Parker? Are we supposed to take his word for it? One politician covering for another?"

Parker looked perturbed. "This is murder, not politics, Stanley. The AG has reasons for clearing the congressman. That's all we need to know right now."

That wasn't a good answer and I told him so. "Besides," I said, "that's the same thing you said yesterday."

"Sorry for repeating myself, Stanley. If we're to know more, I'll let you know. But for right now, get Berrigan out of your mind. Now, go put on a tie, so we can go to that funeral."

St. Cecilia's Catholic Church in Forbes Island was just about large enough to hold all the mourners who came for the Winborns' funerals. It had been a long time since I had been to a Catholic funeral, and it surprised me that both caskets were covered with blue-and-gold trimmed white linen and that Father Hennessy wore white vestments. The little booklet I found in my pew said the white represented the Christian hope for salvation and unity with Christ.

The church itself was about medium size; it appeared to seat about six hundred. I had been to a wedding a few months earlier and that church was modern and round. This church was older and formed in a traditional cross, with most of the mourners seated in the main rectangle. St. Cecilia had a high altar below a life-sized crucifix, complete with Jesus' body, a medium-high, but rounded—not arched—ceiling, and six stained glass windows, three on each side, which bathed the congregation in a warm light.

Most of those attending the funeral were there by the time Parker and I arrived. Michael, as uncoordinated as the night before, entered with the caskets and was seated in the front of the church with the nuns from Anna Marie's convent. Buffy was near the front, seated with Mrs. Roberts and a very color-coordinated Margo. Buffy was still dressed in black, and I could see that both friends were crying intermittently during the service.

I noted that many of the civic leaders who attended the wake Tuesday evening were not present at the funeral, but, to my surprise, Congressman Berrigan was in attendance and was seated with the mayor. Ace Rhodes, of course, was there, and several others I recognized from the newspaper. The funeral crowd, surprisingly, was younger than the crowd for the wake, probably due to the increased participation from Anna Marie's friends.

Father Hennessy's eulogy was short. He spoke of Easter and the Resurrection, life after death, and heavenly reward.

"There are many of you here," he said, "who are asking the same question St. Paul asked: 'What shall we say to this?' You have come here today . . . here today . . . full of faith, anger, and fear. Faith in our own Resurrection and that of Chuck and Anna Marie's, anger over the manner in which they died, and fear over the forces loose that took these souls from us.

"As Christians, we must concentrate on faith. We must concentrate on Jesus' example of victory over death. Isaiah spoke of this victory in describing a place where God will wipe away all tears, and the faithful will be provided a place of joy with him.

"Glory be to God. I know this is a difficult day. A very, very difficult day, for here we see not only the power of God's love, and His love for us. But we also see the power of sin . . ."

I sat uncomfortably in my seat, trying to remember the last time I had been in church on a regular basis, as the priest concluded.

After Father Hennessy, Mother Mary Frances rose to speak of Anna Marie. "She was like a shooting star that dazzles the heavens for one brief, shining instant, whose beauty, exploding in the night, will never be forgotten by any who saw it," she said.

"Weep not for our sister, Anna Marie, for today she has achieved her utmost desire, and our dearest goal, life with Christ, our Lord."

When she finished, Michael, in his uncharacteristically deep voice, spoke of his father. "He was not a man who sought solace from the approval of others. He found comfort in what was right, not popular; in what was good, not pleasurable; and what was honest, not disingenuous. He was a man more concerned with responsibilities than rights, with honor than achievement, and with duty than desire.

"He strove to give strength to the weak, a voice to the mute, and a hand to the helpless. And in the final analysis, he gave himself and his life to this community.

"God has blessed my sister and my father. He has blessed me, too, with their gift. Your prayers and words of support have been most kind."

Michael's tribute to his father had many, but not all, in tears.

After the funeral, a long procession of cars took Winborn's body to the cemetery, while Anna Marie's was returned to the funeral home for transport back to her convent. At the conclusion of the service, there was a luncheon in the basement of St. Cecilia's.

Since Parker insisted that we attend the Winborns' funerals, it was not surprising that he wanted to stick around the church for the food. The lunch was served buffet-style and consisted of soup, sandwiches, potato salad, and pie. Parker made sure he took enough of everything to hold until dinner. That didn't surprise me. What did, however, was Parker choosing to sit with Buffy and Margo at my table, rather than with the mayor and Congressman Berrigan.

"My mother had to leave," Margo said. "She helps in Dad's dental office, and one of his girls is sick today."

"I'm sure she's quite a help to your dad," Parker said, although I didn't know how serious he was.

"Well," Margo said with a blush, "at least she tries to be."

Parker smiled. Then he turned to Buffy. "Buffy," Parker said, then hesitated. "I can call you Buffy, can't I?"

Buffy's blue eyes sparkled as she replied, "Oh, yes, of course you can. Everybody does."

Margo giggled. "Do you remember when we started calling you that?"

"I don't even want to remember," she said.

Margo turned to Parker, "They had reruns of a TV show with a little girl named Buffy. That's just how she looked as a girl." Then she turned to Buffy. "You know, I think it was Anna Marie who started it."

"I think you're right," she said. "Poor Anna Marie."

"I take it, then, that you girls go way back," Parker suggested.

"Oh yes," said Buffy. "We all went right here to grade school. There's no Catholic high school here, so we all went to City High. Those were the days, weren't they, Margo?"

"Boy, you said it. Remember when Anna Marie was picked up after homecoming for speeding?"

Buffy giggled, "Speeding! Like what was she doing? A hundred or something? We all thought her dad was going to kill her. But no, not Anna Marie. She was out the next weekend, her daddy's car and all."

Both girls were obviously enjoying themselves, remembering their friend.

"Did she have any boyfriends in high school?" Parker asked.

"Oh, sure," Buffy said. "She went out a lot, but nothing serious."

"Anna Marie had boy friends, but not a boyfriend, if you know what I mean. She was very popular," Margo said.

"Yeah," Buffy added. "If someone asked her out, she'd go. If he was a good guy. She wasn't a snob or anything."

"That's right." Margo said. "Some of the girls would only go out with the right kind of guy. You know the type; they just want to date the quarterback. But not Anna Marie. She'd go out with anybody who asked, as long as they weren't the bad type."

Buffy nodded in agreement. "Yeah, that's right."

"Tell me," Parker asked, "when did Anna Marie tell you

she wanted to become a nun?"

Buffy turned to Margo. "Oh, Margo, when did we know?"

"I think we kind of knew all along. We all went to different colleges, but Anna Marie went to an all-girls school run by nuns. I think we all suspected by then."

Buffy added, "After we graduated, Anna Marie went to Europe for a year. I think she just wanted to see the world before she left it, so to speak."

"Did she go with anybody?" Parker asked.

The girls looked at one another, then Margo responded, "No, I think they had some family in France or Belgium or something like that, and she kinda stayed with them as she traveled. Why?"

"No reason," he replied. "She would have been what? About twenty-one or -two then?"

Both nodded affirmatively.

"Why, you don't think this has something to do with her death, do you Mr. Parker?" Buffy asked.

I could feel Parker's cool glance and wince at the name thing again. "No. You girls just seemed to enjoy talking about Anna Marie. I just thought I'd indulge you." He smiled, and then was interrupted.

From behind we could hear the voice of Congressman Berrigan. "Parker, how nice to see you again." Parker stood, shook hands with the congressman, and made the introductions. "I hear you've been asking about me," Berrigan said.

Parker smiled.

"Can we talk?" Berrigan asked, and motioned away from the table.

Parker turned back to us, excused himself, and went with the congressman out of earshot.

"I think I'm going to have to leave now," Margo said. "I've got to get back to work. Nice seeing you again, Mr. Stankowski. See ya, Buffy."

I was finally alone again with Buffy, but I couldn't help watching Parker and Berrigan.

"Are they more fun than me?" she asked. I looked at Buffy. She reached across the table for my hand. I smiled. "Okay, captain. What do we do now? When do we go see Mrs. Becker?"

I looked into her eyes and could feel a little tug on my heart. "Right now," I said, and with that, I waved to Parker and left with Buffy.

The trip to Grand Bay wasn't long, and after a short stop so Buffy could make a quick, albeit immodest change, we found ourselves at 122 Prospect by mid-afternoon.

"My mom's not home," a pre-teenaged boy told me after examining my identification, "but I can tell you where she is."

We found Mrs. Becker at the local power company office. I thought it best to leave Buffy behind while I met with Mrs. Becker alone.

"Stan, I'll be good. She'll just think I'm another cop."

"That's the problem, Buffy. That can be considered impersonating an officer. You can't say who you are, because she might not speak freely in front of someone from the newspaper that crucified her ex. Now, be a good girl and wait for me."

She said she had a friend working at a travel agency on the next block and would go to see her. "Maybe we can go to Belgium and investigate what Anna Marie did there. Want I should check flights?" I smiled and watched her trot off, like a little girl.

Inside the power company office, I found Mrs. Becker at thc customer service window. "Mark called and said you were coming. I take it this has something to do with Milo."

When I said it did, she invited me back to a small coffee area. It wasn't very big and looked more like a family kitchen than an office break room.

"We can have more privacy here. I suppose this has something to do with the killings in Forbes Island, too."

I explained that this was just routine, but that we had to check out all leads.

"Well," she said, "it didn't surprise me that someone would try to kill that old, oh, SOB Winborn. I told Milo just before I left that I thought he should leave, too. 'Milo,' I said, 'someday someone's going to try to kill that man, and you'll get the blame.' He just smiled and said he'd be happy to take the blame, if someone else would save him the trouble."

She took a seat at a small kitchen table and pointed me into a chair across from her.

"Sergeant, I know this doesn't look good for him, but Milo is not the type of man to be involved in something like this. He can be a hothead, but he'd never try to actually kill anyone."

"Why did he stay, Mrs. Becker?"

"I think he thought he had more in Forbes Island than he really did. I know that shortly after he lost his job at the dealership he tried to get on at city hall. He knew Tom Foley from the Army and I think he thought his old Army buddy would take care of him."

"Did he talk much about Foley and the Army?"

"No, not really. Just said that he and the mayor were in the same outfit and knew each other. A few stories, I guess. That's about all."

"Did he tell you what he did in the service?"

"Something about artillery. Cannons and the like, I think."

"Did he mention he was in any trouble in the Army?"

She hesitated. After a pause she answered. "Not in so many words. I think he got drunk and was in a fight." She put her hands to her lips. "Oh, dear, it wasn't anything more than that, was it? Maybe I should have known something. Oh, Sergeant, he didn't hurt anybody, did he?"

I pushed on, "Did he have a temper?"

"No. Well, yes . . . Well, no more than most men. He wasn't violent, if that's what you mean."

"He never struck you?"

"No, absolutely not."

"The kids?"

"No. I don't like where you are going with this."

"What kind of people were his friends?"

She paused before she answered. "He didn't have many friends."

"Did he know the police chief?"

"How would he know the police? What are you suggesting?"

"Did he know a man named Costello?"

"From the construction outfit?"

"Yes."

"If he did, it was only to sell him a car."

"Were you aware of a police record?"

She was clearly concerned and growing nervous. "Maybe I've said too much. He still is the father of my children. I don't want to see anything happen to him."

"Mrs. Becker, please understand . . ."

"No, you understand, Sergeant. I once had a family. It wasn't perfect, but it was all I had. We were happy. We all lived together. Then that, that . . . that bastard Winborn took one mistake and used it to rip my family apart. I'm glad he's dead. I'm sorry about his daughter, but he's . . . We're all better off with him dead." She was in tears. I handed her my handkerchief, but she pushed it away, got up, and walked to the corner of the room, where she found a napkin with which to wipe her eyes.

"I don't care what you say. Milo didn't do this. He wouldn't . . . he couldn't have been involved."

I turned around in my chair. "Involved, Mrs. Becker? You make it sound like you might know something. Was there more than one person? What do you know?"

"Nothing, Mr. whatever-your-name-is. Nothing. Now get out."

I stood. "Mrs. Becker, there was a crime for which your former husband has a motive. I have a job to do. There are questions I have to ask."

She gave me an icy look from the corner. "My husband," she said quietly. "We've never gotten a divorce. Now go."

Chapter Nine

After an uneventful drive back from Grand Bay, I dropped Buffy off at her apartment and met Parker at the Family Hour Café across the street from the Forbes Island Courthouse. Parker was already in the smoking section enveloped in a cloud of pipe smoke when I arrived.

"Geez, Parker. Doesn't this smoke ever get to you?"

"Nope. What happened today?"

I told him of my visit with Mrs. Becker and of my growing suspicions about her husband. "She seemed too protective under the circumstances," I said.

"So, what are you telling me, Stanley?"

It all of a sudden struck me as odd that he was so concerned about what name Buffy and the old nun called him, yet he continued to harass me with the name Stanley. "Parker, do you know what irony is?"

"What is ironic about Becker?"

"Not Becker. This Parker thing?"

"What Parker thing? I'm Parker. Stanley, are you feeling alright?"

Sometimes you'd like to slap him upside the head. "Okay, okay. Just never mind," I said.

"Then what did you mean about Becker?"

He could be so difficult to talk to. Sometimes it's easier just to change the subject.

"What I was starting to say is that there appears to be more to this Becker matter than we see. He is the one person who had the means and a motive to do in Winborn. He won't talk to us, and now his wife won't talk either. There's too much smoke here not to expect to find a fire."

"And I take it you are going to follow-up."

"Sure. That's what cops do, Parker." Parker busied himself with the menu. "I had another thought," I said. "Becker tried to get on with the city after he lost his job with the car dealership. Do you think he might have it in for the mayor? Mrs. Becker indicated that he thought of Tom Foley as an old buddy. Foley didn't think of Becker the same way. He didn't live up to what Becker expected. Is it possible that Becker, if he did this, tried to make it look like the mayor was responsible?"

Parker put the menu down. "What are you suggesting, Stanley? That Becker planted the bomb then tried to frame Foley? That's a real stretch."

I pondered that for a minute and thought that Parker might be right. Of course, I'd never tell him so. He picked up the menu again.

"Parker," I interrupted, "if this was Becker, do you think he might be looking at the mayor next?"

Parker looked up and appeared to be interested. Then he buried himself back in the menu. "No. Probably not. Especially not now. But if you are concerned, tell Foley."

I'd have to think on that one a while. "So what did the congressman say?" I asked.

"Oh, that."

Parker decided to order before he answered. The Wednesday dinner special was meatloaf, carrots or peas, mashed potato, and salad. Naturally, Parker talked the waitress into giving him both the carrots and peas. "You can never eat too many vegetables, Stanley."

"Yeah, Parker, your mother would be proud. Now, what did Berrigan tell you? Does it have anything to do with our case?"

"Stanley," he replied, "we've been over this before. He is not a suspect."

"Then why the embargo on his file? And how did he know we had asked for it?"

Parker looked exasperated. "Okay, Stanley, I can tell you this much: He knew we wanted his file because the Attorney General told him. The AG knows why his file is embargoed. So does Berrigan. There is nothing suspicious about this matter."

"Do you?"

"Do I what?" he asked.

"Do you know why the file is embargoed?"

The waitress brought Parker's salad, saving him from an immediate answer. There was an awkward silence while Parker tried to avoid the question.

"Do you, Parker?"

He looked up. "Yes, I do. But I can't tell you now. Maybe in a day or so, but for right now there is nothing I can say."

"Can you tell me if the congressman is under investigation?"

Parker looked at me and appeared to carefully weigh his thoughts before he answered. He took a bite from his salad. He swallowed and looked directly at me.

"Yes, I can tell you," he said. "He is. Now drop it, Stanley."

After dinner we returned to the SuperSaver. I finally had some time to check in with headquarters and to download

Buffy's file. Except for a few speeding tickets, Buffy was clean. I met Parker back in his room. I had just sat down at his table when the phone rang. Parker walked over to the table between the beds to answer it. I could tell from the conversation that it was about Buckwheat Bob, and, despite Parker's representations that the Attorney General was genuinely concerned about his flea-bitten friend, I figured the call was from Mrs. Skosh.

"And how is your dog?" I asked when he hung up.

"He's doing just fine, thank you, Stanley."

"And Mrs. Skosh is looking after things well enough?"

Parker said she was.

"Parker, is there a Mr. Skosh?"

He blushed. It's always fun when I'm able to get his goat.

"In fact, Stanley, Mrs. Skosh is a widow lady."

I started to say something, but he interrupted me. "Now, before you get too comfortable, we're taking a little trip."

"Where to?"

"To see Michael," he said. "Let's go."

It wasn't long before we were at Michael's apartment. He was expecting us, and ushered us into what passed for a combination living room and dining room. There was a scratching sound and a bark from what appeared to be the bedroom.

"What is that I hear?" Parker asked.

"Oh, that's Coco scratching at the patio door. He was really Anna Marie's dog. If I let him in, he'll just jump on you."

I dreaded what Parker said next: "Go ahead. I've got one, too."

That was easy for Parker to say. I knew whom the dog would go to first, and I was right. It only took a minute for me to find my face being washed by a rather large dog.

"What kind of dog is this?"

"It looks like a Labrador, Stanley," Parker said.

"A Chocolate Lab mix, Sir. That's how it got its name, Coco," Michael said as he pulled the dog off me."

"Did you say your sister's dog?" I asked. "You're not telling me that she had it at the convent."

Michael laughed. "No, no. Anna Marie got him from the pound when he was a pup. She had to leave him with Dad. I'd keep him, but for the apartment rules."

"Funny," I said. "We didn't see him the other day."

"Before I left for the hospital, I took him over to Doctor Burnelli's. I knew a lot of people would be going through the house," he said. "Under the circumstances, the manager said I could keep him here until I move into the house."

"You're going to take over the house?"

"Yeah. At least until I decide what to do with it. I can't let it sit empty, and there's a lot of stuff there that I'll have to go through. Might sell it and buy a condo, but it's too early to make any decisions. I got a lot to think about."

"I have a dog, too," Parker said just as I was getting Michael to open up.

"Oh, what kind?" Michael asked.

"A basset hound. His name is Buckwheat Bob."

Michael smiled. "That's a little unusual name, Mr. Noble. How did you get it?"

"I named him after his mother."

Michael looked amused. "What was her name?"

"Buckwheat Betty."

Michael looked at me, shook his head, as if in disbelief, and smiled.

Coco headed for Parker. Coco sniffed and sniffed, then

just lay down at Parker's feet.

"He likes you," said Michael.

Parker just smiled as he fondled Coco. First, it was a scratch behind the ear. Soon Coco was on his back, and Parker was rubbing his belly. Then Coco was up licking Parker's face. Michael finally got Coco settled down.

"Now, Mr. Noble, you wanted to talk?"

"Thus far," Parker began, "we have no end of suspects. That's why I need your help. We have to narrow the numbers down. Tell me this: you indicated Saturday that your dad may have received threats. Did I understand that right?"

Michael nodded. "Well, like I said then, we were always getting kooky letters and funny phone calls. I've not lived here for the past few years, so I don't know what came to the house recently, but we always had some."

"Did your dad say anything about anything recent?" Parker asked.

"Like I said, not that I know. Dad never said anything."

Parker brushed some dog hair off his trousers. "What was your father's relationship with the mayor?"

Michael twisted his face, as if trying to think of a good answer. "Well, he and the mayor used to get along, but, of late, they hadn't. Dad never really said much about it, but I know he would have opposed Tom's re-election."

"Why?"

Michael shook his head. "Don't really know. There was some bad blood there, but I wasn't privy to it."

"What about the police chief?"

Michael shrugged his shoulders. "No, nothing. I think he thought him weak, but that's all. Dad was a kind of law and order guy. I think he thought Edwards a little soft for the job."

"Do you know a man named Costello?"

"I know of him. He's the real estate guy."

"Any reason for your father to try to kill his new development?"

A blank expression took hold of Michael. "Don't know."

"Did your dad know Costello?"

"Maybe, but, if so, not well. He knew almost everybody."

"Does the name Milo Becker ring a bell?"

"Should it?"

Parker nodded towards me. "His picture was taken coming out of a brothel," I said.

"Oh, him. Yeah. Now that you mention it, he did threaten my father. I was there the day he called. Said something to the effect that he'd get even. Do you suppose he did this?"

I asked, "Did anybody else see him make the threat?"

"No," Michael said. "He called on the phone. I was in my dad's office when the call came in. Dad told me about it. Said the guy told him that he'd get even." Michael had a hopeful look. "Does this help?"

Parker assured him that it did, and then had him reconstruct Friday evening's events.

"Well, we picked up Anna Marie in Grand Bay in the afternoon. Then we came straight back here to give Anna Marie a little time to freshen up. Doctor Burnelli came over, and then the four of us went to Christie's for dinner. After dinner we came back here for wine and pie that Doctor Burnelli had brought with him. Anna Marie called Margo, and she came over about half an hour later.

"We sat and talked, and Dad got out some old pictures of the family. There were pictures of Mom and Mrs. Burnelli. That brought back a lot of memories for my dad and Doctor Burnelli, and they talked a lot about when they first moved into this ncighborhood."

"Michael," Parker asked, "did you run into anyone you knew in the restaurant?"

Michael shook his head. "I've been asked that before. Not that I can remember—at least no one came over to the table to visit. But like I said, Dad did know some of the staff."

Parker asked, "How long were you there?"

"Gee, only about an hour or an hour and a half. I didn't keep track of the time."

Parker sat back and looked at me. That was my signal. "When was your sister last home?"

"Thanksgiving. Almost a year. Dad went to Minnesota last Christmas to see her."

"Michael, Margo said that Anna Marie had written from the convent saying that she would be coming home. Do you know if she told anyone else?"

"No, I don't think she did. Sis wanted to surprise her friends. Her schedule seemed to be up in the air. We only knew the date the week before."

"Did she call anyone while she was here?"

"Margo."

"Anyone else?"

"No."

"What kind of pie did Doctor Burnelli bring?" Parker asked.

"Apple."

"One of my favorites," he said.

"Ours, too. He didn't make it, though. Got it at the bakery. But he knew Sis loved it."

"One other thing, Michael," Parker said. "When did you find out your sister had MS?"

"Me? Not very long ago. I think Sis found out in college."

"And your dad's cancer?"

"About two years ago, I'd say. It was something they call non-Hodgkin's lymphoma. It's a slow cancer. He had heart problems, too. I think we were all more worried about his heart than the cancer."

That was it. Not very much new about Friday night, but I, at least, had a little more to go on with Becker. On the way back to the motel, Parker gave me some suggestions on how to follow up on the Becker matter, but they were nothing that I hadn't thought of earlier. He also suggested I pursue the zoning matter.

"Your little friend, Buffy, might be able to help you with that," he suggested. "It's possible that she knows something, but doesn't know what she knows."

"Like something she may have overheard said in the newsroom or city hall?" I said.

"Exactly. Something that may have been said in passing that seemed meaningless at the time. Maybe this girl can help after all." He rolled down the car window and looked outside. "Just maybe," he repeated. We drove the rest of the way in silence.

Chapter Ten

A light rain was falling Thursday morning, so I decided to forego my usual walk. Instead, I sat at the little table in my room, looking over my notes and the reports I had received from headquarters. I made a list of loose ends that needed attention. At the top of my list was the matter of our good congressman. In spite of Parker's assurances, I would not rest until I knew why the congressman was being investigated.

I decided to call Captain Hodges. He was in. I asked about Bert Berrigan but told him to keep it on the QT.

"I don't understand why you can't get the file."

"Neither do I, Cap. That's what's so odd about this matter. I've never heard of a file being embargoed. The Bureau has a field office there. Can you check it out and let me know?"

Hodges said he would, then added, "How's your partner, Stan?"

"Funny, Cap. While you're checking on Berrigan, see if Parker isn't needed back in the capitol. Isn't there some training class somewhere where they need him?"

"Now, now, Stan. Thou shalt not speak evil of the AG's buddy."

"Yeah, gee, thanks. If that's all you can do for me, Cap."

I could hear him laughing on the other end. "Have a

good day, Stan," he said as he hung up.

I turned back to my notes. Becker was next on my list. I was starting to discount any real connection between Becker and Foley as mere coincidence. It may have played into Becker's state of mind after he was fired, but I was doubting seriously if he and Foley had anything more than a nodding acquaintance. But I also could not shake the idea that Foley could also be a target of a vengeful Becker. Parker had told me to convey a warning, if I felt the need. I called Chief Edwards.

"Look," I told the chief, "this may be little more than an overactive imagination, but . . ." I laid out my suspicions about Becker and told him of my conversation with Mrs. Becker.

"I see what you're getting at, Stan. I'll call the mayor and put a uniform on him."

"No, not a uniform. If he's willing, put someone in street clothes with him. If Becker is our guy, let's see if we can draw him out."

Edwards agreed and said he would call Tom Foley. That took me to the next person on my list, Chief Edwards. Parker didn't want to confront him with his record until he needed to do so. Now I understood why. It's much easier to get his cooperation if he doesn't know he's under investigation.

Next on the list was the zoning matter with Roscoe Costello. I wasn't sure yet, but I was beginning to think that there might be a connection somewhere between Costello and Anna Marie's death. That was where Buffy could help. She was my next call.

"Hello," a groggy voice intoned.

"Morning, sunshine. This is your captain speaking."

"Hi!" She perked up.

"Sleeping in late? It's already eight-thirty. Get up, get outta bed."

I could hear her roll over. "How do you know I'm not alone?" she asked.

I felt a twang of jealousy. "I don't. Are you?"

She giggled. "Of course I'm alone. But I needn't be. As long as you're up and running, why not stop by?"

The jealousy left. "Because," I said, "we've got work to do. Tell me, do you know anything about a zoning matter with a Roscoe Costello?"

"Who?"

"Costello and Sons Construction. I thought you said you covered city hall?"

"I did. You mean the zoning thing? I thought that was done."

"No, it isn't. Costello was still pushing it, and Winborn was still opposing it. Anything said around your place about it?"

I could hear her breath on the phone. "That never made any sense, Stan. Winborn was always for development. But I do remember a little about it. A lot happened after I left the paper, though. You want me to do some checking?"

"Yeah, Buffy. See what you can find out for me. Keep it on the QT. I don't want anyone to know it may have any connection to your friend's death."

"Ya know what, Stan?"

"What, Buffy?"

"I think she would be real happy that you asked me to help. Bye."

I told her thanks, wished her well, and opened my door a notch so I could hear Parker when he left for breakfast. Shortly after hanging up the phone, I heard him in the hall. I went to the door and saw him lumbering towards the lobby area, like a skinny zombie only barely alive. He glanced back and saw me behind him. He went through the lobby, speechless, in this catatonic state. He stopped only once, to pick up a morning paper off the rack. Then he pointed over his shoulder at me for the clerk. I felt stupid for doing so, but I paid the clerk for Parker's paper. I had to wait for change but found him, as expected, in the diner next door.

Parker had found a booth, and I took the seat across from him. I knew better than to speak until he at least had his coffee. He looked at me like he wanted to say something, then just opened the paper to the sports page. When his coffee came and he had taken his first sip, I spoke.

"Good morning, Parker."

He looked up from the paper. I noticed his little bow tie was crooked today. He pointed towards the window. "It's raining. That's not good." Then he went back to the paper.

I told him that Buffy was going to check out the zoning matter. He looked and nodded. "I wonder if they still have that three-egg thing," he said.

"I don't know, Parker. Why don't you ask?"

"Okay." He blinked twice, then turned and waved over a server. He asked about the three-egg thing, and she assured him they had it. He ordered it. I ordered oatmeal and grapefruit.

"Parker, all that stuff is going to clog your arteries. You'll die."

"So I die," he said. "I'm going to anyway. May as well go full. What else did you do this morning, besides call your girlfriend?"

"She's not my girlfriend, Parker."

"Oh." Parker went back to the paper. He didn't seem

too interested in what else I had to say. So I told him anyway. Naturally, I left out the part about the congressman, but I did tell him of my conversation with the chief.

Now he was interested. "You told the chief about your suspicions regarding Becker?"

"Right."

"And you told him about your theory that Becker might be after the mayor."

"Right. I let him warn Foley."

"Stanley, I said to tell Foley, if you wanted, not the chief. Did it ever occur to you that if the chief was behind this Winborn thing, he might now find it expedient to do away with the mayor to frame Becker for the whole mess?"

His food came just in time to distract him.

"Parker, let me . . ."

He waved me off with a quick hand motion and a grunt. "Let me think on this while I eat."

We stopped back at the motel before we left on Parker's agenda for the day, and I was able to download the remaining file we had requested. It reported that Roscoe Costello had no criminal or military record. While we were there, Parker called Foley about the Becker matter. I couldn't hear the mayor's side of the conversation, but it sounded to me like the officer Edwards said he would send had already arrived.

"I'm relieved," I told Parker as he hung up. "I really didn't mean to screw things up."

Parker just looked at me. Then he shook his head and muttered something about cops, and headed for the parking lot.

Our first stop was Quentin Collier's office. Parker had

his pipe stoked and fired as we entered. Collier wasn't there but his secretary was.

"Mr. Collier was called to the courthouse on an unexpected matter," she said, handing Parker an envelope. "He said to give this to you. He also left his home number, if you need him after hours."

Parker thanked the secretary and led the way to a small coffee shop in the lobby of Collier's building.

"Should I try that?" he asked, pointing to a chalkboard sign behind the counter.

"Try what?" I asked.

"That coffee."

"The hazelnut?"

"Yeah. Mrs. Skosh says it's good. But I don't know. Something about tampering with God's bean just doesn't seem right to me."

I looked down at him and could tell he was debating ordering something that for him was new. It was hard to suppress a smile. "Go ahead, chance it."

"Think so?"

I assured him it would be all right, and when the girl told him it cost the same as regular, he ordered two cups of the hazelnut coffee, and we took a seat in a small booth.

"Thank you," I said.

"For what?"

"You bought the coffee."

"That's right," he replied, and went back to the counter to get his receipt.

"That's a little funny that Collier would have an unexpected court hearing," I said, when he returned. "Don't you guys always have notice for those things?"

"Not always. Sometimes things come up at the last minute." He took a sip of his hazelnut and looked up to the ceiling while he beat his lips together, as if trying to determine whether or not he liked it. Then he did it again. Then he nodded and took another sip.

"What do you think, Parker?"

He took another sip. "I don't hate it."

I was thinking about what an odd little duck he was, as I watched him open the envelope from Collier and spread the contents over the table.

"Winborn's will," he announced.

I picked it up and started skimming the document. It was only six pages long. I had expected more from a man of Winborn's stature. Winborn had made a few gifts outside the family, the largest being a $5,000 gift to St. Cecilia's. All the rest of his property appeared to be left to Michael and Anna Marie.

"What does the word 'seized' mean, Parker?"

He looked up, and I noticed he was still licking his lips. "Not awful."

"What do you mean, 'not awful'?"

"The coffee, it's not awful."

"Parker, stay with me on this one. Seized, as in 'all the property of which I am seized.' "

"Owned. As in owned outright. In property law . . ."

It was my turn to cut him off. "Parker, I don't want a law lecture. I just want to know what this means."

He put down his cup and looked at the will. "It means he gave everything to his kids."

Why he just couldn't have said that at first beats me. Then he turned to the girl behind the counter, "Hey, are there free refills?"

We arrived at the Forbes Island Courthouse about ten-thirty. Parker said he wanted to catch Collier there, but I think he mostly wanted to take a peek inside the building. Parker walked around the ground floor, looking at everything from the murals painted on the walls to the gargoyles hanging from the pillars. He was standing under the rotunda, looking up into the dome, when we heard a familiar voice.

"Stan. Mr. Parker."

Parker shot me a sideways glance, the meaning of which was perfectly clear.

"I just came from the recorder," she said. "I don't know how to pronounce this, but the name is P-O-R-C-L-A-R Incorporated."

"What, young lady, are you talking about?" Parker asked.

Buffy caught her breath. "The zoning change. At the same time Costello was turned down, another one was approved. It was for land not far from Costello's. Looks like about sixty acres. It's owned by however you pronounce it, incorporated."

Parker took the scrap of paper from Buffy on which she had written down the name. "Porclar, Incorporated," he mused. "Buffy, have you ever heard of this outfit?"

"No, Sir. And I looked it up in the book. Zip." She had a slight twinkle in her eye, as she looked up at me while Parker just stared at the paper.

"Okay," he said finally. "Check into this and the Becker thing. Find out who this Porclar is. And if you are going anywhere, leave me the car." With that he went back to his sightseeing meander.

I looked down at Buffy. "Okay, sunshine, how do we find out who Porclar is?"

She giggled. Her pale blue eyes sparkled as she stepped back from me and struck a model's pose. She was wearing a short, blue jacket, matching slacks, and a light blue blouse opened at the collar. She also had on a small, ladies' fedora.

"We can find out with one phone call," she said, as she slowly made a full circle. Then she lifted her hat. "Like it? I call it my gumshoe hat. I bought it yesterday."

I said I did, and we headed to city hall. The Forbes Island Municipal Building was only a couple of blocks from the courthouse, but the morning's light rain had turned heavy, so we took Buffy's car. Actually, it wasn't a car, but one of those small pickups that were popular a few years ago.

"When I lost my job, I couldn't make my car payments. My brother took my car and the payments and gave me this. It's really in bad shape."

That was an understatement. It belched black smoke, and was so full of fumes it smelled like a truck stop.

"Steve says it needs rings. He works at a co-op and traded a guy a load of manure for it. He always called it his shit truck. He gave it to me, but I can't go far with it. Makes job interviewing tough."

"Do you have any job leads?" I asked.

"No. I get leads from the alumni association, but they're all so far away. With this thing, I can't get there. My brother says he'll lend me my old car, if I can get an interview, but, well, we've been over that."

We pulled up in front of city hall.

"This brother of yours, where does he live?"

"Small place, Atwood, about an hour and a half south. He has a wife and a little girl."

I turned in my seat to face her. "Any other family?"

She shook her head. "My parents were killed in an accident in Spain. It's just Steve and me." She looked at me, and I could see her eyes were beginning to water. There was a long pause, and then she broke the silence. “Let’s go in and I’ll show you what I found.”

Someone named Dennis in the clerk’s office quickly showed us the paperwork on the zoning changes. The land owned by Porclar was almost adjacent to the land Costello wanted rezoned.

“What’s the problem here?” I asked.

“Beats me,” said Dennis. “These are routine matters. Ag land being rezoned for commercial or residential development. Happens all the time. Porclar went through without any objection. Then, just like that, the zoning board kills Costello’s job. Never made any sense to me, but then, I’m not paid to understand, just do.”

“Who is Porclar?” I asked.

“Don’t know. The zoning change was requested by the previous owner. A farmer named MacBee.”

“Where can I find MacBee?”

“Don’t know. He left the area.”

We were getting nowhere fast when Buffy asked, “Who was this guy’s lawyer? Didn’t he have one?”

Dennis started to fumble through his paperwork.

“Good question, Buff,” I whispered. She just smiled and ran a finger across the brim of her hat.

“Here,” said Dennis. “A guy named Earl Marshall from Grand Bay. Here’s his number.”

It didn’t take us long to get Marshall on my cell phone. He was no help.

“All I did was draft the zoning application, file it, and draft the papers of transfer. I never met anyone from Porclar. All I know is that Buzz got his money and retired.”

“Where is he now?” I asked.

“Ireland.”

I thanked Marshall and hung up. “Okay, pumpkin,” I

said to Buffy, handing her my phone, "make that phone call and find out who Porclar is."

"It'll take two. First, to directory assistance. Give me a pencil."

Her second call was to the secretary of state. After a short wait, she wrote something down on a notepad, ended the call, and gave me a provocative look.

"What, Buffy?"

"The registered agent and president of Porclar is Jeffrey Fielding."

"That name rings a bell."

"It should," she said. "He's the business manager of the newspaper."

Chapter Eleven

I thought the Fielding matter should be brought to Parker's attention immediately. I had, after all, opined that there might be some connection between the contractor, Costello, and the car bomb that took Anna Marie's life. When I couldn't locate him by page, Buffy and I took a drive back to the courthouse, where we found him still wandering around, looking at the building.

"They don't build places like this anymore," he said when we arrived.

"Did you ever find Collier?"

"Oh, yeah. Upstairs in the main courtroom."

"Parker, about this Porclar matter, I think we have a lead. Buffy found out who Porclar is."

He looked at me, then at Buffy. "Okay, well that's fine. But I want to look into another matter, too. Collier reminded me of it. It's the matter of the trust that owns the newspaper."

Buffy looked puzzled. "You mean the old man didn't?"

"No," Parker said. "Apparently the ownership was in a trust. You remember, Stanley, our meeting with Collier?"

"Yes," I said. "Collier said that Winborn's financial affairs were run by Jeffrey Fielding at the newspaper."

Parker nodded. "Right. You go do what you will. I'm going to see Fielding."

"Funny you want to see Fielding. That's where we were headed," I said. "Fielding is Porclar."

Parker gave me that look. "Let's go," he said.

Buffy was still hesitant about going to the newspaper office, which was fine with Parker. We found Fielding in his office. He looked much younger than I had expected. "I'm thirty-two," he said in reply to my question. "I'm from the Grand Bay area. I got an MBA from Hobart and moved back."

"Hobart," I replied. "I'm doing some graduate work there myself."

"I was only there for the MBA, did my undergraduate at Central. I worked at Cattlemen's Insurance. Almost stayed, but my mom's a widow and she needed someone closer to home. Winborn gave me a job in the accounting department and the rest, as they say, is history."

Fielding had an easy manner. His demeanor was open and honest, and it was easy to trust him. I figured him to be about five-eight, and a little on the stocky side. His desk was pushed against a side wall, so that when he turned to talk to us, he did so without a desk as a barrier.

I told Fielding what Collier had told us, and that we had a copy of Winborn's will. I asked about Winborn's finances.

"Collier is right, gentlemen," Fielding told us. "Chuck owned only a small portion of the paper. The rest was held by a trust established for the children, Michael and Anna Marie. It was split almost evenly. Of course, now Michael will control it."

Parker asked how much the paper was worth.

"Well, that's hard to say, exactly. The *Independent* is on an almost break-even basis. Most of its equipment is mortgaged. Clear, I'd say it would be about two hundred thousand dollars."

"That little?" I asked.

He nodded. "Well, understand that most of the paper's assets are encumbered. When I say clear, I mean what would be left after paying off the debt. The paper is solid; it's just not going to make anyone rich. But it does pay its way."

"And what was the extent of the rest of Winborn's holdings?" Parker asked.

Fielding then took us through Winborn's finances and, when he was finished, the picture I had of Winborn's wealth had vanished.

"Let me see if I have this right," I said. "The entire estate is under nine hundred thousand dollars?"

"Right," he said. "And that includes the two hundred thousand dollars in the paper trust. His house was clear, that's another one hundred eighty thousand. The rest was in stocks and bonds."

"What about Porclar?" Parker asked.

"That's included."

"What was that, anyway?"

"A land investment. It's worth about four hundred thousand dollars. But its potential was much greater. It could be worth millions someday."

"Do you have any ownership interest in Porclar?" Parker asked.

"No. I just served as its agent. Winborn wanted to keep his name out of the public records."

"What else does it own, besides the parcel on the south side of town?" I asked.

"Nothing. Chuck wanted the property and had me set up the corporation. He transferred the money into it and had me purchase the land."

"Where did the name come from?"

"Beats me. He gave it to me. I didn't ask. I just figured it meant something to him, like those vanity license plates you see all around."

"Where are the corporate records?" Parker asked.

"They're with the attorney I used. He's my cousin. Gary Fielding."

"Can you get them for us?" Parker asked.

"Sure. I'm president, remember? Just tell me what you need."

"Everything."

"No problem. Gary's on vacation this week. Is Monday okay?"

Parker said Monday would be fine. Then we adjourned to the Family Hour Café, where we met Buffy and Parker did his best to clog his arteries again.

Lunch was unremarkable. Parker, as is his custom, ate (and ate) with very little interaction with the outside world, but, in deference to Buffy—not me—he did sit in the non-smoking section. And, as is also his custom, he became more talkative when the last plate was cleared away.

"You don't suppose they have that other kind of coffee here, do you?" he asked.

Buffy gave a quizzical look. I had to explain. "He means hazelnut. He had some this morning at a coffee bar. I don't know, Parker. Just ask."

He did. They didn't. He settled for what he now called the old stuff.

"Okay," he said to us, "where do we stand?"

Buffy answered without missing a beat. "The contractor and Becker did it."

Parker looked a little taken back. "Okay, young lady, explain."

"The contractor wanted the old man out of the way so he could get his zoning through. Becker hates the old man for what he did to him. They got together to plot his death."

Parker just smiled.

I said, "Buffy, you're watching too many old movies. Why would they get together? How would they know each other? Costello builds houses, Becker sold cars. How would they come into contact with one another?"

Buffy sat back in her seat and pulled her gumshoe hat down with a small pout. Parker looked at her and smiled a favorite uncle type of smile. "Go ahead, Buffy. Tell us how they could be connected."

Buffy looked at me, then back at Parker, pushed her hat back, and leaned forward. "Okay, suppose Costello met Becker at the car shop. Costello's looking to buy. Becker is being a good salesman and starts talking about business. Costello says he clears land to build houses. Becker says he was in the Army and knows explosives. Costello keeps that in the back of his mind and calls Becker, when he needs some tree stumps or rocks blasted. Could have happened." She stopped long enough to catch her breath.

"Then they get to talking about the paper. Costello says, 'Why is this guy blocking my business?' Becker says, 'Why did this guy screw up my family?' Then they hatch a plot, and bingo, except they kill the wrong person." She looked at me, then at Parker. "Could have happened."

"What do you think, Stanley?"

I shook my head. "It seems a little farfetched. But from what we know now, both men are still in the box."

Parker nodded. "Coincidences happen all the time. It might not be as farfetched as we think." He paused to restoke his pipe. "Look, you are already looking into Becker and this Porclar thing. Why don't you see if there is a connection?"

With that, he got up, threw a couple of dollars on the table, saying, "I'll take care of the tip," and left, telling us that he had other things to do.

Buffy looked up. "I think he likes me. I wasn't sure at first, but I think so now."

I smiled. "Okay, gumshoe, what's our next move?"

"Well, I suppose we should look to see if there is a link between Becker and Costello."

"And your suggestion as to how?"

She looked up and scrunched her nose. "That I don't know. Don't you guys keep records or something?"

"No, we don't," I said. "At least not those kind of records. But I know who does."

"Who?"

"The guy who pays the salesman a commission. He'd know who bought cars and from whom."

It didn't take us long to get to Stevens Ford. Arriving in Buffy's shit truck caused quite a stir among the sales staff, but they calmed down as soon as they found out that we weren't there to trade.

"But you look like too nice of a couple to drive around in that," one of the salesmen said.

Buffy looked up at me with a mischievous grin and replied, "My husband's such a cheap bastard."

The salesman blushed and started to apologize.

"Oh him," Buffy said. "He's not my husband. He's my lover." The salesman turned beet red.

"We're here to see your boss," Buffy announced.

The man left to find his manager.

"Now, Buffy . . ." I started to say.

She giggled. "You're lucky. I started to say you were my husband's lover."

"This isn't a game, little girl. This is a state police investigation."

"Just the facts, Ma'am," she said in her deepest voice, and giggled again.

I rolled my eyes just as the sales manager approached us. He introduced himself. I showed him my shield, and he took us back to his office.

"My friend here has an odd sense of humor," I said, as I explained our visit and introduced Buffy.

"Russ?"

"Buffy, is that really you?"

Apparently they knew one another.

"Russ was in my brother Steve's class."

Russ was identified by his business card as Russ "Quick Deal" McGraw, sales manager and assistant general manager for Stevens Ford.

"In fact," Buffy said, "Russ took me to a party where I had my first beer. He was the first guy to get me drunk. I think he took advantage of me, but he never would say."

Quick Deal just smiled. "Mr. Stankowski, Buffy was—how would you say it?—ready to try anything."

"That's not true."

"Buffy, I remember you telling me once that you'd try anything twice."

"Twice?" I said.

"Yeah. She said she might not like it the first time."

Buffy blushed. "I liked it the first time."

They smiled at one another. I could feel myself becoming jealous. I could also feel how much I was really starting to care for the little one in the gumshoe hat. I thought I'd better change the subject.

"I remember Becker," McGraw said. "He was a good salesman, although he kind of kept to himself. Not really strange, just a little different."

"Know anything about his personal life?" I asked.

"Knew more about it after the picture incident than I did before. We knew his wife and kids, but not very well. He didn't always socialize with the rest of the sales staff. I guess when you think about it that wasn't really so odd. Most of the salespeople are either single or divorced. Milo had a family to go home to each night."

"Was he ever a discipline problem or cause any trouble?"

"Naw. Only when the picture came. Mrs. Stevens said he had to go, and that was that. He took it like a man, but I couldn't help but to feel a little sorry for him. Most of us weren't close to him, so it didn't affect us too much personally. But we did lose a good salesman."

"Do you have a record of his sales?"

"For how long?"

"How long do your records go back?"

"All on computer. I think we can get you his whole history. I can check."

I asked him to do so, and he left Buffy and me alone. I looked at Buffy. She looked straight ahead, but peeked at me from the corner of her eye. I could see a little smirk starting to tug at the corner of her lips.

"Anything twice?"

She turned and looked directly at me. I could see she was suppressing a smile. "Three times if I liked it."

"And how quick was old Quick Deal in high school?"

She grinned. "Junior high. I had other friends in high school."

"You and Quick Deal, and your best friend's a nun."

"A girl's gotta have fun."

I was beginning to think I was getting into things a little too deep. "How much fun?"

Buffy giggled. "Now Stanley, a lady's got to have some mystery about her."

I couldn't tell if I was turning red or green, but Buffy was greatly amused. She was enjoying this in a way that Diane never would. I was finally saved from digging any deeper when McGraw returned.

"They're printing out what you need now." He led the way to the dealership's business office, where a young girl was just taking our information off the printer. McGraw pointed to me, and the girl handed me the printout. "If you don't need me, I have a meeting."

Buffy took the printout from my hand, and I followed her into the showroom where she spread it out over the trunk of a new Crown Victoria. We both scanned the sheets, although my mind was still elsewhere.

"Here, Stan," she said. "He did sell a car to Costello."

I continued to scan the sheets. "It's more than that, Buffy. He sold one here, too, and a truck to Costello and Sons."

That was almost enough for me to forget about Buffy's rule of twos.

It felt somewhat odd conducting a state investigation out of Buffy's shit truck but, thanks to Parker, it's all we had at the moment. At least it was some transportation. After leaving Stevens Ford, I was more convinced than ever that Becker had something to do with Anna Marie's death. I still wasn't sure about the connection between Becker and Costello, but I decided it was worth another look.

I wanted to see Becker again, and Buffy's little truck could, at least, belch and stammer its way there. We arrived at a quarter to four only to find no one home.

"The curtains are open. Let's take a look inside," Buffy said.

"No, no, Buffy. Legal reasons and stuff. Just leave well enough alone. We'll check at the QuicKing for him."

A few minutes later we were at the QuicKing, and, as I did before, I sent Buffy in for a soda. She came back with two. "He's not there."

"Hmm, not at work and not at home. A Thursday afternoon. I wonder. . . ."

"You don't suppose he took off, do you, Stan?"

I was a little perplexed. I expected Becker to be where he'd ordinarily be. I went into the store myself. "He left. Said he might not be back until Monday, Sergeant," the assistant manager told me.

"When did he say this?"

"Last night. Called the boss and said he had a family emergency. Didn't think he'd be back for a while. Said we'd better take him off the weekend schedule."

"Is he still in town?"

"I doubt it. He has no family here."

I got back to Buffy. "Can this thing get us to Grand Bay?"

"Don't know until we try." She smiled. "We might get stuck and have to spend the night there."

I smiled. "Interesting thought."

"Yeah. I've only tried that one once."

Buffy's truck didn't quite make it to Grand Bay. In fact, it almost didn't make it out of town. I called Chief Edwards, who had no idea where Parker was, but did arrange for me to pick up an unmarked car at the city garage.

We drove directly to Mrs. Becker's residence. It was after the dinner hour when we arrived. There were two cars parked in front. I ran both plates and found what I had expected; one was registered to her and the other to him. We parked where we could see the house, but where we were out of sight.

There were lights in the house but no movement outside. Buffy curled up next to me and dozed off while I kept watch. Nothing moved. Then, about nine Becker emerged and went to his car, took a suitcase from the trunk, and went back into the house. I waited. Then he came back out and moved his car into the garage. He went back into the house. Another forty-five minutes or so went by, and house lights went out.

I woke Buffy. "He's in there for the night, sleepyhead. Let's go."

Buffy straightened up in the passenger seat. "What happened?"

"Nothing. He went in with a bag. Spending the night."

"Is she hiding him?"

"Don't know, Buff. He moved his car out of sight. Let's get back to town."

Before dropping Buffy off, I decided to check on Becker's residence again. Now I wanted to see if anything on the inside could be seen from the yard.

"Why don't you just pick the lock?" Buffy suggested.

"Can't do that. Not without a warrant. Especially with Parker here. See if you can see anything on the inside."

"With what?"

I checked the car. There was a flashlight in the glove compartment, but even with its help we couldn't see inside very well.

"Look," Buffy pointed to an upstairs window. "If you give me a boost, I think I might be able to see in."

Buffy wasn't very heavy, so it was an easy boost. She

climbed up on the top of the front porch and peered in the window.

"Stan," she whispered.

"Yeah, Buff."

"Are you allowed to go in if the window's not locked?"

"No, it's still his house. Police can't do that. Not without a warrant."

She didn't say anything for a few minutes, and it was too dark to read her face.

"Stan, what if a reporter went in?"

"That's trespassing."

"Then you can arrest me later." With that, she slipped out of sight and into the house.

A few minutes later, she was out the front door. "Nothing," she said. "He's gone. Nothing left except the furniture. Bet this was a furnished place. A lot around here are."

We got back into the car. "There's two logical explanations for this," I said. "First, he's reconciled with his wife."

Buffy nodded. "And the second?"

"He's getting ready to run."

Chapter Twelve

Friday was a pleasant day. My morning walk took me back through the little park across from the SuperSaver. The morning traffic was little different from day to day, and I was beginning to recognize by sight some of my early morning walking comrades. I was sure that if this case occupied me much longer, I'd probably get to know the names of the dogs being walked every day, too.

Returning to the motel, I noticed Parker on his way to the diner. That was good. I thought I'd let him beat me there, so I could give Captain Hodges a call. What old Parker didn't know would never hurt him.

"Nothing, Stan. Nadda. Zip. These guys are as tight-lipped as I've ever seen them," he said.

"No indication at all why Berrigan is being investigated?"

"They know, but they're not saying."

As I went to join Parker for breakfast, I kept wondering about our dear congressman. I know Parker said to let it alone, but I couldn't help feeling that something was amiss. That feeling got stronger as soon as I got to the diner. Parker was sitting at a table near the window. I took the seat across from him.

"Let this Berrigan thing go, Stanley."

"Good morning to you, too."

"I mean it. The AG says we're to stay off. We stay off."

"What did I do, Parker?"

"You know exactly what you did. You called to check on Berrigan. Your people called the field office in the capitol. They called Washington. Washington called the Governor. The Governor called the AG. The AG called me, and I am telling you: Let it go."

The waitress brought Parker's breakfast, and I ordered pancakes. "I thought you had eaten already," I said.

Parker looked amused. "Why?"

"You're so coherent already."

I got that look again. I hate that look. "You got in late. What did you find yesterday?"

"Becker is at his wife's in Grand Bay. He's cleaned out the duplex."

"How do you know?"

"Staked out Mrs. Becker. Peeked in the duplex."

"You could tell all that from a peek?"

He looked at me like he knew more than he was letting on. "Okay, Buffy found an open window and checked it out. Are we in trouble?"

"Find any evidence?"

"No."

"Then we're not in any trouble. Anything else?"

"Becker sold Costello at least three vehicles in the last two years."

"So?"

I pondered his "so." I had to agree that wasn't much with which to make a murder connection. "I wonder if Costello even knew about Porclar."

"We've got a couple of things to check out today," he said. "I think Costello should be one of them. First, we need to see Ace Rhodes. He left a message about some more files he's found in Winborn's office. Then I think it's about time to see the chief about the little incident in Durham."

"Parker, we've been here almost a week, and I have the feeling that we're not any closer to solving this thing than when we started."

"Yeah we are," he said.

"How so?"

"We've eliminated the congressman."

When we arrived at the newspaper office, Rhodes was in a meeting. Parker told the secretary that we'd wait. She asked if we wanted any coffee.

"Is it just the regular kind?" Parker asked.

The secretary looked a little bewildered. "The regular kind?"

I had to explain that Parker had recently become infatuated with hazelnut coffee.

"Oh, I'm sorry. We just have the regular kind, Mr. Noble."

He settled for what was available. While we waited, I used a phone in a conference room to call Buffy.

"Hi, captain. What are we doing today?"

"I'm stuck with Parker. Just sit tight."

"I have to. I don't have any wheels, remember?"

"Yeah. I'll call."

"What can I do at home?"

"Okay, Buffy. Just think. You may have overheard a conversation, either in the newsroom or at city hall, that might help. You know what we've found so far; see if something doesn't click."

"Roger."

"Who's Roger?"

"Isn't that what you guys say?"

"No. We just say good-bye."

After I hung up and started to think, it hit me how familiar I had become with Buffy. I had only met her the previous Sunday, and somehow it was beginning to feel like I had known her all my life. I didn't know if she was becoming a substitute for Diane or not, but I was getting a little concerned about some of the information I had shared with her. After all, this was still a police matter, and just because I was on my own, with only Parker for company, didn't mean I should share information with just anybody. I was just starting to ponder a question I didn't want to face when Parker interrupted.

"Let's go, Stanley."

I followed him across the reception area to Rhodes' office, where the secretary held the door open. As we entered, Jeffrey Fielding and Michael Winborn were just leaving. We exchanged a few pleasantries.

"How are things going, Mr. Noble?" Michael asked. "Do you have any leads yet?"

Parker assured him he did. "Our problem, Michael, is that we have too many right now. If you can think of anything that will help, please let us know."

Michael nodded. He looked a little more relaxed than when we had seen him previously. He also matched better today.

"I hope Mr. Fielding was able to help," he said.

"Yes. He was most cooperative," Parker replied.

Michael started to leave, then turned back to Parker. "This girl, Buffy," he said. "I hear she's been hanging around. She and my dad were not on the best of terms. I hope she doesn't need to know too much about my family's affairs."

Parker looked at me, then turned back to Michael. "She was close to your sister. I think she just wants to help. She seems fairly harmless."

Michael pressed his lips together and studied Parker for a long minute. "Mr. Noble, I don't want to tell you how to do your job, but I wouldn't say that Buffy and Anna Marie were that close of late."

"Michael," I asked, "who did your sister correspond with from the convent?"

"Well, there was Dad, and probably Margo. I think she was much closer to Margo than to Buffy. Buffy is a little flighty. She's a nice girl, but not too dependable. My dad tried to help her out, but it just didn't work. Well, if you'll excuse me, Mr. Collier wanted to see me this morning."

Parker nodded, and we all stood at the door to Ace's office, watching Michael cross the hallway and leave.

"Poor guy," Fielding said. "He's so mild-mannered and shy. I don't know what he's going to do."

"You know," Parker said, "I don't remember anybody saying what he does."

"Works here in the accounting office," Fielding said. "Pretty much a bean counter. Talk about getting kicked upstairs."

"What do you mean?" I said.

Fielding shrugged. "I guess he'll take over his father's job, as publisher. He doesn't want it, but I guess he'll try."

"Actually, he'll probably just sit around and collect a paycheck," Rhodes said. "He's not interested in the news, but I can run that. And Jeff takes care of the business end. Payson, the advertising manager, has been here about nine years. That'll run itself. He really doesn't need to do anything. Just keep counting those beans."

Fielding nodded, then excused himself. Ace Rhodes ushered us into his office, which was much smaller and less impressive than Winborn's.

"Found this," he said matter-of-factly, as he reached into his filing cabinet. "Read it. It's a death threat. The old man must have been amused to keep it around."

Parker slowly opened the envelope and began reading. As he finished, he handed it to me. It was written on a yellow legal pad, folded in half, then thirds, and mailed in one of those small, nondescript white envelopes. It said simply:

You'll get yours. God loves fags and queers and He hates you. See you in HELL, you pompous papist.

I looked at Parker. "What's this all about?" I asked.

"From what I can tell by the message and the postmark, it probably has something to do with Jerome Jackson."

"Who?" I asked.

"Jackson was a chemistry teacher at the high school. There had been some rumors about him being gay, and, as you can imagine, the old man was concerned. Well, to make a long story short, some of the stuff got into the paper, and the old man wrote a scathing editorial about it. Jackson's name was never used, but most people knew who the references were about. Jackson ended up killing himself. The letter came about a year ago, right after his death."

"Did you know about this before now?" Parker asked.

"No. I just found it in a file yesterday. Notice it was addressed to the old man at his home."

Parker reached for the letter. "No, you don't," I said. "This is my line now. We might get some prints off this thing. Ace, you have a plastic bag or something?"

Rhodes' secretary carried her lunch and had a plastic

sandwich bag, which worked just fine, crumbs and all. Not having a jacket, I gave the bag to Parker, who put it in his breast pocket.

"Any ideas about this?" he asked Rhodes.

"None. There's only a small gay community here, and they kind of stay to themselves. Most are probably still in the closet."

"No idea about who might make this kind of threat?"

"None."

Parker seemed to let that sink in for a while, then asked, "Tell me about Buffy Coyle."

"Not much to tell. She worked here about two years and quit a few months ago."

"As an employee?"

"She was a pretty fair reporter. Good writer. Short, succinct style. Was always able to put a lot of information into her stories. No complaints that way. In fact, I wish I had another one or two like her. But Michael was right. She was a tad flighty."

"How so?" I asked.

"Buffy, I think, expected more from the paper. She didn't understand that the *Independent* belonged to Chuck, and he could do what he wanted with it. I think she thought of the paper as more of a public utility, not a private enterprise. She was frustrated and left."

"Any bad blood between her and Winborn?"

"He never said anything, but I think there was. Hard-nosed, conservative businessman and a flighty, idealistic young girl. Talk about bad chemistry. She was a good reporter but just didn't fit Winborn's style."

I asked, "What was her relationship with Michael?"

"None. They spoke and were friendly, but they weren't friends. He was just her friend's brother."

"You know," Parker said, "he does seem like a strange little guy."

"Naw, he's not strange. Just shy and awkward. Socially retarded, you might say. Kinda withdrawn. Would melt in a crowd, if he didn't look so odd. I think he may be a tad color blind, which doesn't help his appearance any. Poor kid."

We started to leave, but Parker stopped at the door for a final question. "How long was this Jackson at the school?"

"About twelve or thirteen years."

Parker thanked Rhodes and we left. When we were back on the street, I asked, "What are you thinking, Parker?"

"The man was at the school twelve or thirteen years."

"Yeah, so?"

"That meant he probably taught Anna Marie and Buffy."

Chief Edwards was just returning from the sheriff's department when we arrived. He escorted us into his office.

"We need to talk to you about three things today, Chief," Parker started. "The first two are Jerome Jackson and a zoning change involving a Roscoe Costello."

Edwards leaned back in his chair. "Let me take the second one first. Costello has been doing business around these parts for at least thirty years. He is one of the leading builders in what we call the Tri-County area. He's been in and out of court over the years, but they've all been civil matters: you know, unhappy customers. Nothing to become suspicious of.

"He's involved with some pretty rough characters, mostly union leaders and the like, but that's just part of the construction business. I know he had been trying to build on some land, but the city had it bottled up. Don't know much more than that. I don't get involved in those matters."

That reminded me of something both Buffy and Tom Collier had mentioned. "Chief, do the unions representing the construction workers that work for Costello have anything to do with the unions involved in the tractor strike?"

"They're all separate unions, but they have a local union council they call the Tri-County Labor Confederation. It's kind of an umbrella group, but it's mostly political."

I asked, "Have you ever had any labor violence around here?"

"Only with the tractor plant strike. None of it really got out of hand. Some of the hotheads threw rocks at trucks. One tried to fire-bomb the guard house, but failed."

"Who was he?"

"Don't know. Never caught him. Strike ended shortly after that, and the union was pretty much broken."

"Anyone around Costello or the union that would be interested in seeing Winborn dead?" I asked.

Edwards smiled. "Plenty. But you're asking the wrong question. You want to know if anyone would actually try to kill him. That I can't answer. I doubt it, but who knows? Winborn engendered strong feelings."

"And Jackson?" Parker asked.

"High school teacher. Committed suicide after he was outed as gay. Very traumatic for the kids at the time, but they got over it. What's his connection to this?"

Parker gave Edwards the letter and asked him to run it for prints.

"Sounds like that Right Way group," Edwards said.

"Who?"

"Militants. Most are from Grand Bay. They broke into a Catholic church over there, protesting the church's stand against gay marriages. Spray-painted slogans like these all over the inside. Stuff like, 'God hates you, but loves queers.' That kind of thing."

Parker asked, "Are they militant enough to try to kill?"

"Well, I wouldn't put it past them to threaten or damage property. But to kill is another matter. I suppose some might. But, for the most part, these are not violent people. They just want to be left alone."

"But the militants," I said. "There are hotheads all over. And, from what we can see, Winborn was the type to set them off."

Edwards sat quiet for a second. "You know, it just occurs to me. The victim was a Catholic nun, and she was the daughter of their nemesis."

Parker glanced at each of us. Then he said, "Then we may be back to square one. Just who was the intended victim?"

"Yeah," I said to Parker, "but then you still have the question of who knew Anna Marie was in town."

Parker lifted his pipe out of his pocket and motioned towards Edwards. The chief nodded and Parker lit up. "Have your men found anything?"

"Nothing. We have checked with nearly all her old friends. No one knew she would be home. A couple of close ones thought she might come but didn't know the date. You talked to one, Margo. No one heard anything that night. There are no prints on anything. The powder could have been purchased at any sports shop. We are at a dead end. I was hoping you'd bail us out."

"Could the powder have come from a construction site?" I asked.

Edwards fanned away some pipe smoke. "Oh, probably not. You'd find dynamite there. Chase and the ATF guys would have noticed the difference."

"Can we get the police report on the Jackson suicide?" Parker asked.

Edwards picked up the phone. "Sure. I'll have Sherry get it for you." He ordered the file, then turned back to Parker. "You said you had three things."

Parker looked directly at Edwards. "Tell us about your stint in Durham."

Edwards went pale. His mouth dropped, and he had the look of a man who was hit in the head with a two-by-four. There was a long pause. When he finally spoke, it was in a slow, measured cadence.

"I was dismissed after an altercation with an African-American. They claimed I used excessive force. It wasn't true. I was a pawn in a political war. I was sacrificed. That's as simple as I can put it."

"And your ex-wife, Peggy?" Parker asked.

Edwards clenched his jaw. "Am I never to live that down?"

"In this state, that is domestic abuse. You can't be a cop with that on your record," Parker said.

"I can have my lawyer contact you," Edwards said. "I think he can answer all your questions."

"Do you have your application for the Forbes Island department?"

"I'll have Sherry get that for you, too. Anything else?"

Parker took the pipe out of his mouth, looked at me, then back at Edwards. "No. But for right now we're holding this as confidential. It is on a strict need-to-know basis. Okay?"

Edwards looked a little relieved. "Okay. Thanks for that much."

I got the files from Sherry and met Parker back out on

the street. He was just standing there, looking in the direction of Billy's Dugout. "We eating?" I asked.

Parker just stared at the restaurant. "You know, Stanley, there's one thing that bothers me."

"What is it, Parker?"

"Edwards had covered his tracks fairly well. He was genuinely surprised that we knew about Durham."

"So?"

"Sometimes things revolve around things that don't happen or questions that aren't asked."

"What's your point?"

He turned to me. "Edwards never asked how we knew."

Chapter Thirteen

Parker, to my surprise, found a booth in the non-smoking section of Billy's Dugout. When I asked about his change of habit, he replied only, "It's starting to bite."

"Well, you know, Parker, it's probably better that you not smoke. You'd live a more healthy life."

He just grunted something about pipes and spit, then turned to the menu. The lunch special was a fish sandwich, tartar sauce, fries, and a drink. Parker ordered the special with an extra sandwich and a root beer. I ordered a club sandwich, coffee, no fries.

Parker took the Jackson file and opened it. On the inside there was a picture of Jackson. It looked like one of those shots taken for a school yearbook. Inside the folder was the written report on the teacher's death, complete with notes of interviews taken at the time. Inside a manila envelope were graphic photos of the scene of death and the autopsy, all of which Parker dumped onto the table.

"Parker, we're getting ready to eat."

"You obviously have never had to prepare a witness over lunch."

"No, I can't say that I have. Put the pictures away."

He gave me that look, but this time I held my own with what I thought was a strong glare back. He shook his head, put the photos back in the manila envelope, and handed me

Edwards' material. "Here. See what he put on his application."

Edwards' application was pretty straightforward. It listed his early schooling, his associate degree from a community college in Ohio, and his police work from Ohio on. What it did not mention was his service in Durham. In fact, for the four-year period from high school until college, it listed only his National Guard service and an employer called Hexigraph Services. Under remarks was written: "Delivery driver. Company failed. Out of business." I pointed it out to Parker.

"Sure, a good way to cover the years. Who would go looking for an out-of-business firm this many years later? The guard he'd have to list, too easy to trace, but this Hexigraph would be a good cover."

"But, Parker, why would the record we have show the gap?"

"Someone must have tried to check out this Hexigraph later. Probably when he was being promoted to chief. They couldn't find Hexigraph, so they just listed it as unknown."

"Then he lied on his application. Isn't that grounds for termination in and of itself?"

"No, not by itself. He would have been covered by civil service, and that wouldn't be enough to do it. But covering up a prior disciplinary action would. The gamble for him was an easy one to take. No one here would check for this Hexigraph place. They'd only check his immediate job references and for a criminal record. Back then, he could hire on here from a smaller force with little or no problem."

"But if this came out?"

"Like I said, his biggest problem is the domestic abuse thing. You know, he could be right about the racial thing. It happened back then. He could have been sacrificed to keep some protesters silent. That would have been easy to do, especially since they already had the wife thing against him."

"Okay, Parker, why didn't he ask where we got the information? Did he assume we got it from Winborn?"

"He may have made that assumption. After all, he almost said as much when we first met Saturday. Remember, he said something to the effect that Winborn had something on everybody. But he was surprised today. Do you want to bet that means he didn't know Winborn had it?"

I pondered that for a while, as Parker went back to the Jackson report. He appeared deeply engrossed with it when our lunch arrived. "Hey," the waitress said, pointing to the yearbook shot of Jackson, "that's Mr. Jackson. He was my teacher."

Parker looked up. The waitress was a large girl but still didn't look much older than high-school age. "How long ago, Miss?"

"Two years ago. I had him the semester before he died. What are you doing with that stuff? Are you police or something?"

Parker looked at me; that was my signal to show her my shield. "I'm Sergeant Stankowski from the state police. This is Mr. Noble from the Attorney General's office."

"Why are you looking at that stuff? Wasn't it supposed to be a suicide?"

"Could you answer some questions for us, er, ah, Miss . . . ?" Parker started.

"Bobbie. Bobbie Douglas. Sure. Let me take care of something and I'll be right back."

True to her word, Bobbie was right back. She pulled up a chair from a neighboring table. "I never thought he killed himself. I think someone done him in because of that gay stuff."

"Bobbie," Parker started, "what did you know about Mr. Jackson?"

"Well, everyone knew he was gay. I mean, that's kind of hard to hide, isn't it? He was real nice and everyone liked him. But then there were them rumors going around, and the newspaper wrote some stuff about it, and everyone in school knew it was about him. Then, one day they made an announcement and said he had passed away."

"Did you know anything about his private life?" Parker asked.

"No. He just lived in an old house with his mother. Anytime we saw him outside of school, he was either alone or with her. He used to come to all the games and things. But he was usually alone."

A burly man wearing an apron approached. "I'm Chad, Bobbie's dad. I own this place."

"Not Billy?" I said.

Chad smiled and pulled up another chair. "I bought it from Billy. He played a few years with the old Washington Senators farm club. That's how it got its name. I just kept it."

"I was with Detroit, played in Erie," I said.

"Not with the Tigers?" Chad asked.

"Pitched against them once."

He looked like he was sizing me up. "Yeah, you look like a pitcher. An exhibition game?"

"Against their Triple-A."

"How'd ya do?"

"Good enough to go up."

"Injury?"

"Second year."

"That's too bad. A lot of good ones get cut down before

they have a chance. I think that was old Billy's deal, too. Bum knee."

"Arm."

"That'd do it for a pitcher." He looked sympathetic. "I only managed a little high school ball. Football was my sport. That was too many years ago. Anyway, Bobbie says you're interested in that queer school teacher."

"Daddy," Bobbie said, slapping her father's leg, "we don't use those words any more."

Chad shook his head. "Well, whatever you call them. It was a damn shame. Nobody had any beef with him. He used to eat in here. Quiet. Kinda guessed he was, you know, different, gay." He turned to his daughter. "Is that the word they use? Anyway, he was never any trouble. Too bad about him."

"Mr. Douglas," Parker asked, "what was the community reaction to all the rumors?"

"Hell, nobody gave a damn. So, he's queer. Live and let live, I say. What he does in his own life is his business. We should have all just left the man alone. But not that newspaper. They had to get all over the thing. Everyone knew who they were talking about. Hey, that's it, isn't it?" Chad exclaimed. "You guys are here about that Winborn stuff. Do you think this is connected?"

"We're only checking out loose ends," I said.

"Say, you don't think it was really murder, do you? The Jackson thing, I mean. Bobbie always said she didn't believe it was suicide."

"Why, Bobbie?" Parker asked.

"I don't know. Just a feeling. He never seemed to be the kind of guy who would do something like that. I don't know. It just didn't seem right to me."

"Who would have killed him, then?"

"That's just it. Nobody would have. Everybody liked him. Except if he was leading some kind of hidden life."

Parker smiled. "Then he might have been the suicidal type. What do you think, Mr. Douglas?"

"I think the cops had it right. Poor guy was embarrassed. Might have lost his job. Just decided to hang it up." He turned to his daughter, "I know Bobbie doesn't want to believe it, but I think it's true. He killed himself."

That was it. We thanked them for their help, then turned back to the file.

"Oh, Bobbie, just one more thing," Parker said.

Bobbie turned around and returned to the table, "Yes, Mr. Noble?"

He lifted up an empty coffee cup. "Do you have hazelnut?"

Parker was back to his usual moody self on the way back to Costello and Sons. He had picked up one of those free advertising newspapers at Billy's Dugout and was reading it in the car.

"What are you looking for, Parker? There's only ads in that thing."

"Yeah, I know. If you must know, I'm in the market for a used, heated dog bed for Buckwheat Bob."

"A heated dog bed, Parker?"

"Yes. I figure it'll get him off my couch."

"Just push him off."

"I can't do that. He loves it there. It's warm, you know."

The conversation went like that, driving me crazy for another fifteen minutes, until we pulled up in front of Costello's. Roscoe was out, but his nephew, Peter Costello, was there.

"My uncle said you'd been here," he said. "What else can we do?"

We asked about the zoning change.

He leaned against a filing cabinet and folded his arms. "He probably told you as much as he knew. It just wouldn't go through and was holding up our project."

"How much money is invested in something like that?" Parker asked.

"Right now it's just the land costs. If we could get it rezoned, there would be a couple of million in it."

"And your payroll?"

"A project like that? Heck, it would be huge."

"Did you know who owned the land just to the south and almost adjoining yours?" he asked.

"Yeah, a farmer named MacBee. We tried to buy it. Wouldn't sell."

Parker looked at young Costello, as if trying to take the measure of him. "Then you didn't know MacBee had sold it to an outfit controlled by Winborn?"

Costello's eyes widened. "Now things are starting to make some sense. Let me call my uncle; he's about five minutes from here."

Roscoe arrived, and Peter explained the MacBee sale. Roscoe took us into his office. "I'll be," he said to Parker as he stood behind his desk. "I knew there must have been some reason he was blocking our zoning. That's it. He owned a competing project."

Parker shook his head. "It wasn't competing yet. I'm given to believe he had plans to do so, but what his timing was, I'm not sure we'll ever know."

"Uncle Roscoe said they couldn't keep the zoning change from us permanently," Peter said.

"That's right," Parker replied. "But he only needed to

keep it from you long enough to get started with his project. Mr. Costello, am I right in assuming that the city could probably only support one project like yours?"

"Absolutely. Eventually both would go as the area grew. But, for now, once one got the jump-start, the other would be out. I can see what he was doing now. If he could delay our zoning long enough to get his project started, it would be the only one for some time. We could get ours sold, but probably not for another eight or ten years."

I asked Costello, "Had you any indication that Winborn was involved in any type of development?"

"No. This comes as a complete surprise to me. I didn't even know he owned the land."

"It was a corporation he controlled, Porclar. Does that name mean anything to you?" Parker asked.

Both Costellos shook their heads. "Sorry fellows," Peter said.

"By the way," I asked, "where do you fellows buy your cars?"

"Don't know about Peter, but I've been buying from Stevens Ford for years."

"Know the salesman?"

"Yeah, now that you mention it. It was that fellow who left. Becker? I think that's his name. This guy was in the paper for patronizing a cathouse. Gone now. You don't think this is all related, do you?"

I told them I didn't, and Parker asked them to call if they thought of anything. They agreed, and we left.

Clay Spencer did not fit the image of a labor boss. The first thing you noticed about him was his tailored dress shirt with sleeves rolled up a quarter, and a silk tie that probably came from a designer's rack. The next thing you noticed were the certificates on his office wall: a diploma from a private college and a CPA certificate. It was a small but impressive office. Spencer sat behind an executive desk. Parker and I took the two guest chairs in front of it.

"We don't really consider ourselves like the other unions," Spencer said. "We're building trades. We represent, for the most part, very skilled workers. Some require state or local licenses. Our philosophy is that we are more of a partner to business than an adversary."

"That seems unusual," I said.

"Not really." He leaned back in his chair. "When you think about it, business has to be really good for our people to work. When business is down, building is off. When business booms, we work. If it isn't good for business, it's not good for us."

"Some of your people might say you've been co-opted by management," I replied.

Spencer smiled. "You might think that. But then remember that some of our people, electricians, for example, own their own businesses. We facilitate putting knowledge and skill with capital to get a job done. We make sure our guys get a fair break, but we do work closely with industry. We have to. Capital, not labor, creates jobs."

Parker leaned forward. "We were told that the labor council here harbored some hard feelings about the newspaper because of the tractor strike."

"There was. But in many respects it was the strikers' own damn fault. The farm economy was in a recession. The company had asked for concessions to keep everyone working. The union refused. The union lost. End of story. Those guys think differently than we do over here."

He turned to me. "Sergeant, you noticed my CPA. I'm the local business agent here. The rest of our business staff members all have some kind of degree, at least on the associate level. Our state president holds an MBA. A couple of years ago, our president had a Ph.D. in economics. Our board of directors is made up of electrical and structural engineers, a college professor, a retired general contractor, and a disabled bricklayer who now sells real estate from his wheelchair. This is not your normal union group. In the other union hall, the best you might find are a few GEDs. Not here. We understand money first. That way we know how to fit people into the mix, so they can take their share."

"Mr. Spencer," Parker intoned, "are you aware of a pending zoning change requested by Roscoe Costello?"

"Yes. I thought it was dead."

"How does that affect your people?"

"Right now, it doesn't. We're spread across three counties in this area and, quite frankly, we're short of skilled tradespeople. Costello's project would be nice, if we could get to it. Right now, no. These guys really need to get their projects to the point that we can work indoors during the winter. Unfortunately, even if he could get the change he needs, nothing could be done until spring. Then all hell breaks loose, and we'd be scrambling to get him enough labor."

"Are you a member of this Tri-County labor deal?" I asked.

"Sure, but that's mostly a political organization. We let them do their own thing. We usually end up supporting Republican candidates. Big business and all. The other unions are usually on the other side."

"Who was the leader of the tractor plant strikers?"

"Fellow by the name of Black. After the union was broken—and don't get me wrong from what I said; we don't approve of breaking unions. We honored the picket lines and shut down the plant remodeling that was going on at the time. Of course, our people just went to work on other jobs at different sites, so we weren't hurt. But, anyway, Black is gone. Left after the union lost."

"Hard feelings?" I asked.

"You bet there were. All around."

"About the newspaper?"

"Especially about the newspaper. That guy Winborn helped do in the strikers. It wasn't fair, even if the strike was stupid to begin with. Those folks had families and a story to tell, too."

"What about the fire bomb at the guard house?" Parker asked.

"Word on the street was that it was Black. No one was ever arrested. But, outside of a few picket line scuffles, it was a pretty calm affair. The union liked Tom Foley, but he laid down the law about violence, and they took him at his word."

"Know where we can find Black?" I asked.

"I'd check the state union records. Probably using his card somewhere, doing the same thing."

"First name?"

"Phillip. Phillip Black."

Phillip Black was easy to locate. Spencer was right, state union headquarters was able to locate him for us. He was in the capitol working for another tractor plant. Spencer was right about another thing; Black was still using his union card. I called headquarters and had them pull his file, if he had one, and made a note to check for it in the morning.

Parker settled into his easy chair at the SuperSaver and popped the top off a soda can that he had purchased from the motel's machine.

"We've had a long day here. I would like to try to get a hold of Mabel Crane tonight," he said.

"Who is Mabel Crane?"

"Oh, I'm sorry, Stanley. That's Jerome Jackson's mother. You didn't have time to look at that file. After dinner, we'll give her a call."

He paused long enough to take a drink of his root beer. "I was thinking. One of us should go home for the weekend. We're not both needed right now, and one of us can check out this Black character."

"Yeah, Parker, and I'm sure Buckwheat Bob misses you, too."

"Well, suit yourself. You can go. I think one of us ought to stay, though."

"Parker, did it ever occur to you that I can have an agent there interview Black and e-mail us his notes?"

"That's fine, Stanley, if you trust that electronic stuff." He suggested that I call around to see if I could find where Becker banked. "We might want to monitor his account. See if he taps into it. If he's going to run, he'll want whatever savings he has."

When I left Parker, it was about four-thirty. He told me not to come back until six. He wanted to take a nap, he said.

I got to my room and called Hodges and told him what we needed. Then I called Buffy. There was no answer. Getting back to business, I called the assistant manager at the QuicKing and asked if Becker's payroll was on a direct deposit and, if so, to what bank. She said she'd check and call back.

I turned to the Jackson file. The scene photos clearly indicated that Jackson's death was a suicide, and so did the autopsy report. Everything was consistent with suicide, including a note. According to the file, it was addressed to his mother and students. It simply said, "I'm sorry for the embarrassment I've caused. I love you all. We will meet again in a better, kinder place. Please forgive me."

The report and the interviews painted a picture of a simple, kind man who never advertised his homosexuality but never denied it, either. There was nothing in any of the materials I had in front of me to indicate that he would have been connected in any way to the militant gay group, Right Way. Also included in the file was a copy of the editorial written by Winborn, calling on the school board to rid the schools of their "homosexual and perverted" staff members. "This is an abomination against nature," the editorial said, "and this scourge of perversion and sexual deviance must end, or our schools will surely fail in their most basic task: the production of God-fearing, clear-thinking, and value-driven young men and women who will someday assume the mantle of civic and business leadership."

Strong stuff, I thought. Since it was strong enough to push poor Jackson into suicide, I wondered if it was strong enough to push someone else into murder. I started to think again about what the chief had said. Right Way had vandalized a Catholic church. We were dealing with the death of a Catholic nun. Parker had mentioned something earlier about someone trying to get their revenge on the old man by killing the daughter he loved. If so, that would be a two-for-one shot for the bad guys.

I raised Parker at six, and we went next door to the diner for dinner. Parker after a nap was much like Parker in the morning. He really didn't say much of anything until he had his coffee, the old kind.

When he got his bearings, I summarized the Jackson file for him. He just looked at me, and every once in a while would say, "I didn't know that."

"Of course you didn't, Parker. You didn't have time to read the whole thing. Not while you were chatting with Chad and Bobbie. But don't you think it's now more important than ever to find out if anyone knew Anna Marie was coming home?"

He agreed. "Didn't you say Buffy knew? And Margo knew? Ask them again. But we've been over this, and there doesn't seem to be anyone who knew the exact date. Just the family."

I added, "And Doctor Burnelli."

"Yes, and, along with the congressman, we can rule him out, too."

The trip to Mabel Crane's was uneventful. It was even more uneventful when we found that she wasn't at home. With time on our hands, Parker, to my surprise, suggested a quick stop for a drink. We found a small neighborhood tavern near the Crane residence. Parker ordered Scotch and, after listening to "anyone who drinks beer will steal," I ordered a cold draft.

"Hey, Parker," I said. "When we were driving up here last week, you started to tell me a story about a newspaper editor getting killed in Booneville. You never did finish."

He smiled and took a sip. He loved telling stories, especially about his career.

"Wasn't much of a story. This guy owned a bar and didn't close for Good Friday. The editor made some derogatory comments about it, which irritated the bar owner, who said he was as good a Christian as anyone and killed the editor to prove it. Kind of an open-and-shut case. What was interesting about it was what happened afterwards."

Parker stirred his Scotch and took a drink, then continued his story.

"The guy had a court-appointed lawyer who convinced the jury that his client must be crazy. So instead of getting convicted, he was found insane and committed to a state mental health hospital.

"Well, a few years later, the mental hospitals are so overcrowded that the legislature passes a law that lets them replace their patients. All they need is a facility that will accept them, and the approval of a panel of psychiatrists who say the guy is not dangerous."

He took another drink.

"Well, this panel of shrinks says that this guy has some kind of God complex and is only dangerous to newspaper editors who write about him. So they release him to this hospital up north, run by an order of monks. Now he spends his time in meditation and baking bread. They even call him Brother Bill.

"That was one of my first cases, and I don't think I'll ever find anything to top that."

"Do they still do that, Parker? Put people out like that?"

"Nope. Then the legislature approved gambling, built a new hospital with the tax money, and repealed that law." He finished his drink. "Let's check out Mabel again."

She still wasn't home. Parker said that was okay, since Friday was a good night on the Nashville channel. So we headed back to the SuperSaver. Parker went right to his room, but I stopped by the lobby for a paper. The clerk waved me over and gave me a message. It was from the QuicKing assistant manager. I was to call her at home.

"No direct deposit," she said. "But he did cash a check in the register. It's on County Bank and Trust. Know where that is?"

I said no.

"It's easy. It's real small. They have only one branch. It's on the square right next to the mayor's insurance office."

I thanked her and decided to turn in early.

It was still dark when I heard the pounding on my door. It took me a minute to get my bearings. My watch said four-thirty. The pounding continued. I got to the door. It was Parker. His hair was mussed, and he looked terribly stupid in pajamas with little sailboats on them.

"What is it?" I asked.

"Get dressed, now!" he said urgently. "Margo Roberts just called. Buffy is missing."

Chapter Fourteen

The fear that something may have happened to Buffy stirred something in me that shouldn't have been there. Whether it was because of Diane, or in spite of her, I had allowed this girl to get too close to me. Whatever had happened to her, I couldn't help but to feel that I was somehow responsible. After all, it was me who, against all good police practice, took Buffy into my confidence and let her help with the investigation. And it was me who exposed her to the risks of tracking down a murderer. In short, I had no one else to blame for whatever hazard might have befallen her.

Parker and I rushed to Margo's. On the way, Parker told me all he knew. Margo had called and said that Buffy had borrowed her car to help the police. After waiting all night, and unable to reach her by phone, Margo called Parker.

"That's all we know right now, Stanley. Just that she's missing and Margo is worried."

"Have you called Forbes Island PD?"

"No. After our little confrontation with the chief yesterday, I thought it best to keep this between ourselves until we know more."

Since I had been to the Roberts' home before, it didn't take me long to find my way back. Margo and her parents met us at the door. I quickly introduced Parker to Dr. Roberts. Mrs. Roberts brought us coffee as Margo started her story.

"She called me at work yesterday. Said something about needing my car to help the police with Anna Marie's case."

Parker wanted to know why she didn't use her own car. I had to explain about the shit truck and how it came to rest at the police garage.

"That's exactly what she told me," Margo said. "She said her little truck had broken down, and you guys traded it for another police vehicle at the garage. She said Stan was using his car, and she needed one but couldn't get a city car because she wasn't a cop."

"What do you think, Mr. Noble?" Mrs. Roberts asked.

"I want to hear more," was his answer.

Margo continued, "Well, I picked her up at lunch and let her take my car. I even gave her my cell phone. She dropped me off back at work, and Dad picked me up later."

"Did she tell you where she was going?" I asked.

"No. Just something about watching a suspect. Some kind of stakeout. She was going to watch somebody and report back to you."

I looked at Parker. "Becker. She's gone to watch Becker."

We got the description and license number of Margo's car, and her cell phone number. "Have you called the number?" I asked.

"Yes. Several times. That's what has me worried. There's no answer."

"Miss Roberts," Parker said, "did she say when you could expect her back?"

"Late Friday night. She said something about being done by the time the bars closed. She also said she'd call if anything held her up."

We thanked the Robertses and left. Before starting to Grand Bay, I went to the trunk of the car and retrieved my service revolver, holster, and a light jacket I could wear over it. "I hope you won't need that," he said, as I got behind the wheel.

"I hope so, too, Parker. I know where she is."

"Tell me."

"I told you, Thursday night we watched Becker's place in Grand Bay. Becker left his job, cleaned out his place in Forbes Island, and moved in with his wife. I'm sure Buffy was left with the impression that Becker was our man. She probably went back to watch him for me."

"Rhodes said she was flighty. How flighty, Stanley? Would she do something as stupid as confronting Becker?"

"I doubt that, Parker. But she might be seen loitering around his wife's house. He might remember her from the newspaper. Might have seen her with us, for that matter. If he is guilty or hiding something, the sight of her might cause him to panic."

"Amateurs. Why do they always try to get involved in this kind of thing?"

For the first time since I heard that Buffy was missing, I relaxed and had to smile. "Listen to what you're saying, Mr. Private Citizen."

"Ahhh, but Stanley, crime is the business of the Attorney General."

Parker had one-upped me again, but this time it didn't seem to matter. My thoughts drifted back to the little one in the gumshoe hat and I started feeling guilty again. Parker seemed to sense my feelings.

"Don't blame yourself, Stan. It's not your fault." It was the first time I had ever heard him call me Stan. That worried me even more. It was as if Parker was trying to soften the blow that he thought was coming. "She'll be okay," he said.

I hoped he was right. I mindlessly pointed the car in the direction of Grand Bay and thought of Buffy. I could picture her sitting in her chair, venting her hatred of Winborn the first day we met. I could see the tears in her eyes that night at the bowling alley. My mind continued to replay the last week: Buffy comforting the old nun, crying at the funeral, modeling her hat. I could see Parker's expression when she first appeared at Billy's Dugout. I was starting to wonder if I'd see Buffy any more or if she would become just a memory.

The sun was rising as we entered the city limits of Grand Bay. It didn't take long to get to Mrs. Becker's place.

"There's the house, Parker. We parked over here." I drove around the corner, but there was no car matching Margo's.

"Try the phone," Parker suggested. "Maybe this thing is over now."

I called Margo's cell phone. There was no answer.

I drove around the block and stopped a few doors away from Mrs. Becker's home. "I'm going to the house. You wait here."

Parker reached over and grabbed me. "Are you crazy? If she's in there, you'll just put her in more jeopardy than she is already. Think with your head this time, Stanley. What would a cop do?"

"Call for help."

"We can't do that. Second option."

"I'm blanking, Parker."

"Okay. Tell me this: Are all the right cars at the Becker house?"

"That's Mrs. Becker's car. Becker put his in the garage."

"Okay. Let's find out if his car is still here. Can you slip a peek into the garage without waking the whole neighborhood?"

"Sure." I drove the car around the block again, so I'd be on the garage side of the house. It only took me a minute to check out the garage and return to Parker.

"His car's still there."

"Okay. Then where would Margo's car be?"

"Well, if he found Buffy, he'd have to dispose of the car. Couldn't keep it here."

"Let's start moving. I don't like sitting here as the sun comes up. Let's make concentric circles around this place and see what we find."

"Parker, I think he'd move the car farther than that."

"Do you have any better ideas?"

I drove as Parker directed. He didn't have the best police sense in the world, but right now I knew I didn't have any.

We hadn't progressed very far, when Parker motioned for me to stop at a small gas station. It was one of those places that have six or eight pumps and a tiny building in the center, where coffee, soda, and a few staples are sold. At first I thought Parker wanted to stop for coffee.

"Stop. Now, pull over around the side. Look at the car parked on the far side."

I could see what was attracting Parker's attention. It was a car that closely resembled Margo's. I pulled around to where we could get a good look at the license number.

"Bingo! That's Margo's," I said and pulled into the drive towards Margo's car. Parker was out of the car almost before it stopped. I wasn't too far behind. It was Margo's car all right, but Buffy was nowhere in sight. The car was locked, but we could see inside. On the seat were Buffy's purse, a coffee cup, and Buffy's gumshoe hat.

"There's no sign of anything funny," Parker said.

"What now?"

"Well, Stanley, I don't know what a cop would do, but I think I'll just mosey on over to the office there and ask if they know anything."

I felt rather foolish but followed Parker into the small store. There was a plump, middle-aged woman inside behind the counter.

"We're looking for the driver of that car out there," Parker said pointing to Margo's car.

"Are you here to tow it away?"

"No, Ma'am. We're looking for the driver. A small, young woman about twenty-four, but looks younger."

"That little wildcat! Little thing? About five-four, one hundred and five soaking wet?"

"Yeah, that's her," I said.

"Are you with her? I'm calling the cops."

"We are the cops," I said, flashing my shield.

"Well, then you know where she is. They took her away. You sure you're a cop?"

I gave her my identification. "State police? What's the state police want with her? I knew it. She's in big trouble, isn't she? I could tell. She's a wild one. You could see it in her eyes."

Parker stopped her. "Hold on here. Just tell us what happened."

"She broke into the store and I found her. I called the police and that Sergeant Brookman came. He's black, you know. I'm not prejudiced, mind you; I have a black friend. Her name is Jerri."

"Back to the story, please," I said, trying to hurry her up.

"Well, Brookman came. He's a big guy. Keeps all those gang people quiet, so you know he can handle himself. And she screamed and cursed. Why the things that came out of that little mouth would make a Marine blush. She was all he could handle. He looked like he was wrestling with a greased pig. Took him the longest time to get the cuffs on her. All the time she was screaming, claiming she was on an official investigation. She even bit him. Cut clean through his shirtsleeve. Why, I never heard or saw the likes of it."

"Did they take her to jail?"

"Reckon so. Where else would you take her? Oh, she was a wild one, that one. What you want her for? Hey," she said pointing to Parker, "you don't look much like a cop. Who are you?"

Parker gave her his business card, the one with the gold Department of Justice seal on it. She studied it and looked at Parker. "Should have figured this was something big. State boys, Attorney General's office. She's on drugs, isn't she? This is about a drug ring, isn't it?"

Parker thanked the woman, and I followed him back to the car. "Seems like your little girlfriend has gotten herself into a wee bit of trouble."

"I don't understand it, Parker. Buffy breaking into a gas station? Think they have the right person?"

"We'll find out soon enough."

I didn't know whether or not I wanted the girl arrested in the gas station to be Buffy. Why would Buffy try to rob that little store? And if it wasn't Buffy, who was it, and where was the real Buffy?

We arrived at Grand Bay PD shortly after eight-thirty. I showed the desk officer my identification, introduced Parker, and asked about Buffy.

"Buffy? I don't have a record of a Buffy. When did she come in?"

I explained about a black sergeant named Brookman and

the scuffle at the gas station.

"Oh, that. Yeah. Brookman's here. Was in first aid. Got bit by that girl. Gave her name as Frances something. Said we should call someone from the Attorney General's office. Hey, is that you?" he said to Parker.

"I think I may be. Can we see her?"

The officer called Bookman met us. He was a big man. It was easy to see how he could keep gang peace all by himself. He spoke softly and appeared gentle, but he didn't look like the type you'd want to cross.

"Got a call just after six. Woman, Mrs. Simms, we all know her, was reporting for work and found your little she-devil inside the store. Mrs. Simms says the girl just screamed at her. When I arrived, the little one was cowering in a corner and wouldn't come out. When I tried to grab her, all hell broke loose.

"Why, she's like a rattlesnake, that one. She scratched, bit, fought, screamed. I don't mind telling you guys, she was more than one cop could handle. I almost had to call for help. Just as I was backing off, she lost her balance, and I literally had to sit on her to cuff her."

"That doesn't sound like the Buffy I know," I said.

"Is she really with you guys? She kept screaming something about the Attorney General."

I shook my head. "That's our girl."

"Well, then, I wouldn't brag about it," Brookman said. He led us back to the holding cells. "You sure you want to see her? She just quieted down. We had a drunk driver in there when we brought her in. Had to release him; he said he'd sue us for exposure to *that.*" Brookman winked. "He's a regular. Sent him out for breakfast. He'll be back."

Brookman opened the door to the holding area. Buffy was sitting in one of the two cells. She had her feet on her cot and was holding her knees to her face as we entered. She looked up.

"Stannnnn, get me out of here. Mr. Parker, please, tell them I'm with you."

She ran to the door of the cell and reached through the bars for me. "Get me outta here. Oh, Stan. Get me outta here."

"Whoa, slow down," I said. "What happened? Why were you in the gas station?"

"Oh, Stan. Oh, Stan. It was horrible. Oh Stan."

"Buffy, tell me what happened."

"Oh, do I have to stay in here? Can't they let me out?"

I looked at Brookman, who nodded and got the key for the cell. Buffy ran to me as soon as she was out. "Oh, it was so horrible, Stan. And they treated me like a common thief. Me! Frances Jean Coyle. Like a common thief."

"Calm down, Buffy. Just tell me what happened."

She looked up at me, then at Parker. She took his hand, "Thank you, too, Mr. Parker, for coming to get me."

Parker looked at me, but this time I didn't care. I was just starting to feel relieved that Buffy was all right.

"I came out here last night to watch Becker," she started. "I parked over by the house just like we did the night before. I didn't want him to run." She looked up at me with her big, pale blue eyes, "I wasn't going to do anything. Just watch. Honest, Stan. I was just going to watch and call, if he made any suspicious moves. I just wanted to help out."

"Okay, Buffy, but how did you get into the station?"

"Well, about eleven o'clock Becker left. He had his kid with him, so I figured he'd be back. I followed him to that little station. He came out with a bag of stuff, so I figured he'd be going home. So, after he left, I went and got one of those big cups of coffee. I figured I'd need it to keep me awake. So, I went back to Becker's. His car was there, so I just stayed and watched and drank the coffee."

She stopped long enough to see that everyone was listening. Parker shook his head and tried to suppress a smile. Whatever he was thinking went right over my head. "Go on," I said.

"Well that was it. I drank the coffee."

"So?"

"So, then I had to pee! It was almost two o'clock, so I went back to that little place to use the little girls' room."

I was starting to catch the drift. "Buffy, when we're on a stakeout, we usually use a tree."

"Well, paaarrdooon me! If you haven't figured it out by this time, Mr. State Policeman, I haven't got the plumbing for tree-peeing."

"Finish your story, Buffy."

"Well, I got back to the store. It was still open, but no one was there. So I used the girls' room. When I came out, it was all dark and I was locked in. I couldn't call, because the phone was on the counter behind the glass and the pay phone was outside. I left Margo's cell phone in the car. I knew I blew it, so I just sat down and cried. I must have fallen asleep, because the next thing I know there's this fat hyena screaming at me like I'm a criminal or something. I tried to say something and she just ran at me, screaming and pushing me with a broom."

She pointed at Brookman. "Then this hairy beast comes at me. Chases me around and corners me next to the milk. Then he jumps on me and shackles me. Why, he touched me in places no lady should be touched!"

Brookman just looked amused.

"Yeah, grin, you son of a . . ."

I grabbed Buffy as she lunged at Brookman. Then she started crying. "He told me I was under arrest, and I had the right to this and that. I tried to tell him I was with you and didn't mean any harm; but, whoosh, he just drug me from the milk cooler and threw me into a squad car. Brought me here and put me right next to a drunk."

Parker looked at Brookman. "What are the charges, Officer?"

"Right now, just trespassing. Mrs. Simms said nothing's missing. Her story about being trapped could be on the level. The place closes at two Friday nights. There's a little room behind the counter with the safe. Night man was probably there when she came in."

"Resisting?"

"Could, but won't." He looked at Buffy, who by now had both arms wrapped around me so hard it was difficult to breathe. "Tell you what. I know the owner. As long as the Attorney General wants this little rattlesnake out of here, I can get him to drop the trespassing. But you have to make me one promise."

"What's that?" Parker said.

"You have to promise you'll never bring her back."

We agreed. I pulled Buffy from the cell area, still hissing at Brookman, and down to the street.

"In the car, young lady; we're taking you home," I said.

She stood on the curb outside the police station with a defiant look. "No," she said, crossing her arms.

I could feel the blood rushing to my head and my face becoming flushed. "What?" I screamed.

"I can't right now," she said. "I have to pee again."

Chapter Fifteen

It was almost eleven in the morning before Parker and I arrived back at the SuperSaver. We had left so fast that we both wanted a chance to clean up a little. Parker also wanted to catch up on his sleep. He suggested that I grab a bite to eat and visit Mabel Crane. I was still too keyed up from the morning's scare to be really hungry, so I skipped the meal and instead called Captain Hodges.

"Can't find this Black fellow," he said. "I sent Dale over to interview him, but he's not home. Neighbor says he's been gone a week. They don't know when he's coming back. We'll keep looking."

"Yeah, thanks, Cap. Say, did you get anything on his record?"

"Military, Army grunt, minor record, mostly intoxication and DWI. We've got it for you to download. Nothing spectacular." I downloaded the file on my way out, before heading for the Crane residence.

Mrs. Crane looked like a woman in her late seventies or early eighties. She was small, thin, and spry. As soon as I told her who I was, she invited me in and gave me a seat in her parlor. It was a spacious room with large windows, giving it an airy feeling. Lace doilies covered the end tables, and an arrangement of cut flowers was on the coffee table. An upright piano held several photographs and knickknacks.

"I was thinking, Mr. Stankowski, that it's just about time for tea. Would you please have some tea with me?" It was hard to refuse an invitation as nice as that. She brewed some type of herbal tea that I had to admit was quite good.

"Yes, my Jerome, he was a wonderful son. Jerome, isn't that such a nice name? I saw it on your identification. Your name is Jerome too, isn't it?"

I admitted to the name. "But everyone calls me Stan."

"Well, why is that, Jerome? Jerome is such a nice name. Stan is harsh. You should be Jerome. I'm going to call you Jerome."

I suddenly realized how lucky I was last night when Mrs. Crane was out. I couldn't imagine all the names I'd have to go by if Parker were here. I tried to turn the attention to her son.

"He was a wonderful boy. Took after his dear, departed stepfather. Kind and quiet. Would do anything for you. Not his father, mind you. His stepfather, my second husband. My first husband, Mr. Jackson, was Jerome's father. I wish not to talk about him, so don't you dare ask. Would you like more tea, Jerome?"

This woman was too refreshing and real to say no. "Sure, Mrs. Crane. I'd love more tea."

"Would you like me to fix you something to eat, too? I can make you anything you'd want."

"No, thanks, Mrs. Crane. Just the tea."

Mrs. Crane told me about Jerome at the school. "He just loved it there. Loved the students and they all loved him. I thought everyone knew my Jerome was gay. I did. He didn't tell me, but mothers know those things. He was gay all right. But that doesn't make a person bad, does it, Jerome?"

I said no.

"Good. I knew it didn't. Well, one day he came home

very nervous and started to cry. He said, 'Mother, why can't people accept me?' Why, it was enough to break a mother's heart. I told him everything would be okay. He seemed to perk up for a while; then, there was that newspaper stuff.

"My poor little Jerome," she started to sniffle. "Excuse me. My poor little Jerome. He was just so crushed and hurt. It was like a knife in his heart, and mine, too. I hadn't seen him like that since Mr. Crane died. He just adored his stepfather so. Do you get along with your father, Jerome?"

I said I did.

"That's good. And your mother, too?"

I couldn't help but to smile. "Yes, my mother, too."

"That's good. Now, where was I, Jerome?"

"The newspaper articles."

"Yes. Those darn—excuse my language—darn newspaper articles. Why you'd have thought Jerome was a Communist or something. He wasn't a Communist. He was just gay. Anyway, he left a note and that was that. I hope he is happy. Probably with Mr. Crane. Mr. Jackson is in the other place. I won't say its name, but he's there all the same. Devil's got him, you know."

I asked about Jerome's associates and friends.

"Everyone was my Jerome's friend. He didn't have an enemy in the world. That's why I can't understand why they did this to him. Do you know, Jerome?"

"That's part of what I need to find out, Mrs. Crane. Did your son belong to any organizations?"

"Oh, yes. The teachers' group and the Triple A. When he was in college, he was a Young Democrat. Is that what you mean?"

"Well, I'm looking for other organizations. Does the name Right Way mean anything to you?"

She excused herself. When she returned, she gave me a stack of newsletters called *The Right Way.*

"Is this what you are looking for, Jerome?"

It was and I told her so.

"Why, you just look those things over, and I'm going to get us some more tea. And you know what? I have some sugar cookies. You have been a very nice boy, so you get some sugar cookies. Now, you just sit."

I paged through the newsletters. The leader of the Right Way group was a Paige Singlehart from Grand Bay. The newsletters contained the usual stuff you'd expect to find in a newsletter of this sort—list of meetings, activities, and the like. There was nothing militant about the newsletters, except for the last one, dated the month after Jackson's death. In it was a lengthy article about Jackson, and an edited version of the editorial that appeared in the *Forbes Island Independent.* The newsletter ended its article with a warning to the newspaper publisher. "We will avenge our brother," it said.

Apparently Jackson had been receiving the newsletters for about six months before his death. I wondered if perhaps his joining the group, or its interest in him, was what may have triggered the public flare-up.

"Here you are, Jerome, tea and sugar cookies."

"Mrs. Crane, did Jerome belong to this organization?"

"Well, I don't know if he did or not. He never went to any meetings. What does all this mean?"

"Mrs. Crane, I'm here to investigate the car bombing that took the life of the daughter of the man who ran the newspaper. I was trying to determine if there was a connection between what happened to your son and this man's daughter."

She nodded and rocked in her chair. "I see, Jerome.

Why, that would be logical. Someone vengeful?"

"Yes, something like that, Mrs. Crane. Do you know of anyone who might seek vengeance against the newspaper man?"

"Why, yes, Jerome, I do. It's me."

I smiled. "I mean someone who would actually do something against the paper."

"Well, Jerome, I'm guilty."

"Guilty, Mrs. Crane? What have you done?"

"If I tell you, you'll have to arrest me, won't you, Jerome?"

I smiled. "I'm investigating a murder, Mrs. Crane. I'm afraid if you didn't murder anybody, I won't be arresting you."

Mrs. Crane smiled back. "Then I can tell you. Every day I go to the newspaper box on the corner. I put in one quarter but I take two papers." She smiled smugly. "Would you like another sugar cookie?"

It was after two before I left Mabel Crane's. I was starting to feel a little hungry but wanted to check in with Captain Hodges first. Parker was out when I arrived back at the SuperSaver. The desk clerk said he was at the diner. I went to my room, called Hodges, and asked for Paige Singlehart's file.

Since it was midafternoon, the diner was almost empty. Parker was sitting in a booth in the corner all by himself. He wasn't wearing a jacket, just a short-sleeved, white shirt with his ever-present little bow tie. Today, he also had matching suspenders.

He looked up from a bowl of cheese soup. "Did you see that Crane woman?"

"Yeah, Parker. She was some help. Gave me these."

Parker started perusing *The Right Way* newsletters. Finally, he returned them and went back to his soup. "Learn anything?"

I told him what I knew about Jerome Jackson, Mabel Crane, and the events that led to Jackson's death. "I just called headquarters. They're running the leader, this Paige Singlehart, for me."

"Call Brookman," he said.

"Buffy's friend?" I smiled.

"Yes. These people are from Grand Bay. That woman at the gas place said something about Brookman working with gangs. I'd call him, if I were you." He reached over and took the newsletters back, then started looking through them more earnestly. "Not much of what I'd call hate in here," he said.

"Yeah, but Parker, this is the stuff that outsiders could see. We don't know what they planned at their meetings."

Parker finished his soup, mumbled something incoherent, and started looking for his pipe. "Spoken like a true suspicious cop, Stanley. Betcha I left my pipe in my jacket."

"You should quit anyway."

"Been thinking about it some. You know, they start to bite after a while. I was thinking about a cigar."

"Let me help you find your pipe."

We went back to Parker's room and I called Grand Bay PD. Brookman was off-duty, but the desk officer said he would be at a basketball game at Junction City later. "It's a youth thing," she said. "He helps coach some of the minority kids. Keeps them off the street."

"Junction City is due south about thirty minutes," Parker said. "Why don't you take a trip down there and see him? I want to check into this matter a little more and talk to that priest. I'll meet you for a late dinner. First, before you leave, call Michael Winborn. See if he knows anything about this Right Way group."

Parker called Forbes Island PD for a uniform to take him to the station. He said he wanted to meet with the local guys handling hate crimes. I called Michael, who wasn't able to tell me much more than we knew.

"Mr. Jackson? I remember him. Killed himself about a year ago."

"Yeah, Michael. Do you remember your dad getting some mail from a group called Right Way?"

"Those the gay guys?"

"Yeah. Remember anything?"

"Like I told you before, we got lots of hate mail. Dad pretty much ignored it. I can't say for sure that we got anything from them, but we did get our share."

"What was your dad's problem with Jackson?"

"None really. I don't think he even knew Jackson. I never took a class from him. I think he just didn't like homosexuality getting into the school. Seemed like it came up all of a sudden. He spoke his piece in the paper. There was some public debate, and then Mr. Jackson died, and it was over."

I was beginning to wonder if this Jackson thing wasn't another dry hole. Then I looked at my watch and realized that if I wanted to catch Brookman before his game, I'd better be on my way.

"Singlehart? Yeah, I remember her," Brookman said. "You think that little thing you were with today was a hellion, you wait until you meet Paige Singlehart."

Brookman's team was warming up, and his attention was divided.

"Good kids here, just from problem families."

"You seem to enjoy what you're doing," I said.

"I enjoy life. I enjoy police work. I enjoy working with the kids. Never knew my dad. My ma died in what we'd call a crack house. She was a prostitute. I was raised by my aunt and uncle. I was lucky. I had a family to teach me right and wrong.

"Most of these kids today don't. No father. Mother either drinks, sleeps around, or is working too hard to teach them how to take responsibility. It's hardest on the boys. Too many black boys without fathers. First time someone calls them a nigger, it's them against the world. We got to stop that. God gave me something. I'm just trying to pass it along."

"Doesn't look easy."

"It's not. Too much booze and too many drugs. And it's not just the inner-city kids. The white folks would be appalled if they knew how much went on in their neighborhoods. But I do what I can."

"You're a good man, Brookman."

He smiled. "It's Bob. I take it you're Stan. Isn't that what she called you today?"

"Yeah. By the way, how'd you get the owner of that station to drop the charges?"

"Well, Stan, he's Polish, so he's not too smart." I could see Brookman grinning at me.

"We had a pope."

He laughed. "I bet you haven't seen the inside of a church since you were a kid. Anyway, I asked how your little rattlesnake could get in past the night man. He said there's a bell on the door that is supposed to ring, but it's broke. I said he might be liable for a lawsuit, and he said he'd forget the whole thing."

"Well, I think you scared the hell out of her."

"Sorry if I got a little rough with her. My, she was a feisty one. Anyway, you want to know about Singlehart. One of those lesbos, led that little group called Right Way. Real odd monkey. I remember arresting her at a protest. She and her girls stripped outside city hall. What a sight. That woman never shaved. She had more hair under her arms and on her legs than I did."

I asked if he knew anything about Jerome Jackson.

"Just what Forbes Island PD told us. We were asked to make a check of things after his suicide. It was all just routine. Best we could tell, he was never part of that group. Tell you the truth, most of the gays around here aren't. They think Right Way is a little too weird. Gives a bad name to all the gays."

"How about the church vandalism?"

"Oh, that stuff at St. Theresa's? I don't know if that was Paige or not. We never did find out. I think that group's mostly out of existence. I haven't seen Paige in months."

"Were these the type of people who might seek revenge with a car bomb?"

"Your guess is as good as mine. Paige is the type to have blown herself up to make a point. I know they hated a lot of people. Don't know about a car bomb, though. We have her prints on file, if you want to try and match anything."

I thanked Brookman but declined his offer to watch the game. I had just enough time to make it to the little steak house where I was to meet Parker.

Parker's choice for dinner was a little, out-of-the-way steak house with the imposing name of Rothchild's. I beat Parker and ordered a beer at the bar while I waited for a table. It was after the dinner rush, so the wait wasn't long. I took my beer to the table and started going over my notes, trying to see if anything fit; but, of course, nothing did. I was just starting to enjoy the quiet when Parker arrived.

"Find out anything, Parker?"

"Probably nothing we can use. Forbes Island PD doesn't have anything on this Right Way group. Suggested we look at Grand Bay. No prints on the letter Rhodes found."

"Parker, don't you think you're a little out of place in here with a suit and bow tie?"

"A man can eat, no matter how he dresses, Stanley. What did you find?"

"Besides a sociology lesson, nothing more than you did. The leader of this group is a little radical, but it's an open question if she, or any one of them, would stoop to murder."

"And Michael?"

"He just said what he's always said. His dad got a lot of hate mail. He can't remember anything specific."

"So where are we now?"

"Beats me, Parker. I'm beginning to wonder if we'll ever solve this thing. They're going to want us back in the capitol before long. If we don't get a break soon, we're going back empty-handed."

A young woman came for our order.

"Well, Stanley, there's one thing that can help us now."

"What's that, Parker?"

"Food. I'm ready to order."

The rest of the dinner was uneventful. Parker filled himself with steak, salad, potatoes, lima beans, pie, and ice cream. The only thing it seemed that Rothchild's didn't have that Parker wanted was hazelnut coffee. Tactfully, he never mentioned our morning outing to Grand Bay.

It was nearly nine-thirty when we arrived back at the SuperSaver. We were almost through the lobby, when I heard someone clearing a throat. We turned to look. It was Buffy, looking very sheepish but dressed to kill in a short, black cocktail dress.

She smiled. "You guys still talking to me?"

"How did you get here?" I asked.

"Margo's car. She had a date and said she wouldn't need it until afternoon."

"You look like you're dressed for a date, too," I said.

"I was hoping to have one. I haven't been dancing in a long time." She blushed, and then turned to Parker. "Gee, I'm awfully sorry about this morning. Things just happened so fast. And I even bit a cop."

Parker just smiled and took her arm. "Young lady, over the years I've worked with a thousand cops, and, I daresay, better than half of them should have been bitten by someone."

Buffy smiled.

"Now," he said, "if you'll excuse me, I'm not much for dancing, but Stanley here just might be."

Chapter Sixteen

Saturday evening was relaxing. It was the first time since arriving in Forbes Island that I was able to just let my hair down and unwind. Buffy was a wonderful date. She was fun, pretty, a good conversationalist, and knew the right place to go for good music. I found we had something in common: we both liked jazz.

She took me to a little nightclub with a four-piece jazz band. She surprised me when she ordered a fuzzy naval rather than a beer. "Anyone who drinks beer will steal," she reminded me. I had to smile; she said it much cuter than Parker ever did. I had a draft anyway.

We sat, she told me the story of her life, and I listened.

"I was only seventeen when my parents were killed in Spain."

"I had the impression you were older."

"No. They were there with a church tour. My brother, Steve, had just finished at the community college and was working for an implement dealer. They called the priest to tell us. Steve moved back home and took care of me until I graduated. Mom and Dad left us some money. It wasn't enough for me to go to college with, so Steve gave me his share. You have any brothers or sisters?"

"Only child."

"You'll miss something. I don't know what I would have

done without Steve. He's my rock. He and Anna Marie. She used to come over all the time. Those two got me by. I love them both. I miss her so much." She looked like she was getting a little misty again. She looked up, dabbed her eyes with a napkin, and smiled. "Tell me about your girl."

I wiped my mouth with my handkerchief. I looked at Buffy, not knowing whether to tell her the story or not.

"Go on," she said. "It might even make you feel better."

I started to smile. "Her name was Diane. I knew her from college, but we never dated then. She was from a prominent family; her dad was a heart surgeon. Anyway, I ran into her shortly after I got my release from the Tigers and we just sorta hit it off. We started dating, and one thing led to another."

"How long ago?"

"A week ago. I should be on my honeymoon right now."

She looked a little startled.

"I travel in my job. She didn't like that. I think there might have been something else, but she called it off a few days before. Everything was ready."

Buffy took a deep breath. "Gee, I don't know what to say. I didn't think it was so soon."

"When she called, she sounded cold. Almost clinical. She said she wanted a man at home every night. Maybe there was someone else; I don't know. I was just stunned. I tried to call her back, but the line was busy."

"She broke the engagement by phone?"

I nodded. We were sitting in a curved booth. She slid down next to me and put her head on my shoulder. I put my arm around her. For the next twenty minutes she didn't say a word. Once in a while she'd take a sip of her drink, look at me, and smile, then tuck herself back under my arm again.

The band stopped, the bar closed, and I took her home. After making sure Margo's car was returned and Buffy was home safely, I headed back for the motel and a good night's sleep. The thought of Buffy so quiet intrigued me. She obviously felt comfortable with me. I did with her, that was for sure. She almost seemed a pleasant change from Diane, who always seemed a little too preoccupied with social standing. It made me wonder how much I'd miss Buffy when the case was over.

The next morning, I felt the weight of the world had been lifted from my shoulders as I took my morning walk. It is amazing what a little R&R, good conversation, and a good night's sleep can do for an attitude.

Parker and the car were gone when I returned. I was sure he was at church. I checked for any downloads from headquarters, but, as expected, there were none. I grabbed a copy of the *Sunday Gazette*'s state edition, took a booth at the diner, and waited for Parker.

He arrived in another rumpled suit, bow tie and all, a short time later. Since he had been up for a while, I expected him to be more coherent before breakfast than he usually was.

"Good morning, Parker."

"Hi ya, Stanley."

"My, you're chipper this morning. Good news from home?"

He smiled and ordered before answering. With Parker, it was always first things first. "Nope, Stanley. I'm just beginning to think we can piece this thing together and get out of here. And, as long as you asked, Buckwheat Bob is fine."

I felt a twinge of remorse. I was beginning to hope the

case might drag out for at least a little while yet. "Tell me, Old Wise Man, whodunit?"

He just smiled. "Not yet, Stanley. There are still a few loose ends to take care of. I want to visit with Doctor Burnelli. Did you say he takes an afternoon break at some eatery?"

"Yeah. Last week at the hospital they told me he stops at the Pancake Inn after his rounds."

"Good, we'll plan on meeting the good doctor there. I want Buffy, too. We can have dinner with her later. I want to get to the bottom of this Jackson thing, and I think they can both give us some information. The doctor from Winborn's perspective, and Buffy from both."

"Did you talk to the priest, Parker?"

"Yes. Didn't know much. Said Winborn thought the church too liberal. Apparently they didn't see eye-to-eye on too many things. Said Winborn could be brusque, but we knew that."

"Okay, Parker. What else?"

"I'm waiting for a package from Durham about the chief. And I want you to get the Porclar documents from Fielding's cousin tomorrow. I'm almost sure everything else is a wash. We're just looking to pare things down."

Parker's food came, so he stopped. He took a sip of his coffee. "I like the hazelnut best. Maybe we'll have to stop by that little coffee place in Collier's building tomorrow."

"You really like that stuff, don't you?"

"Yeah. It's better than I thought."

"You know you can buy it in the store and take it home with you."

"You can? The hazelnut stuff to put in your coffee?"

"No, Parker. It comes in the bean. You just make it like regular coffee."

"Really? Well, I'll be. By the way, how was your date last night?"

I was wondering when he was going to ask. I started telling him about this little jazz place she took me, but he picked up my paper, took out the sports section, and started reading. I stopped talking. He looked up from the paper.

"Uh-huh. Go on. I'm listening. Music."

I shook my head. "We eloped, Parker."

He turned to the inside of the sports section.

"Good, good. I'm glad you had fun." Then he looked up. "Make it like regular coffee, huh?"

Parker suggested that we not call Dr. Burnelli first. He thought catching him off-guard would be best. That seemed a little odd to me, since Dr. Burnelli was the last person I'd suspect would keep anything from us. But I went along with his little plan.

We found Dr. Burnelli just where we expected to find him. "Hello, gentlemen. Here to join me?"

I said yes, and we engaged in a little small talk.

"Doctor," Parker said, after a bit. "I think you can help us tie up a few loose threads. Some of these questions may seem unrelated, but bear with us, okay?"

"Proceed, gentlemen. I am completely at your disposal. That is, until my pager goes off." He smiled.

Parker started. "First, can you tell us anything about Winborn and a group named First Way?"

"Right Way," I corrected.

"Right Way," Parker repeated.

"Is that that gay group?"

Parker nodded.

"I don't remember much about it, except for what Chuck said. I guess it was some type of militant homosexual group. Or at least that's what Chuck thought. There was an occasion last year when he thought they were trying to infiltrate the schools and recruit members that way.

"I tried to tell him that people just don't choose to become gay, but he would hear nothing of that. He had read a magazine article on the subject and thought it could be a learned lifestyle. There was a teacher at the school who was supposedly passing around gay literature. I don't know if it was true or not, but some of the town folks started to get worried."

He took a drink from his coffee, and continued.

"I remember when it came out in the paper. A lot of my patients were worked up over the issue, too. I tried to tell them the same thing I told Chuck, but they listened about as well as Chuck did. Then the matter came to head when the teacher involved took his own life. That was that; then it died away."

"Did Winborn know the teacher?" Parker asked.

"I don't think so. I'm not sure he even knew which one it was. Just heard rumors and printed them."

"Is Michael gay?"

"Heavens, no! He's had a few girlfriends. But he thinks like his old man on the subject. In fact, I was surprised how callous he was about the teacher's suicide. Chuck, at least, felt a little bad about the whole episode. Michael didn't. Told me one day there was one less fag in the world, and that suited him fine."

"Kinda harsh, isn't it?" I interjected.

"Well, remember what I told you last week? Michael adored his father. His father had condemned those people, and Michael wouldn't do any less. Don't get me wrong. He's not an evil boy, just afflicted with the same prejudices as his father."

Parker continued, "Doctor, do you have any information that the teacher's death was anything other than a suicide?"

He shook his head. "Again, no. It was a pretty clear case. Hell, he left a note."

"Were there any repercussions from the suicide?"

"No. Things kind of died down after that. A few people felt sorry about the whole thing. I think everybody learned something from it. But when it was over, it was over."

"Did Winborn ever tell you he received a death threat from this Right Way group?" Parker asked.

"No. Wouldn't surprise me though. He was receiving hate letters all the time."

"How was his health?"

"Oh, he was going to be around for a couple of years. Had non-Hodgkin's lymphoma, low-grade lymphoma; but at his age, he'd die of something else first. I think I told you before, he had a bad heart. When we found the cancer, we thought his days were numbered, but not really. He easily would have had a couple more years. Hard to tell about those things. Hell, he was a stubborn old bastard; those kind tend to outlive themselves."

"How about Anna Marie?" he asked.

"Well, you know she had MS. She was diagnosed after she came back from Europe. It's not fatal. She might eventually have been put in a wheelchair, but that's speculation. MS is a funny disease. You can go long periods with no symptoms, and then one day you can't get up from the dinner table. It's treatable. There are good drugs, kind of expensive, but they're around. Of course, Chuck saw to it that Anna Marie had whatever was necessary."

"When did she first want to go into the convent?"

"You know, with Anna Marie I think we just always expected it. She was like some boys who you know will go into the priesthood. It was always there, and I think she knew early on. I can tell you this: it was no surprise to me. But I do remember the day Chuck told me she was going. He broke down and cried. He thought this was the greatest thing for his family."

"Was he a religious man?"

"Very. Very conservative, however. I sometimes thought he would have been better in one of those far right religions. Lot of times he didn't get along with the priest. He sometimes thought the church was a little too liberal. But if he was anything, he was a religious man. And a family man. He would have done anything for either of his kids."

"And Michael?"

"He and his father were almost inseparable. He worked for the paper. Chuck was grooming him to take over. I'm not sure Michael has the talent for that, but I do know some of the people over there. The paper's in good hands, and Michael's smart enough not to rock the boat."

"What was Michael's relationship with his sister?" Parker asked.

Dr. Burnelli paused and took another sip of his coffee. "Pretty much like any brother and sister. He was excited to have her home for the weekend. He didn't want our little party Friday night to end." He took another sip of coffee. "Everyone loved Anna Marie, and Michael was no exception."

"Do you know anything about a land development called Porclar?"

"Never heard of it."

Parker sat back, as if he were finished. "Anything else, Stanley?"

"A couple of things. Doctor, how well did you know Anna Marie's friends?"

"Oh, I'd see them come and go. I knew Margo Roberts fairly well. Her father is a dentist. I'll see him at the hospital once in a while."

"A dentist?"

"Oh sure, they're there all the time. People in the hospital need dental work, and some dental work requires hospitalization."

"Anyone else?"

"That little Buffy. I've seen her around lately."

"Is there anything that you know about Anna Marie, or her friends, that might make you think she was the target of the bomb?"

"No. With Anna Marie you got what you saw. Just a nice, decent girl. Always was. Her friends, too. They never seemed to be in any trouble, always clean cut. Never came to me for pills, pregnancy counseling, or because of drugs. I can't say that about the rest of the kids nowadays, but Anna Marie was a good girl, and had good friends."

He took another drink from his coffee, and then pointed at me.

"You know, I even remember Chuck mentioning how nice the kids' friends were. He was proud that they kept such good company."

"Buffy worked for the newspaper. Did you know that?"

"Yes. Chuck said she quit. I think he felt bad about that."

"Was it possible, Doctor, that someone else could have known that Anna Marie was coming home last week?"

"I doubt it. We knew she was going to come home before she took her vows. They were scheduled for next weekend. We had planned to go up for it. But as far as her coming home, we only knew the date about two weeks ago."

"Who was going with you to the convent?"

"The three of us: Chuck, Michael, and me."

"Any of her friends?"

"I never thought of it. I guess so, probably. I'm sure they all knew about it."

Now I was finished and sat back in my seat.

Dr. Burnelli looked at both of us. "Well, if that's all, gentlemen, I have some reading to do."

I watched him leave and turned to Parker. "Well, what do you think?"

He reached for the menu. "I think I'll have some pie."

By now, I should have known how to frame my questions better. "Someone knew she was coming home."

"Yeah," he said, "we knew that. The chocolate cream looks good."

"No, that's not what I mean, Parker. Look here, this is something we missed. Burnelli says the date for Anna Marie's thing, whatever they call it, was next weekend."

"So?"

"So, that was a date anyone could find out. I bet if you called the paper two weeks ago and asked, they'd tell you. Her friends must have known the date. Anyone who wanted to hurt her could have found out."

"What's your point, Stanley?"

"Just this: There was a window of opportunity for somebody who wanted to harm Anna Marie. Her friends knew she was coming home, just not when. But she had to do it before next weekend. And it would probably be for a weekend. Don't you see?"

Parker ordered his pie. "Yeah. We did miss that. If somebody was after the girl, they might not know when she'd be home, but they'd have some pretty good ideas."

"Right. And if you were part of a small band of crazies

who wanted revenge, it would be easy to stake out the Winborn residence."

"So you think Anna Marie was the target?"

"It's a strong possibility. Don't forget Parker's first law: Never rule out the obvious."

He smiled. "You may finally be catching on, Stanley. So, what are you going to do about it?"

"This Right Way thing. I'm going to try to track it down."

"Okay, that's why I wanted to meet with Buffy later. You don't think this pie will spoil dinner for me, do you?"

Chapter Seventeen

It was about four o'clock Sunday afternoon when we arrived back at the SuperSaver. Parker wanted to get out of his suit and into something more comfortable before we met Buffy for dinner. As soon as I got into my room, the phone rang. It was the desk clerk.

"I tried to catch you as you went thorough the lobby. You're to call Officer Eaton at the police station."

When I reached Eaton, she said I was to call Brookman at his home in Grand Bay. She gave me the number.

"Did a little checking on your girl. A girl we think is Paige Singlehart is wanted for questioning in connection with the bombing of a Baptist church in Omaha. At least the description matches."

"Good. Anything else?"

"We won the game."

"I kinda figured you would. You were playing a white team, weren't you? What is it they say about white kids jumping?"

"Damn Pollock." He paused. I smiled.

He continued. "I got to thinking about your problem and did a little checking this morning. Paige hasn't been seen around here for about two months. I do have an arrest record for one her friends, a woman by the name of Grant. Paula Grant. She was picked up at one of those titty bars, protesting the exploitation of women. We let her go and dropped the charges, but the note says she was in your area last month. Some scuffle with some anti-abortion people. Might mean Paige is around. Thought you'd be too stupid to figure it out for yourself."

I could hear him chuckling on the other end.

"You'll never guess who I'm having dinner with."

"Yeah, well, just don't bring her back here. We don't have any restaurants that serve raw meat."

"Hey, Bob, thanks."

"I figure it never hurts to have you state boys owe me a favor."

I sat down on my bed and took out one of those yellow legal pads Parker is always using. I started a "Who's Who" of suspects, listed the pros and cons for each, and began a winnowing process. Then the phone rang again.

"Dale at HQ. Got the skinny on your boy Black, if you're still interested."

"Shoot."

"He was in the Harden County poky. DWI. Served seven days for third offense. Started last Friday and was released Thursday. If I can figure your timetable right, he's out."

"Thanks. You're right. Don't waste any more time on him. He wasn't rigging any bomb here from a county lockup way over there."

"Captain says you're having fun with your roommate."

"Aren't you funny."

"He wants to know when to expect you."

"Well, I'm having so much fun with Mr. Noble, I thought we might stay another two or three weeks."

He laughed. "I'll tell him you don't know, then. Later, dude!"

I went back to my Who's Who and the phone rang again. This time it was Buffy wanting to know when we were picking her up. I had almost forgotten that she didn't have any transportation right now.

"Where's the best place around here on a Sunday night?"

"Like Italian?"

"Is the Pope Catholic?"

She giggled. "Marcella's. But it closes by nine."

I gave her a time and went to tell Parker. He was ready at the appointed hour. His idea of something more comfortable was a pair of slacks, a long-sleeved, striped shirt and his little bow tie. He was sitting under a cloud of pipe smoke when I stopped in for him.

"No TV?" I asked.

"I was thinking, Stanley."

I didn't want to ask about what. So I told him about the calls from Brookman and Dale.

Marcella's was not crowded when we arrived. We were seated at a table near the center of the dining room. A waiter took our drink order. Buffy ordered a wine cooler, Parker ordered a Scotch, and I ordered a brew.

"Anyone who drinks beer will steal," Buffy giggled, to Parker's approval and my annoyance. She said anything on the menu was good. She and I decided to split a pizza. Parker ordered the lasagna.

"What toppings do you like, Stan?"

"Sausage. You like mushrooms?"

"Isshey," she said and scrunched her nose.

"Good. Neither do I."

That out of the way, Parker asked Buffy about Jerome Jackson.

"Yeah, that was really sad. Mr. Jackson was my chemistry teacher when I was at City High. He had Anna Marie, too. Almost everybody knew he was gay."

"What about Winborn and the paper?" I asked.

"Gays? Winborn hated them. He hated a lot of people."

"You were at the paper then. What happened?"

"Yeah. I didn't have anything to do with the school stuff. But someone said that there was a gay group trying to get into the high school, and Winborn went berserk."

"Was there any indication there was an active gay group in the area?" Parker asked.

"Yeah. Something called Right Way. Real weirdoes. I mean, these guys are more than gay. They are just plain weird."

"Does the name Paige Singlehart ring any bells?" I asked.

"Sure does. But I thought her first name was Penny. Penny, Paige, whatever, she was one of the leaders. A real dyke. Sad thing was, I knew a lot of gays and lesbians in college, and none were like these guys. That Right Way group gave them all a bad name."

The waiter brought our drinks. "What are we drinking to?" Buffy asked.

"I hear you're looking for work," Parker said. "We can drink to your luck."

"Thanks," she said. "I'm going to need a break soon. I've been out of work for three months, and, thus far, I haven't gotten so much as a nibble for all the letters I've written."

"Are you drawing unemployment?" he asked.

"Are you kidding? Winborn put a kibosh on that. All he had to do was to say that I quit, and I was out. If it wasn't for my brother, I don't know what I'd do."

"How did Winborn take your leaving?" he asked.

"Well, you saw how I get when I'm angry. I didn't bite

him, but we did have words. I told him what I thought of his ethics, and he said it would be a cold day in hell before I got another job in a newsroom."

"Did you know Anna Marie wanted to call you Friday night?" I asked.

Buffy nodded. "Margo told me the story. It was nice to know Anna Marie wanted to see me her last night." She dabbed her eye with a napkin. "I'm sorry. You guys must think I'm just awful, but this still gets to me."

"Buffy," Parker started, "did you know when Anna Marie was going to take her vows?"

"Sure, next weekend."

"How many others knew that?"

"Gosh, I suspect most of her friends. Margo and I weren't her only ones, but we were probably her closest. We had even talked about driving up for it."

"Had you talked about Anna Marie with any of her other friends lately?"

"You mean before she came home? Sure. A few. Why?"

"Did they know the date she was taking her vows?"

"I guess so. We spoke about it. I assumed they did. Gee, anybody who wanted to know that could have just called Winborn or Michael. It was no secret. Old Man Winborn was really proud of her. He'd tell anyone who asked. Why?"

"Bear with me a little longer," Parker said. "Who knew Anna Marie was coming home for a visit?"

"Well, I guess we all kind of knew. Just didn't know when. Why?"

Parker looked at me. That was my signal to break the bad news. "Buffy, this may be hard to believe, but there is a possibility Anna Marie was killed as revenge for your Mr. Jackson's suicide."

"What!"

"This group Right Way vowed to avenge Jackson's death. They wrote about it in their newsletter. Shortly after the suicide, a death threat—or what seemed to be a death threat—was sent to Winborn. He must have assumed it was directed at him and ignored it."

"Yeah, he got those all the time. We all knew that."

"Well, this was sent to his home. I've got a copy of it. It said something like, 'You'll get yours. God loves fags and queers and hates you. See you in hell, you pompous papist.' "

Buffy looked stunned. "Anna Marie?"

"It's possible, honey. This group could have singled out Anna Marie to get revenge against Winborn."

"No. No. That can't be. What about Becker, and the other guys you're investigating?"

Parker, in his best favorite uncle manner, reached across the table and took Buffy's hand. "We don't know, Buffy. But it is possible that Anna Marie was the intended victim. After all, they hated Catholics and Winborn. Killing a nun who's the daughter of a man they hate is revenge in anybody's book. It's also possible that her dad was the target. We don't know yet. We might never know. But we do need to know what you know about this group. You were in Winborn's office at the time of the suicide. You knew Jackson and his students. What can you tell us?"

Our food came and sat, untouched.

"Those were weird people. They might have done anything. But how would they know when Anna Marie was home?"

"A stakeout, Buffy, just like we did the other night," I said. "You've confirmed my suspicion that anyone who wanted to know Anna Marie's date could find it out easily enough. It also appears that it was fairly common knowledge that she would be home for a visit before that date. It wouldn't take much to figure it would be a weekend visit. That eliminates a lot of possibilities and makes it easy for somebody, like one of these Right Way people, to find her quickly."

"My God, Stan," she said. "I'd never have thought anyone would deliberately try to kill Anna Marie. She was an angel. We all loved her so. I can't imagine anyone sitting outside her house like that."

"Wouldn't need to," Parker said. "They knew where she was coming from. It would be easy to watch the Grand Bay airport. They were from Grand Bay. Now, let's eat before it gets cold."

The table was quiet for a long while as the three of us ate in silence.

"Are they still around? The Right Ways?" she asked.

"Yeah, Buffy," I said. "Grand Bay PD reports a Paula Grant was in the area recently. She was part of Singlehart's group. She was picked up there and here. Singlehart herself is suspected in a church bombing in Omaha."

"Jeepers. Well, what about Becker?"

"He's still a question mark, too," I said.

"What else do you need to know?"

"I think you've told us all we need right now," Parker said.

"Good," she replied. "Then can we change the subject?"

Chapter Eighteen

There was a chill in the air as I took my walk around the little park across from the SuperSaver on my second Monday in Forbes Island. I couldn't help but feel that Sunday was a breakthrough day in our investigation. By the end of the day, I had pared the suspect list down to Milo Becker and the Right Way group. I had some lingering doubts about Chief Edwards, but they were fading. We clearly could eliminate Phillip Black, even though he wasn't really ever a suspect. And I saw no reason to continue any notion that Mayor Foley or Roscoe Costello had anything to do with Anna Marie's death. I was kind of pleased with myself, as I entered the diner for breakfast with Parker.

"Good morning, Parker."

He looked up from his paper, blinked twice, and went back to reading.

"Parker, I think this thing is getting narrowed down. We have no physical evidence yet, but I think we're looking at either Becker or this gay group. I'm starting to lean to the group myself."

"I was reading, Stanley."

There was no way to answer that, except to sit quietly until the waitress brought our meals. It was a long wait, and I could notice the difference between quiet with Buffy and quiet with Parker. With Buffy it was nice. With Parker it was just strange. About halfway through steak and eggs, he looked up. "You have to get that Porclar stuff today from what's-his-name. That's important."

"Got ya covered, Parker. It's already on my list."

He looked at me, shook his head, mumbled something I didn't understand, and went back to his steak and eggs.

"How long do you think we'll be here?"

He looked up, swallowed, appeared irritated, and said, "Don't know."

"Are you awake, Parker?"

No answer.

"Earth to Parker."

"Stanley, I'm eating."

I made a mental note to myself to tell Captain Hodges that next time he had a case the AG wanted his friend involved in to look elsewhere. Finally, Parker finished eating. "Parker, I'm going to the police station. Can I drop you anywhere?"

"The paper."

I think he was finally awake by the time I dropped him off at the newspaper office. We arranged to meet at ten-thirty at the coffee bar in Quentin Collier's building. That was Parker's idea. It didn't surprise me.

At the station I went immediately to Chief Edwards.

"I'm looking for a Paige Singlehart. Know her?"

"Yeah, wasn't she with that Right Way group?"

"Right. The leader. If you check your bulletins, you'll find she's wanted for questioning about a church bombing in Omaha."

"Ouch. That may answer the question you asked the other day."

"Sure does. Got a second name, too, Paula Grant. One of Singlehart's lieutenants."

"I can bail you out on this one," he said. "She's in the county jail, waiting for trial."

"For what?"

"She got into a small altercation outside a doctor's clinic with some abortion protesters. She was released on her signature and ran. When she missed her preliminary, the judge issued a warrant. Unless she makes bail, she's not going anywhere."

"How long?"

"Oh heck, it was such a minor matter I didn't pay any attention. I'll have Sherry check. Hang on."

"Chief, see if she can check on her visitors, too. They do keep a log here, don't they?"

"Sure do. I'll be back."

I began to feel a little sorry for Edwards. Since we arrived, he had been nothing but cooperative. Yet, whoever put that bomb in Winborn's car also put a time bomb in Edwards' career. His office was not a big one, but it did have the usual personal artifacts that give an empty room the personality of its occupant.

"Got it," he said, coming back.

I pointed to a photograph on the wall. "Is that your son?"

"Yeah. Timmy. I guess I can't call him Timmy any more. He'll be going to college next year."

"Where is he?"

"City High. Why?"

"Oh, nothing. I just got the impression that he lived with a mother somewhere else."

"No, Stan. I was one of the lucky ones. He came with me. I know what it's like as a struggling single father. It gives me some empathy for our single moms out there."

I couldn't help but to feel another twinge of remorse for

Edwards. The irony was cutting. This was a big case and Edwards and his department were doing their level best to help solve it. Yet the successful conclusion of the case might just end his career.

"Here's what you want. Paula Grant has a prelim at ten-thirty tomorrow morning. She's had one visitor three times, a Penny Squires. No attorney. Been in twelve days."

"That would put her in just before the Winborn thing. Penny Squires. Do you know that name?"

"Does nothing for me."

"Somebody last night called Paige, Penny. I wonder if it might be an alias. Let me use your phone."

It only took a minute to get Brookman on the line. I asked if Paige Singlehart ever used an alias. It didn't take long for him to call back.

"Peggy Simmons, Patty Squires, Penny Smith, and Paula Staples. At least those are the ones reported. Apparently uses them for business purposes, whatever that means."

"Can you wire us a mug?"

"Sure thing. I'll get it out now."

"Thanks, Bob. Good luck with the hoops."

"You, too, fella." I hung up the phone.

"If Grant has a hearing in the morning, and Squires is Singlehart, I wonder if she'll come. And if she does, I wonder if she'll be up to anything," Edwards said.

"I'd suggest you take some precautions."

"You're right. I'll have some extra men in the courthouse. I'll put them in uniform. I'd rather prevent something ugly than take any chances with the public."

"I think that's right. I'll cross my fingers."

"You won't be the only one. By the way, what do you want me to do with the extra man with the mayor?"

"Let's play it safe, Chief. Let's keep him in place for another day."

Parker was sitting alone in the coffee bar when I arrived.

"What did you get, Stanley?"

"I think this Singlehart is in town. Her friend Paula Grant has been in the county lockup since just before Anna Marie was killed."

He looked interested and stopped playing with his coffee.

"Hazelnut, Parker?"

He nodded. "Go on."

I gave him a rundown on my meeting with the chief and my latest phone call to Brookman.

"Nice work," he said. He started to get up, but was stopped. It was Quentin Collier, dressed rather casually in a designer sport shirt and slacks.

"Nice to see you again, Parker." He held out his hand to shake.

"Counselor, nice to see you again. You remember Stanley."

"Yes, Mr. Stankowski. How are you? Let me grab something and join you for a minute. I'd like to know how things are going."

"Try the hazelnut, it's very good," Parker said.

Collier ordered cappuccino.

"You are looking rather informal today," Parker said.

"Only one thing today. I'm getting the Winborn inventory ready to file. Michael is coming by in the morning to sign it and take it to the courthouse. I'm just here to see that it is ready for him. Then I'm off to Chicago."

"Pleasure?" I asked.

"A bit. I'm part of a symposium at Northwestern Law

School, my alma mater. I'm the moderator of a panel discussion. 'The Law and Economic Development,' they call it. Moderator is the job to have at one of these things. You don't have any lines to learn and can just wing it from the stage."

Parker smiled. "Counselor, can you tell me what Porclar is?"

"Strange thing, Porclar. It was a land deal Winborn was working on. I must say, it was out of character for him but, as I told you earlier, I didn't handle his investments. What do you know about it?"

Parker ignored his coffee. "Just that Fielding set it up for Winborn. Fielding was president. We're getting the paperwork from his attorney today."

"Who'd he use?"

"Gary Fielding, his cousin."

"Oh, sure, I should have made the connection. Say, you wouldn't mind giving me a copy of those papers, would you? I'd like to know if we're going to need to amend the inventory."

"Sure," Parker said. "We're going to a preliminary tomorrow; it may be related. We'll be at the courthouse about ten-thirty. If Michael is going there anyway, he can pick the stuff up then."

"Thanks, I'm sure he'll appreciate that." Collier looked at his watch. "Oh. Gotta run. Thanks again, Parker."

He watched Collier leave. "That wasn't hazelnut was it, Stanley?"

I smiled. "No. It wasn't. Parker, what's an inventory?"

"Oh, it's just a listing of the things a decedent owned when he died. You file it with the estate."

"Ahhh. So, that's how the heirs know what's coming to them."

"No, Stanley. That's how the state knows how much it'll be getting in taxes."

Parker went back to the courthouse. He wanted to check out the file on Paula Grant and talk to the prosecuting attorney. I called Fielding to make sure his cousin was expecting me. He said he was and gave me directions to the office, and I went out to pick up the Porclar papers.

Gary Fielding was young, probably about twenty-seven or -eight. He was located in a small strip mall on the far west side of town and was easy to find. His two-room office was small but neat. It contained only him and his secretary.

"I spent a year as a corporate attorney in the capitol," he said. "Made a lot of money but, quite frankly, the lifestyle was not for me. It was too rushed and too demanding. I grew up not far from here, so, with family in the area, I moved back. I love it."

"Have you gotten much business from Winborn?"

"No, not really. Jeff, my cousin, does his best to throw some work my way. I've handled a few things for the paper: collection work, things like that. The paper has some warehouse space north of the city. I handled the leases. Jeff gives me what he can, and I appreciate it. But I've done nothing for Winborn personally."

"What do you know about Porclar?"

"Just what I needed to know to get it started. Jeff said Winborn needed a vehicle to hold some land he was thinking about buying. The guy didn't want his name connected with the thing, so Jeff was to set up a corporation as a front."

"Did you ever meet with Winborn?"

"Yeah, but not about this. Jeff told me what Winborn wanted, and I did it. Technically, Jeff was the client, not

Winborn. So there was no need to meet with anybody but Jeff."

"Did you have any special instructions, or did anything seem odd to you about Porclar?"

"Well, there are always special things you do for each client. But, if you mean anything out of the ordinary, then the answer is no. I guess the only thing was the name. Never could figure it out. Usually the name is either obvious, like Fielding Incorporated, or the client explains its significance. But with this, Jeff didn't know and I could never figure it out. But then, who cares? As long as the name was clear, there seemed to be no legal significance."

"What do you mean by 'clear'?"

"The state won't let you use a name that is already being used or is too close to that of another corporation. A phone call to the secretary of state will tell you. Obviously, this one cleared."

I guess that made sense. "Didn't hiding the land ownership strike you as odd or funny?"

"No. Should it?"

"Well, here's a prominent man trying to hide his ownership in some land prime for development. Does that seem right to you?"

"Why not? It's done all the time. Someone knows an important person is behind a purchase offer or contract, and the price goes up. Business people use attorneys and agents all the time to transact business. It's one way to keep the competition from knowing what you're up to."

He made a good point and I had to concede it. "What kind of records are we talking about here, Mr. Fielding?"

"Call me Gary. Jeff said to give you everything, so I had LuAnn copy the whole notebook."

"Notebook?"

"Yeah. There are commercial kits we use for these kinds of things. All the forms and certificates you need are provided. Everything is designed to go into a notebook. LuAnn just copied all the pages for you. I can show you the originals, if you wish."

"No, no. The copies will do."

He handed me a large, manila envelope.

"This doesn't seem to be too much," I said.

He smiled. "No. And when you get into it, it'll seem even smaller. The articles of incorporation are about four pages, and the bylaws are about twelve. Most of that is all standard. The rest of the stuff—minutes, stock records, and the like—is only about four or five pages."

I slid the papers out of the envelope and started looking through them. I didn't want to tell him that I didn't understand what he had just said. I knew Parker would understand and would call Fielding if he had any questions. I slipped the papers back into the envelope, thanked him, and left.

Chapter Nineteen

After I left Gary Fielding's office, I went to pick up Buffy before meeting Parker for lunch. She was ready when I arrived, dressed in slacks, a sweater, and, of course, her gumshoe hat.

"I was hoping you were going to take me home alone last night," she said as she got into the car.

I smiled. "What was I supposed to do with Parker?"

"Do we ever get to go anywhere without him?"

"You're lucky he didn't sit in the front seat between us."

"What's the difference? I had to sit in the backseat alone."

"You didn't seem in the best of moods after dinner."

She turned in her seat to face me. "That whole thing about Anna Marie still bugs me. It's so hard to believe that someone might have wanted to kill her. And all because of Mr. Jackson. How could anyone be like that?"

She sat quietly for a minute. Then she picked up the envelope Gary Fielding had given me. "What's this?"

"Oh, that's the stuff about the corporation, Porclar. Remember?"

She sat back and took the papers from the envelope. "Looks like a lot of legal mumbo-jumbo."

"That's what lawyers get paid for," I said.

Since Parker was at the courthouse without a car, we had

decided to meet at the Family Hour Café, across the street from the courthouse. Buffy and I arrived first and took a booth in the non-smoking section.

"This will kill Parker," I said.

"You know, I haven't seen him smoke his pipe lately. He isn't trying to quit, is he?"

"Actually, the other day he was talking about switching to cigars."

"Isshey! Those things are gross."

We waited for Parker to arrive before ordering. A young waitress made sure we had plenty of soda and quiet while we waited. Buffy went back to the Porclar documents.

"What are articles of incorporation? Is that what you write to start this off? It was first."

"I don't know, Buffy. What else is there?"

"Something called bylaws, minutes from some board meetings. Look, this is a meeting with just Jeffrey Fielding. He calls it together, elects himself, and does everything. And here's one with just Winborn. He elects Fielding. This sounds so stupid, Stan."

"Well, I'm sure it's done for some legal purpose. Ask Parker, when he comes."

"Here's a stock ownership report. What does 'J-T slash R-O-S' mean?"

"Ask Parker."

"What are preemptive rights?"

"Where did you see that?"

"Here. It's in the articles of incorporation."

"I don't know. Ask Parker. He's a lawyer."

"Yeah, but he just does criminal stuff, doesn't he? He wouldn't know this stuff, would he?"

"Ask him. Here he comes."

Parker joined us and waved for a menu. The daily blue

plate special was chicken-fried steak, carrots, mashed potatoes, gravy, and a small salad, with the drink of your choice. Parker ordered the special with a root beer. Buffy ordered a chef's salad, and I had a club sandwich.

"What did you learn about Grant?" I asked Parker.

"Not much more than we already knew. Her preliminary hearing is at ten-thirty. The prosecutor says she ran before her last preliminary, and that's why they're holding her. She's only charged with a simple assault and failure to appear. He expects her to plead to both and take some type of suspended sentence."

"What's a preliminary hearing?" Buffy asked Parker.

"It's a court hearing where the judge determines if there is enough to hold a person for trial. Most are fairly routine. The defendant pleads guilty or not; and, if not guilty, a trial date is set."

"What if they plead guilty?"

"Then it's over. I thought Stanley said you had a degree in journalism. Didn't they teach you court procedures?"

"Yeah. But not this stuff."

"No lawyer worth his salt would let you miss this stuff."

"It was Doctor Sawyer. I don't think he was a lawyer."

"What was he a doctor in?" Parker asked.

"I suppose journalism. He had a Ph.D."

I was sorry she got Parker off on academia. "Well, there's your problem," he said. "Colleges don't recognize anything except Ph.Ds. That course should have been taught by a J.D."

"What is a J.D.?"

"It's a law degree. *Juris doctor.*"

"Is it as good as a Ph.D.?"

"It means doctor of jurisprudence. It is a doctorate, like a Ph.D."

"Is that what you have?"

"All lawyers do."

"Should I call you Doctor?"

"No. We're not as filled with ourselves as your professors are."

"Don't you teach?"

"Yes, but it's something different. I teach at the police academy."

"Did you teach Stan?"

Parker looked at me and paused a minute. "No. He'd be a better cop, if I had."

"Hey," I said, "I thought I was a pretty good cop as it was."

Parker smiled. "I teach them evidence and procedure. How to testify in court, and things like that."

"He also gives seminars all over the state about new court rulings and things we need to keep up on," I added.

"Do you ever get back into court?" Buffy asked.

"Oh, sure. But not often. My title is still Deputy Attorney General. I help with some investigations, like this one, but I'm still a state lawyer."

"Would you prosecute this case?"

"No, the local prosecutor would."

"When would you?"

Parker was in his element talking law. "Well, the Attorney General has the authority to prosecute any crime, but most crimes are prosecuted locally. We prosecute when asked by the local prosecutor. Most of the criminal work in the AG's office is concerned with appeals."

"Oh," she said. By then our food came and ended that discussion.

Partway through the meal, Parker said, "I saw an old friend of mine at the courthouse today. An old classmate,

David Connors. Judge David Connors. He's here today and tomorrow for motions."

"What's that?" Buffy asked.

"Motions are when the lawyers ask the court to do something outside of trial. For example, you need a different trial date or want something dismissed. You don't do that at trial; you do it before. It's called a motion."

"And a judge has to come special for that? Why can't Judge Harrison do it?"

"Who's Judge Harrison?" he asked.

"He's the one who has all the traffic stuff."

"No. There are different kinds of judges. Some only can handle small things, like traffic and small claims. In criminal law they can only handle misdemeanors, the lesser crimes. Other judges have authority to hear larger cases, like malpractice, and felony criminal cases. Big cases and small cases. Your Judge Harrison is a little judge; my Judge Connors is a big judge. It is just a different role they play, that's all."

"What does 'preemptive rights' mean?"

"Where did you see that?"

"In the papers on Porclar," she said.

"Let me see those."

Buffy gave him the papers. He asked me if Gary Fielding had shed any more light on the Porclar business.

"Nope, just gave me these. He never even met with Winborn about it. Everything was handled through his cousin Jeffrey."

"As well it should. These papers indicate that Fielding was the sole director and president," he said. "Preemptive means that each stockholder has rights of first refusal, if the corporation sells more stock."

"Oh," she said. "It looked like there was a bunch of

stock. See the articles of incorporation. It says one hundred thousand shares. But, if you look here, Winborn and Anna Marie had only one hundred."

Parker looked at the corporation's stock ledger. "That's right. Just because a corporation can issue a lot of stock doesn't mean it has to."

"And the articles. What are they?"

"That's the paperwork you file with the state to organize the corporation."

"Do you have to do that? Can't you just start one?"

Parker smiled, ever the teacher. "No. Corporate status provides certain privileges for the stockholders. For example, they cannot be held personally liable for corporate debts. In order to avail yourself of that protection, you have to file the right papers with the state."

"Oh, I see. What does 'J-T slash R-O-S' mean?"

Parker handed her the papers. "Show me where you saw that."

"Right here on the stock ledger. It says 'one hundred shares for Charles Winborn and Anna Marie Winborn, J-T slash R-O-S'."

Parker took the stock ledger from her and pondered it for a minute. "It means they held the stock together. They jointly owned the stock. If something happened to one, the stock would belong to the other. It's called 'joint tenancy' and it means the survivor inherits the whole thing."

"And what are all these meetings with only one person?"

Parker handed back the meeting minutes and smiled. "The law requires that the stockholders have at least one meeting per year to elect directors. The directors then must have a meeting to select officers. These look like pro-forma minutes entered in the record to show Winborn and Fielding complied with the law."

"Gosh," she said, "I think I learned more about law in a half an hour with you than in a whole semester with Doctor Sawyer."

Parker smiled, obviously pleased with himself.

Parker asked us to drop him back at the SuperSaver, saying he was expecting a package. Afterwards, we took a trip to the QuicKing, where Becker worked. The same assistant manager who was on duty Friday was there when we returned.

"Was my information helpful?" she asked.

"It sure was. I wanted to see if Becker had come back to work."

"Nope, and he won't. Called this morning and said he had to quit and gave me a new address for the company to send his last check."

"Let me guess. One-twenty-two Prospect, Grand Bay."

"Right, how'd you know?'

"I'm a cop, remember? Did he say why?"

"No." She smiled. "Is there anything else I can get for you?"

Buffy spoke up, "Two sodas."

After leaving the QuicKing, Buffy and I drove back downtown to County Bank and Trust. County was on the square right across from the courthouse and next to Mayor Foley's insurance office. Buffy and I went into the bank. It was a spacious and modern office. The teller windows formed an "L" against the back and side walls.

"Hey, Buffy."

"Hey, Suzie." Buffy pulled me to one of the teller windows. "Stan, I want you to meet Suzie Clayton. She went to high school with me and Margo and Anna Marie."

"Pleased to meet you, Stan," she said. "He's cute, Buffy.

Maybe you want to open a joint account?"

Buffy and Suzie giggled. "Maybe." Then they both started giggling again.

"I heard you were seen around town with a big, handsome guy. This must be him. Way to go, Buff!"

Buffy took me by the arm, and I know I turned a dozen shades of red.

"You know what I always say; he'll do until something better comes along."

They both started giggling again. Then Suzie said, "Men are like buses; there will be another one any minute."

"Well," Buffy said, looking up at me, "maybe he's a little too big to throw back." They both started laughing again.

"What is your last name, Stan?"

"Stankowski."

"Stan Stankowski!" They continued laughing.

"No. No," Buffy finally said. "It's Jerome Stankowski. But we all call him Stan."

"And what do you do, Mr. Jerome Stankowski?"

I started to reach for my identification, but Buffy saved me the trouble. "He is a state police detective. He is working directly for the Attorney General himself on Anna Marie's case."

"I am impressed. Sad thing about her. She was really nice. I couldn't make it to the funeral, but I sent Michael a card. Wasn't that her brother's name, Michael?"

"Yeah," Buffy said.

"Didn't you work for her dad, Buffy?"

"Yeah."

"Too bad about him, too. But you know, Stan, no one around here liked him. Someone said you quit the paper, Buffy. What are you doing now?"

"I'm helping Stan solve the case."

"Good luck. Most anyone around here would have liked to take a shot at that guy. My parents just hated that man," Suzie said. "Well, what are you doing here?"

"Well, Ms. Clayton . . ." I started.

They both giggled again. "Suzie," she said.

"Okay, Suzie. I am looking for some account information on one of your depositors, Milo Becker."

"I remember the name. Isn't he that guy whose picture was in the paper, Buffy?"

"That's him," she said.

"You don't think that he was the one who did in Anna Marie, do you?"

I shook my head. "We really don't know right now. We are just putting things together."

"Okay. I can do that. But I have to ask the witch first."

"Oh," Buffy said, "is she still here?"

"Yes. Making everybody's life miserable."

"Who's this witch?" I asked.

Suzie answered, "Oh, that's Old Lady Parsons. Remember what she used to do at Halloween, Buffy?"

"Do I? Stan, she was the meanest person in town. She'd turn off her lights and threaten to call the police on you, if you came into her yard. How do you work with her?"

"Well, normally Mr. Miller is here and he is fun to work for. But he's out of town this week and she's in charge. Let me get her for you."

We watched Suzie walk back to a small cubicle and talk with someone who was hidden from our view. Shortly, a tall woman made her appearance at the counter.

"Do I hear you want to look into someone's account?" she said with authority.

I explained who I was and handed her my state identification. She put a pair of glasses, which hung by a small chain around her neck, up to her eyes and examined it. She let the glasses fall back on her breasts and handed me back my identification.

"What is it you want to see and why?"

"An account history for Milo Becker. It's police business."

Mrs. Parsons was as tall as I and could look me right into the eye, which she did. "Can't do it."

"Mrs. Parsons . . ."

"The answer is no."

"It is rather important that I have that information."

She glared right into my eyes. "Listen, mister, I'm not getting anything for you. Banking records are confidential. If you want them, there's a courthouse right across the street. You go over there and get yourself a court order, and I'll give you anything you want. But, without it, you get nothing. Is that clear?"

I said it was. Buffy and Suzie meekly said their good-byes, and we left the bank.

"See why we call her the witch? She's always been just like that."

Back out on the street I looked across at the courthouse and pondered my next move. Buffy went back to the car. "It's locked, Stan."

I went to unlock the car for Buffy, and I noticed one of the reasons I had locked it: my laptop was on the floorboard in the backseat. That gave me a quick idea. I grabbed the case and took it into the mayor's office.

"Is he in?" I asked.

His secretary called him. As soon as he saw me, he pointed to a young man sitting next to his office. "Is this your handiwork?"

"Sorry, I'm afraid it is. I asked the chief to assign somebody to you. Just a precaution. Just a little longer, please."

The young man looked up from a magazine. "I'm Officer Davidson."

I smiled and nodded towards the officer. I asked the mayor if I could use his phone line to connect my computer with headquarters. Pleasant as always, he took me into a small conference room.

"Just plug the phone back in when you are finished. I'll leave you two alone."

I gave Buffy the connection to plug in and with a few keystrokes was on line with the state computer. I entered my password, and a beep told me there was a file waiting for me. It was Paige Singlehart's. I downloaded it into the laptop.

"What's it say?" Buffy asked.

I looked. It said more than we knew. She was now wanted for more than questioning in the Omaha bombing. An arrest warrant had been issued. She also had various altercations across the Midwest that had come to the attention of the authorities. Most, a quick glance indicated, were the result of some radical political activity.

"This is good, Buffy. This is just the kind of stuff we need."

I knew Parker would want a hard copy, so I asked the mayor's secretary if I could use her printer. In a few minutes I had my printout, and we were ready to leave.

"Hold on," Buffy said, stopping halfway through the door.

"What's up?"

"The witch. She's walking down to the pharmacy. Wait here."

With that she slipped out of the mayor's office and back into the bank. I chatted with Davidson while waiting for her to come back. I barely had time to find out that Davidson was married and had a baby on the way, when Buffy was back.

"Let's go," she said, brushing the brim of her gumshoe hat.

Chapter Twenty

I would have liked to have spent a little more time with Buffy, but I was paged to go to the police station. I took Becker's banking history and dropped Buffy at her place. When I arrived back at the police station, Parker, Deputy Chase, the chief, and a Dr. Warren, the county medical examiner, met me.

"We have the autopsy on Charles Winborn," the chief said. "Mr. Noble wanted you to hear from the doctor yourself."

"To put it in lay terms, Mr. Winborn died of a heart attack," the doctor said. "It appeared the attack was brought on by a sudden event consistent with what you already knew was his reaction to his daughter's death. What was interesting was that we found additional cancer that had spread to a fairly advanced stage."

"Doctor," Parker said, "would Winborn have known that?"

"It's possible, Mr. Noble. Patients oftentimes know they are in more serious medical trouble than their tests and physicians tell them."

"How long would he have had?"

"Probably less than two years. Eighteen months. Maybe."

Parker turned to Chase. "Anything new for Stanley?"

"No. Just as we thought, the black powder is too common around here to have anything definite. It's also possible that it was purchased somewhere else and brought here."

"Like Omaha?" I asked.

"Anywhere around the Midwest."

Edwards said, "My men haven't found anyone who heard or saw anything out of the usual. We've interviewed all the neighbors, all the newsroom employees, and anyone else we thought might have a grudge against Winborn. We have nothing."

I pulled out Singlehart's printout. "I just got this today. It looks like our friend Singlehart is into a little more than we thought."

The doctor asked if he was needed. We said no. He left a copy of his report and took his leave. Parker, Chase, and Edwards took turns looking through the Singlehart report.

"Everything here is connected to something political," the chief said.

Parker, who was sitting in one of the chief's guest chairs, loaded his pipe.

"You're back to that," I said to Parker.

Parker looked. "Huh?"

"Never mind."

He got up. "This is more than political. It's radical stuff. Gay rights are one thing; blowing up churches is another. But one thing is clear, she is not afraid to use violence."

"You think she might show up for her buddy's hearing tomorrow?" Chase asked.

"She might," the chief said. "We always have some men over there for something or other. I'll just add a few more, and no one will notice anything."

"I'll tell the sheriff," Chase said. "We're normally responsible for courthouse security, so I think he'll want to send a few more men, too."

"Good," Parker said. "Then until tomorrow, gentlemen."

I waited until we were back in Parker's room at the SuperSaver to tell him about Becker's bank records. I thought it might look a little funny, Buffy getting them and all.

Parker just shook his head. "My friend David Connors is here, remember? One phone call, and I could have gotten you a warrant for this stuff. You realize that there may be an evidentiary problem with this, don't you?"

"We didn't have a problem when Buffy went into his house."

"That's because he moved. He wasn't there anymore, and there was no evidence taken. This may be a little different." He took a deep breath. "Okay, the fact is, you have it, so let's see what it tells us."

"By the way, Parker, did you get the stuff from Durham?"

"Yeah. It's here, and I was going over it when the chief sent for me."

I told Parker that Becker had quit his job this morning. He didn't look surprised. He just spread the bank records out on his table. What we had were computer-generated copies of his bank statements for the last six months. There were a few things that we could tell from the statements that were helpful to us. First, he didn't seem to spend much money. The checks that cleared his account each month were for roughly the same amounts, indicating recurring bills like rent and utilities.

Second, the amounts deposited varied slightly, indicating that his paycheck either varied from period to period, or he would keep differing amounts of cash when the checks were deposited. Third, there were no automatic teller withdrawals. This didn't mean that he didn't have an ATM card, just that he didn't use one. It increased the likelihood that if he wanted his money, he'd probably have to go to the bank personally for it.

And the final matter of interest was the balance. Milo Becker had over seven thousand dollars in his account.

"What do you think, Parker?"

"I think if he's going to run, he's going to want his money."

"The manager said he wanted his last check mailed to his wife's residence. Maybe he's not going to run."

Parker looked back through the records.

"I wouldn't worry about that, Stanley. She could deposit it into a joint account in Grand Bay. If he needed the money, she could always forward it to him."

He took Singlehart's record back from me. Then he started over his copy of Winborn's autopsy. "That Porclar stuff, Stanley, hand it to me, would you?"

I did. He started fumbling through it, too.

"Somewhere in all of this stuff is our answer, Stanley. I just wish I knew what we were looking for."

"You don't think Becker is going to run?" I asked.

"Didn't say that. Just that I wouldn't worry about the last payroll check, if I were him. That's pocket change compared to what he has in the bank. If he is going, I don't think he'll have any problem leaving the check for his wife. What he will want, however, is that seven thousand dollars."

He asked me to have Buffy check to see if Becker had an ATM card, then announced our dinner plans.

"I've heard about this little place on the east side of town. It is supposed to have the best barbecue ribs in town." He smiled. "And Monday is all-you-can-eat night."

While Parker was getting ready for dinner, I called Buffy and asked if her friend knew if Becker had an ATM card. Just before we left for the barbecue place, she called back.

"She doesn't know, but she said if there are ATM withdrawals, they'd show up on the statement. But she'll check in the morning and call me."

Parker was unusually quiet on the ride to dinner. Usually he has something to say, even if it is dumb or trivial. On this ride, however, he just puffed on his pipe and looked out the window.

"Crack the window, would you, Parker?"

He grunted and wheezed a little, but did as I asked.

"You're in deep thought tonight, Parker."

He looked over at me, then out the window. "There is just something not right. I haven't got it figured out, but I know it's there. There is something we can see but don't understand. We've got it. We just don't know what the 'it' is."

"Well, let's try to think it through, Parker. It seems we are down to two suspects, Paige Singlehart and Milo Becker. We know Paige has it in her to do something like this, but we're not so sure Becker would. In any event, we can't prove either."

"Don't be too quick to think Singlehart would kill someone. If Omaha is right, she bombed a building. That's radical. But was she trying to hurt anyone? That's the question. You can't make the leap that because she would harm a building, she would also harm a person.

"Of course, I grant you, both have the means and the

motive. But every time I think about them, there's something that doesn't fit. Unfortunately, Stanley, on the basis of what we have now, we couldn't convict either one."

"What about the Durham material?"

"I've only had the briefest opportunity to look that over. I don't think it will affect our case at all. I think after dinner I'll just settle in with all that material and read."

"There's a lot there, Parker."

"Yeah, but that's how I prosecuted. I would get the documents, grand jury testimony and the like, and just read them. I would read them and read them until they were almost committed to memory. Then, when something would come up at trial, I'd be able to go right to what I needed."

We pulled into the parking lot of the barbecue place. "Parker, that may be good at helping you present a case in court, but will it help you solve one? What you presented in court was material gathered by somebody else. It was based upon a lot of legwork and interviewing. Evidence was sifted; the good was kept and the bad was discarded. You were able to rely on the word of others that your case was solid. This is a different ball game, Parker. This is gut-check time in the trenches. This is the infantry. You've always been the Air Force, the glory boys, just fly in and fly out. This is real. This is the front line. This is where war becomes hell."

He smiled. "I don't know if that's a chewing-out or not. But there is one thing that will help me a lot."

"Let me guess," I said. "Food?"

Watching Parker eat ribs was a lot like watching a hungry dog devour a can of dog food: You know he's going to do it, and you know it isn't going to be a pretty sight.

The ribs, to be sure, were good. Parker took advantage of the Monday night all-you-can-eat to fill his plate twice. I was lucky to get through one plate. I, at least, tried to be a little neat, but Parker had the sauce all over everything. The restaurant had rolls of paper towels at each table, and I think Parker went through at least half a roll.

While he was eating, Parker was his usual quiet self, more concerned with his stomach than his case. After he finished, he became a little more talkative again, as usual. This time, however, he didn't mention the Winborn case once. But he did tell me more than I wanted to know about Buckwheat Bob, Mrs. Skosh, the Statler Brothers, and car racing.

"I still can't picture you as a car racing fan, Parker."

"Yes, I like to watch it on TV."

"Why? What's the appeal?"

"They never stop," he said, lighting his pipe. "Think about it, Stanley. Once those guys start the race, they go until someone runs the correct distance. If they stop, it's at their own peril. There is no half-time, no between-innings to sit and think, like you had. It's just go. If you're not ready when they start, it's hard to get ready during the race. There's no half-time analysis. It's kind of like life, Stanley. Once you go, that's it. If you stop, others will pass you by. You run the race to the end as hard as you can."

"I still can't picture you a race fan."

"Yes. I've always wanted to go to the Daytona Five Hundred."

"Well, why haven't you, Parker?"

He didn't answer, just shrugged his shoulders. Then it hit me. He didn't go because he had no one in his life to go with.

On the ride back to the SuperSaver, Parker had me stop at a convenience store, so he could get a big cup of coffee.

"They didn't have hazelnut," he said, as he got back into

the car, "but this will do."

"You're going to float away Parker, like Buffy almost did. Why do you want all that coffee?"

"Stanley, I think I've got everything we need. Tonight I'm going through all the paperwork we have, my notes, crime-scene photos, and your printouts. I'm going to sit up until I have this thing figured out."

"You don't mind if I sleep, do you?"

"Suit yourself, Stanley. I'll probably be at this quite a while."

As we crossed the lobby in the motel, the desk clerk waved for us. "Here, this is for either one of you. She said it was urgent."

Parker took the note, looked at it, and then handed it to me. It said simply, "Call Buffy."

"You can call from my room," he said, as he opened the door.

I went to the phone and watched as Parker carefully lined up the various documents and notes into several small piles on his table.

"It never hurts to be neat, Stanley. Now, call your girlfriend and see what she wants."

"She's not my girlfriend, Parker."

I turned back to the phone as Buffy answered.

"Remember the first time we went to Grand Bay?" she said.

"Yeah."

"And I went to visit my friend at the travel office, while you saw Mrs. Becker?"

"Yeah. Go on, Buffy."

"Well, I told my friend what I was doing. I hope you don't mind, do you?"

"It's a little late for that now, isn't it?"

"Well, she called me tonight. Milo Becker was in to see her today. He bought an airplane ticket. He leaves tomorrow at three. One-way to Los Angeles. There he connects with a flight to Mexico City."

Chapter Twenty-One

Buffy couldn't have told me anything better designed to keep me from sleeping than that Becker was planning a flight to Mexico. I tried to sleep, but my mind kept repeating words I've heard Parker say many times: "Evidence of flight is evidence of guilt."

It was about two o'clock, when, after staring at the ceiling for better than an hour, I decided to take a walk down the hall to the soda machine. I made my selection; then, on the way back to my room, I noticed that there was a light under Parker's door. I didn't know if he was asleep or not, so I stopped and listened. I could hear a slight ruffling of papers. I decided not to go in, but to try to get some rest instead.

There was nothing to amuse me on TV, so, when I finished my drink, I headed back to bed. I don't know if it was the drink or the thought of Parker still working, but I was finally able to get to sleep.

Tuesday morning I woke after eight, much later than usual, so I decided to forego my morning walk. I dressed and headed for the diner. With luck I would still beat Parker.

I stopped in the lobby to get a morning paper. The desk clerk handed me a note. "Your friend left in a police car about half an hour ago. He said for you to pack and for me to give you this."

I opened the note. It read: "We're done. I'm getting a warrant from David Connors this morning. Meet me at the courthouse at ten-thirty, P.N."

I was dumbfounded. "Did he say anything else?"

"Nope. The manager says you can leave your bags in the room. We don't have any reservations for it."

This was mind-boggling. We had been here eleven days, twelve if you counted today. And for at least nine of those days we had no idea what was going on. Now Parker says it's over and I'm to pack. I didn't know what to think. I went back to my room and called Chief Edwards. He was out. I tried Deputy Chase. He was out, too. I called Buffy.

"Hello?"

"Wake up, little girl. We have to go to work."

"Want me to fix you breakfast?"

"No, Buff. Looks like we're almost done. Parker said to pack."

"Pack?" I could hear her voice start to crack. "You mean you're leaving me?"

"Not you, the case. Get ready. I'll pick you up. We have a date at ten-thirty."

By the time I got to Buffy's, her friend Suzie had called. "She said there was no record of an ATM card issued for Milo Becker's account."

"Good. Call her back and give her my cell number. Tell her to call immediately if he tries to make a withdrawal."

"It's Becker, isn't it?" she said. "I knew you had it right from the beginning. Becker. You know, I sort of feel sorry for him."

"How's that, Buffy?"

She tilted her head and looked at me sideways. "It was Winborn who ruined his life. Winborn's death is almost poetic justice. But now Becker will hang for killing Anna Marie. It's all kind of sad."

"Life, Buffy. We don't hang people in this state."

"Well, it's still sad. You know what else is sad? You're going to leave and I'll be here alone again." She put her arms around me and started to cry. I'm a cop; she was once just an interviewee. I shouldn't have feelings for her. I didn't want to have feelings for her. But I held her close anyway; I could feel the little tremble in her body as she cried. It would be hard going back to the capitol, I thought. I would miss the little one in the gumshoe hat.

"Better call your friend," I said, wiping away a tear from her eye. "We still have a case to wrap up."

We drove to a donut shop for a quick bite and coffee. I tried my calls again, all with the same result. I called Captain Hodges.

"Any word from Parker?" I asked.

"No, Stan. Did you lose him?"

"I wish. No, I just thought he might have called in."

"No, he wouldn't check in with me. Call the AG's office. If he was checking in, that's where he'd call. What's up? Are you near the end?"

"Yeah, Cap. Can't talk right now. I think we're coming back today."

"Good. I can't wait for your report."

I ended the call and suddenly realized I had no idea what was happening. Here I was, the only state police official assigned to investigate this crime, and the investigation appeared to be over, and I'm sitting in a donut shop with a girl I don't want to leave while my case was either ending or getting blown, and I still don't have the foggiest idea what is going on.

"Let's go," I said.

"But I'm not finished with my donut."

"Bring it with you."

It was almost ten when we reached the courthouse square. I circled the building, but it did not appear that anything unusual was happening. I parked in front of the mayor's office. His secretary was at her desk, but I couldn't see either the mayor or Officer Davidson.

I sent Buffy into County Bank to see if anything was happening there.

"Suzie says nothing yet. While we were talking, she checked his balance. It's still there, so nobody got it before she got in."

We took a walk to the Family Hour Café to see if Parker was there. He wasn't. I tried my phone calls again, this time adding the mayor; still no luck.

"He said ten-thirty. It's a quarter past. We may as well go."

"Stan, you sound like you don't know what's going on. Do you?"

"Of course, I do, Buffy. Parker is getting a warrant for Anna Marie's killer. We're going to meet him in the courthouse, go and serve the warrant, and take the scoundrel into custody."

"Which scoundrel?" Buffy asked.

I looked down at Buffy. She had a worried look on her face. "That's what we're here to find out," I said.

We entered the courthouse from the door directly across from the restaurant. All looked quiet. Then my cell phone went off.

"Yeah."

"It's Suzie. He's here."

Buffy knew from the look on my face what the call was.

"Show time, little one. Wait here."

"No, I'm coming, too."

She followed me as I exited the courthouse through the doors facing the mayor's office. Suzie called none too soon. Becker was just leaving the bank and walking towards his car when I spotted him. I ran to the curb. He was now directly across the street, unaware, reaching for the door of his car.

"Freeze, sucker!"

I looked down. It was Buffy yelling. Her feet were planted shoulder-width apart, her arms were pointed at Becker, and she was holding a can of mace.

"Buffy, what are you doing with that? It's not a gun," I whispered.

"He doesn't know that. Get him."

Becker, by now, had his hands in the air and was walking towards us. Buffy put her hands down, so he couldn't see she what she had. He spoke to her. "You here to arrest me?"

She nodded towards me. Becker looked me square in the eye. I didn't know what to do, but thought it best to keep Becker with me.

"No," I said.

"Then I can go?"

"No, Mr. Becker. I'm holding you as a material witness in the death of Anna Marie Winborn. Please come with me."

I thought that would suffice for now. He didn't put up a fuss, just followed Buffy, who led the way back into the courthouse. We re-entered the building.

"Mr. Stankowski?"

I turned. It was Michael.

"Mr. Collier said I was to meet you here and pick up some papers."

Good grief, I thought, that's all I need right now. "Hang on, Michael, Parker is coming."

Then, like a scene from an old movie, a scuffle broke out near the magistrate's courtroom. Three city patrolmen and a deputy wrestled a woman to the floor. She was putting up a pretty good fight, but she was finally subdued. The chief, dressed in civilian clothes, came out of the courtroom and led the officers and their captive over to me.

The chief handed me a copy of a mug shot. It was the one Brookman wired to us of Paige Singlehart. There was little doubt that the woman now held in custody was the woman in the picture.

"What is going on here?" Becker demanded.

Buffy looked at him with an icy stare that shut him up better than I could have done. Just then the bell rang on the elevator. The doors opened and Parker, with two deputies trailing him, walked out and approached us.

"Do you have it?" I asked.

Parker just nodded and tapped his suit jacket where his breast pocket would be. He turned to Becker.

"Going somewhere, Mr. Becker?" Becker didn't say a word or move a muscle. "We hear you're going to Mexico," Parker said.

"So, what if I am? Nothing illegal about that."

Parker smiled. "Don't drink the water, Mr. Becker." Then he nodded towards the door, and Becker slowly inched towards it. Then he turned and walked away.

Parker turned back to the prisoner. "The elusive Ms. Singlehart, I presume?"

"Penny Squires," she replied.

A small crowd was beginning to gather. Parker looked at me and I held up the mug shot.

"Good likeness," he said, and then motioned for the officers to take their charge to the jail. He looked at me and smiled. Then it hit me. I knew who the killer was. I felt some new confidence.

"Parker, do you have some legal papers?"

He nodded, reached inside his suit jacket, and gave me a single document. I opened and read it, then re-folded it. Michael and Buffy both had pensive expressions on their faces. Buffy's eyes were pleading, and for a brief moment I wondered what life would be like without her.

Then I turned to Michael, and handed him the warrant. "Mr. Winborn, you have the right to remain silent. . . ."

Epilogue

It was almost eleven as Parker sat in the Family Hour Café. Dressed in his best rumpled suit and bow tie, he had made a beeline to the nearest eatery shortly after the chief and I took Michael into custody.

"I'm not sure whether I want a late breakfast or early lunch," he mused as he examined the menu. I sometimes forget what Parker's real priorities are. He ordered scrambled eggs and bacon—for Parker, a light meal. "Slide over," he said. "Your girlfriend is coming."

"Parker, she's not . . ."

"Quiet," he said, "here she comes."

The first words out of her mouth were, "Why Michael? He was the last person I suspected."

I gave a smug smile. "I think I'll let Parker answer that."

"Well," Parker said, "I think our suspicions started when we first met him in the hospital. He never once mentioned his sister, only his father. He was the same way at the wake and the funeral; he only mentioned Anna Marie in passing. Despite what Doctor Burnelli said, Michael didn't seem to feel any loss for her.

"So we had to ask why. Why would he be so alienated from his sister, and would that be enough to kill her? Then it came to me last night. It was that Porclar thing. We've been saying it wrong. We've been pronouncing it as two short syllables, almost spitting out the word. As I was getting tired, I started to hear it differently in my mind. Say it to yourself, elongating the vowels and separating the syllables into words."

Buffy tried. "Poor claar?"

"Try it again."

"Poor claaar. That's it: Poor Claire, the saint, Saint Claire. The nun with Francis of Assisi."

"Right. He named his corporation after a saint who started an order of nuns. Why? He wanted the benefits of the corporation to go to Anna Marie. That's why he put the stock in her name, too."

"Okay, but why?" she asked.

I answered. "She had MS. We know that from the nuns and Doctor Burnelli. Winborn was using the corporation, which would have become rich when the land was fully developed, to pay for Anna Marie's care. Remember, Buffy, the old nun saying something about how kind Winborn was and what he was doing for the order?"

"Yes, at the rosary."

"Right. That order could not have afforded Anna Marie's treatments. I bet that money was a condition for Anna Marie's remaining there," I said.

"Wait a second," she said. "What about insurance?"

Parker took a break from his food. "She had no insurance. She spent a year in Europe after she graduated from college. Most family plans will cover a child in school. But she inadvertently lost her insurance with her travel. She didn't find out about the MS until she returned. Thus, the MS was a pre-existing condition, which any insurance company would have excepted from coverage."

He motioned the waitress for coffee. Then he continued.

"Winborn, knowing he was a dying man, needed a fast

way to provide for her. The land deal was perfect. Once he had the land, all he had to do was to keep Costello from being able to market his project. That left Winborn, through Porclar, with a monopoly."

Parker's coffee came and he momentarily stopped talking.

"But, one thing I don't understand, Parker," I said. "When Winborn died, his will said all the property would be split between Michael and Anna Marie, right? So, did the corporation change that?"

"Yes. Buffy asked the right question yesterday." He turned to her. "Remember, you asked about the initials J-T and R-O-S? Winborn held the stock for Porclar in a joint tenancy with Anna Marie. If anything happened to him, as he expected, the result would be that all would go to her, not Michael. R-O-S is right of survivorship. It would bypass the provisions of the will. Michael was left with only half of everything else, which basically was the paper, heavily encumbered, and the house. All he really got from his father was a job."

"So you figured it out from that?" Buffy asked Parker.

"Well, once I had a motive and the right victim, it was easy to view the facts as evidence. For example, there were no breakfast fixings in the kitchen when we arrived. Margo said something about a 'mini-breakfast' before everyone left Friday night. Michael knew his sister would want to cook breakfast for her dad. She liked doing that, remember? So, he knew she would be using his car the next morning.

"Then there was the matter of the dog that didn't bark. No one heard anything the night before Anna Marie died. Didn't that strike you as a little odd, considering Coco would have been in the dog pen next to the garage as the bomb was rigged? Coco didn't bark, because he knew the person rigging the bomb: Michael."

"Well," Buffy said, "at least I asked one right question."

"You asked more than one, gumshoe," I said. "You pointed out something else that was helpful. You were the one who noticed the color of the wires in the Winborn car, remember? The black wire under the dash and the red wire on the seat-belt mount."

"Yeah," she said.

"Well, the bomb wouldn't know which wire was which, but any normal person would have automatically used the red wire as the positive lead under the dash, and the black as the ground on the seat-belt mount. That's how most wiring is done. Look at your car battery: the red is positive and the black is the ground. But Michael didn't do it that way. Why?"

"Because he's color blind," Buffy said.

"Right. Mrs. Roberts hinted at it at the rosary. And his clothing, well, you can judge that for yourself."

"But I knew that," Buffy said. "I thought everybody did."

I smiled, "Well, it took some of us a little longer to figure that out."

Parker gave me a wink as Chief Edwards, still in civilian clothing, entered the diner. He came straight to our table and shook my hand, then Parker's. "I can't tell you how much we've appreciated your efforts here. Thank you both very much."

"What will happen to Michael?" Buffy asked.

"That's what I wanted to tell you," Edwards said. "We took him back to the station and he gave us a statement. That's murder one; he'll spend the rest of his life in prison."

"And what about Paige Singlehart?" I asked.

"We're holding her for Nebraska authorities to pick up."

Parker looked at me. "Why don't you call Mrs. Becker and tell her she can have her husband back?"

"Good idea." I called while Parker and the chief chitchatted. When I finished, the chief had left.

"By the way, what will happen to him?"

"The domestic abuse? It was dismissed. His attorney sent me copies of all the court documents. Seems his wife made the charges in a custody fight. The judge believed him and dismissed her complaint."

"That's why he has custody of his son," I said.

"Right."

"Okay, Parker. The congressman. What was with the congressman?"

He smiled. "I guess I can tell you now, since everyone will know tomorrow. He is being appointed ambassador to the United Nations. The FBI was doing a routine background check, when this came up. His uncle had been an assistant U.S. attorney years ago, and he was helping him with a drug investigation. That's how he came to be involved in the chief's file. The investigation came to naught, but when his appointment was pending and you started to look into him, someone at the Bureau panicked and withheld his file."

"And the mayor?" Buffy asked.

"He'll probably run in the special election for Congress. He certainly has the name for it. A few years back, the Speaker of the House was named Tom Foley," Parker said.

"This all seems so complicated," Buffy said. She turned to me, and I could see a little tear in her eye. "I guess this means you will be going now."

"I guess it does, gumshoe."

"Oh, that reminds me," Parker said. "Ace Rhodes gave

me this for you." He handed Buffy a small piece of notepaper.

She opened it. "It says George Ackerman. Isn't he the editor of the *Capitol Gazette*?"

"That's him. Ace says he needs a good general assignment reporter. Are you interested?"

She was speechless. "Yes! Yes! I'm more than interested."

"Good. Ace says you have an appointment at ten-thirty tomorrow."

"Oh, oh, oh." Her hands went to her face. Tears started rolling down her cheeks. "Oh, thank you, Mr. Parker. Thank you, thank you."

She reached for a napkin and started dabbing her eyes with it.

"Oh, Stan. Oh, how do I get there? Oh, oh. Can you fellows take me back? It'll only take me twenty minutes to get my stuff together."

Parker held up his hand. "Okay, okay. You and Stanley go get your stuff. I can wait here for you."

"Oh, Mr. Parker, thank you so much. You are so kind."

Parker took her hand. "It's Noble, Buffy."

"Yes, Mr. Parker. It is so noble of you, too."

I hate that look Parker gives me.

About the Author

Mike Manno is a practicing attorney in central Iowa, where he also teaches college courses in law and government. He is a former newspaper editor and has authored numerous op-ed and feature articles for the local news media. He has served on the Polk County District Court Mediation Panel and for two years was editor of the Iowa Bar Association's *Bankruptcy and Commercial Practice Newsletter*. He is also a past member of the Davenport (Iowa) City Council. He and his wife, Luanne, an accountant, live with their best four-legged friend, Bo, in West Des Moines.